R<
Paul DeGeorge
73,100 words
World rights

A Writer's Engagement

Written by:

Robert E. Wacaster

Edited by:

Paul Alan DeGeorge II

A product of Golden Paradise Publishing LLC.

Cover by Robert Wacaster

Copyright 2010
Robert E. Wacaster
Paul A. DeGeorge II

No part of this book may be reproduced or transmitted in any form, or by any means, electronic or mechanical, including photocopying, recording, or by any information storage and retrieval systems without the written permission of the author, except under fair use
for critical reviews, where only brief passages may be quoted, or where prohibited by law.

This book is a work of fiction. The characters, places and situations are all fictional. Any resemblance to any persons living, dead, past, present, or future is purely coincidental.

One

The plane landed. Robert gathered both his and Katie's carry on bags from the overhead compartment. He followed her through the skyway and out into the airport.

"You've told your sister about my promising to marry you, right?" Robert asked.

Katie glanced at him, "No. Not yet."

"You didn't tell her? Katie, I thought we agreed you would before we flew back here."

"I wanted to tell her in person!" Katie said with a huge smile. "I wanted to see her face when she finds out we're engaged!"

"It was just a promise, Katie. I haven't proposed or even bought you a ring yet."

"You always keep your promises." Katie beamed, "I expect your proposal any time now."

"Yeah. Any time now…" Robert repeated.

"Katie!" Jill yelled as they approached baggage claim. "Katie, over here!"

Katie waved and ran towards Jill. The two sisters hugged and Jill turned towards Robert, "Well sex fiend, back again I see?"

"Uh…yeah, back again." Robert said with half a smile, "How's school life?"

Jill sighed, "School's out in two weeks. I'm trying to decide what classes to take during my time off. So how were things in California?"

Katie smiled. "Oh my God, Oh my God, Oh my *God*! Guess what?"

The smile fell from Jill's lips as she pierced Robert with accusation. "What did you do?"

"We're going to get *married*!" Katie gushed. "Robert promised to marry me!"

Jill's face filled with shock, "You proposed to her…after only two weeks?"

"Well…I…you see…we actually weren't going to…ah…"

"He hasn't proposed yet but he promised he would in a couple months!"

Jill put her hands on her hips and glared at Robert, "Did he now? I guess Robert and I will have to have a little talk, won't we? Do mom and dad know about this?"

Katie's eyebrows pursed at the though. "No, I haven't told them. Do you think dad will be really mad?"

"I don't know. I'm certainly glad I won't be the one telling him." Jill said with a small smile, "I guess we should get your luggage, shouldn't we?"

Robert loaded the bags into the trunk of Jill's car as she stood next to him.

"So…What went on out there in California?"

"Well…I'm writing again!" Robert beamed, "I started on the sequel to the first book."

"That's not what I meant and you know it!" Jill crossed her arms. "What went on between you and Katie?"

Katie walked up to the other side of Robert, "Oh, just tell her we had non-stop sex and she'll be happy! Yes Jill. I slept with him in California!"

Jill glared at Robert, "Is that so? And during the sex you made her a promise I take it?"

"Yes. That's exactly it!" Katie giggled, "Right in the middle he screamed, 'Marry me Katie, I never want the sex to stop!'" She continued to giggle as Robert finished with the bags and closed the trunk, "Don't tell her anything, sweetheart!" Katie laughed.

Robert opened the passenger door for Katie and helped her into the backseat. Instead of getting into the backseat with her, he climbed into the front. Jill climbed in behind the wheel and started the car. Robert looked around, "Very nice, I like the car."

Jill stared at the steering wheel, "Yes, it's very nice and I appreciate you buying it for me. Thank you." She sounded cold and unemotional.

"I sat up here because I know you're curious about what went on between Katie and me. So ask me whatever you want."

Jill looked at him as she backed the car out of the parking space, "What went on is really between you and Katie. It's really none of my business."

"You see, it's none of her business!" Katie said from the backseat.

Robert turned around, "You be quiet back there! She's your sister, and she deserves to know what happened!"

Jill glanced at him, "Did it really happen during or because of the sex?"

"No." Robert answered simply.

"So...you really had a serious discussion about this? You two talked it out and decided you wanted to get married?"

"I asked her at the airport in California just before we got on the plane. I asked her what she wanted to do: Move in together, travel, or whatever. She mentioned that we could do anything. It wasn't as if we were married. I asked if that would be so bad. I promised to propose to her in about six months if we were still getting along the way we are now and were still in love."

"I see...and Katie took that to mean she was engaged?"

"I don't like your tone!" Katie protested.

Jill looked at Robert and waited for an answer.

"I do love her. You believe that, don't you? And yes, I think I will end up proposing. I know it seems pretty early, but it just felt right."

"Well: I guess we'll have to see what mom and dad have to say." Jill said with a smile.

Two

Jill and Katie helped Robert take the luggage into the house and up to Katie's bedroom. Katie let out a happy shriek as she picked up the watch Robert had bought her when they had first met. It was still sitting on the night stand where she forgot it for her trip to California. She placed it on her wrist, threw her arms around Robert's neck, and kissed him.

Robert looked at Jill, "You don't mind me staying here for a bit, do you?"

"Oh, you're almost family, right? No. I don't mind you staying."

"I can get a hotel if it bothers you having me here."

"You will *not* be going to some hotel somewhere!" Katie fussed.

"No, it's fine. Katie's a grown woman. If *she* wants you here that's fine by me." Jill answered.

"I'll probably just sit here and write while you two are at work."

"Not a problem. Do you have a typewriter or something?" Jill asked.

"He writes on his own laptop!" Katie responded.

Robert looked aggravated, "Yes, I write on my own laptop. Katie, I can answer Jill myself, ok?"

Katie opened her suitcase and began to put away clothes. Her bottom lip pushed out just a bit, "Fine. Answer her yourself!"

Robert sighed, "Do you have anything to drink?"

"Just diet coke and some milk." Jill answered, "Would you like something?"

"Yeah, milk sounds good. Are you thirsty, honey?" Robert turned to Katie.

"No. I'm going to put our clothes away. You go ahead and tell Jill all about our private stuff!"

Robert took a hold of Katie's hands. "Look…I just thought she should know, ok? Do you really mind me talking to her?"

Katie took a deep breath. "No…I guess not. I'm just tired. And I just…I just want everyone to know how we feel…that you'll really marry me."

"Don't you ever worry about that, ok? Yes, I'll really marry you! Let's just take our time, ok?"

"I love you." Katie said. Robert leaned over and kissed her gently but firmly.

"Ok, ready for the milk now." He smiled at Jill.

They walked into the kitchen. Robert sat down at the table while Jill poured him a glass of milk.

"There's not much more to it than that." He said, "I promised to marry her and I mean it. We just need some time together before I propose."

Jill sat down next to him. "I guess there are worse people she could marry. So things went pretty well in California, huh?"

"Yeah. Once she got there, things just seemed to click into place for us. I started writing again. Everything seemed so perfect."

"So will you be moving in here?" Jill asked.

"I don't know. I was hoping you wouldn't mind if I stayed for a while. You know, just to see how things work out with Katie?"

"It will be nice to have a man around the house."

Robert smiled and drank his milk.

Three

Robert, Katie, and Jill sat in the living room watching TV. Jill sat in a chair while Robert and Katie cuddled on the couch. After watching some TV Robert looked at Katie.

"You were going to call your parents, weren't you?" He asked.

Jill laughed. "She won't call until tomorrow. Not until she thinks dad's gone."

"You're afraid to tell your dad about us?" Robert asked, concerned.

"No, not at all," Katie smiled, "Jill doesn't know what she's talking about! I was going to call, I just forgot. I was unpacking all our stuff, remember? I had to clear out some room in my closet for your clothes."

"Well, it's not so late yet, is it? Go ahead and call them now."

"Now?" Katie asked, looking worried, "What's the hurry?"

Jill laughed again. "Better to talk to dad now, and get it over with!"

"He's not some monster!" Katie sat up and found her cell phone. "He'll understand that Robert and I are in love! He'll be happy we're getting married!"

"Sure he will Katie." Jill said with a smile.

"Katie, if you don't think he'll understand…" Robert started.

"Its fine honey, I'll call him. I'm a grown woman after all!" Katie dialed her parent's number, got up from the couch, and walked into the bedroom, leaving Robert behind.

"Is it really going to be that hard to tell her dad she's engaged?" Robert asked Jill.

"No. The hard part is to tell him she got engaged to a guy she's known less than a month. He won't like that at all!"

"Hello." Jim Benson answered.

"Hi Daddy, it's me!"

"Sweetheart, how've you been? I was hoping you'd call and talk to me! Your mom said you were in California!"

"I was...but I'm back in New York. I just got back today. Is Mom there?"

"You can't talk to me?" He asked, "I haven't talked to you in a month. I want to know how my girl is doing!"

"I'm fine Dad. I just...I have some news and want to tell Mom first."

"News you can't tell me? It's something I won't like then, isn't it? How about I guess what your news is?"

"Daddy, you don't have to guess..."

"You haven't lost your job, have you? No, if that was it, you'd sound a lot sadder. Let's see...I'll bet it has something to do with a guy by the name of Robert, doesn't it?"

"How did you know that?"

"Your mom told me you were all shook up over some guy named Robert. So what happened? He took you to California?"

"Well...yes, he did fly me out there. I had a great time."

"And what's the rest? I know there's more, you sound so nervous."

"Mom isn't there?" Katie asked, trying one last time.

"Katie, why don't you ever trust me enough to tell me things about these...men you find?"

"I trust you Daddy, I just...I don't want you all upset."

"I see, he hit you, he slept with you, and then threw you out? What happened Honey?"

"Oh Daddy, you always think the worst of people! Robert isn't like that! We've decided to get married!"

"You've..." Jim Benson floundered for words.

"Daddy? Daddy, are you ok? Daddy!"

"I'm fine, Katie. Did you just say you *married* this guy?"

"No, we aren't married yet. But we want to get married in a few months. Robert's promised to propose to me when we've decided we're ready."

"Oh thank God! So you aren't married right now?"

"Can I please talk to Mom?"

"Yeah, sure. What's this guy's name? Robert? And what's his last name sweetie?"

"Do you know his birthday or maybe his social security number? If you can find his wallet and tell me something like a driver's license number that would help too."

"I don't want you doing a background check on him, Dad! That's not why I called! You always do this! Will you *please* let me talk to Mom?"

"Fine, I'll just ask your sister, she's always helpful. Here. Talk to your Mother…"

"Katie?" Her mother's voice came over the phone, "Oh honey, it's so good to hear from you! How was California?"

Jill's cell phone began to ring. She gave it a bored look and then picked it up. "That'll be dad. Obviously Katie didn't tell him enough about you so he's calling me."

"But isn't Katie talking to him right now?" Robert asked.

Jill sighed and answered her phone, "Hi Dad. How is everything in Florida?"

"Hi Sweetheart, I was wondering if you could help me out? I was just talking to your sister, and…"

"Sorry." Jill interrupted him, "I can't help you. If you want to know about Robert, you'll have to ask Katie."

"Honey, I just worry about you girls!"

Jill took a deep breath and pulled the phone away from her ear. "Would you mind talking to Dad? If you don't, he'll just drive both Katie and me nuts asking questions."

"Sure, I'll talk to him." Robert held out his hand for the phone. "Hello?"

"Who is this?"

"Uh…my name's Robert Wacaster. I'm the one who's promised to marry your daughter, sir."

"Wacaster, huh? How long have you known Katie?"

"Around two and a half weeks."

"Two and a half weeks and you're ready to marry her, huh? Do you even know anything *about* her?"

"Yeah, I do. I know she loves clothes. She likes to dress me up and put ties on me. I know she doesn't really like to eat meat. I know she's not very handy with tools or fixing things. I know she's not very handy with electronics either."

"Well...I'm sure you figured all that out in the two weeks you've known her. What do you *really know* about my daughter? After two weeks you think you know enough about her to get married?"

"I know I love her and I know she loves me too. We aren't rushing into a marriage, if that's what you're thinking. I promised to marry her if things keep working out between us. If we still feel the same way about each other in about six months then, yes, I plan on marrying Katie."

After a long pause, her father spoke again, "I...see. Ok, for now I'm satisfied. You can call me Jim, by the way. Is there any chance I can get you to come down to Florida so I can meet you in person?"

Katie came out of the bedroom beaming, "I talked to Mom, and she said..."

"Shhhh!" Jill put a finger up to her lips.

"I think that sounds good. I'd like to meet you too, Jim. Where are you in Florida?"

"We're down in Tampa. It's a nice, little, community."

Katie's face turned to shock, "Is that Dad on the phone?"

"I'll talk to Katie. I'm sure we can set something up pretty soon. Do you need us to stay in a hotel?"

"Absolutely not. You're both welcome to stay right here in the house with us!"

"Ok. Well, she's giving me a frightened look right now, so I guess I'd better let you go. It was nice to talk to you. I'll get with her about the trip and have her call you back, ok?"

"Ok; and Robert...?

"Yes?"

"If I find out you mistreat my daughter in any way I'll have you killed. Do you understand that?"

"I understand. I can see where Jill gets her charm from. Bye now." He handed the phone to Jill.

"That was Daddy?" Katie asked.

"Yeah"

"And what did he say?"

"He invited us to Florida."

Katie broke into a smile, "He did? That's wonderful! So he didn't threaten you or anything like that?"

"Oh yeah, he said if I mistreat you, he'd have me killed."

"Yep, that would be our dad." Jill rolled her eyes.

Four

Robert lay in bed next to Katie. She was on her back, staring at the ceiling.

"Are you ok?" He asked. "Usually you want to cuddle and fool around."

"I was just thinking. You don't really want to go to Florida, do you?"

"Sure, why not? Wouldn't you like to see your parents again?"

"I just don't want daddy running you off honey. I know he'll get all nasty and try to push you around. I'm just worried, ok?"

Robert smiled and moved closer to her. He kissed her gently and then looked into her eyes. "Do you remember our first date, Katie? How you invited me home for ice cream? Jill sat at the table glaring at me and wanting me to fix her car?"

"Yes."

"Did she run me off? Did anything she *say*, or do, come between us?"

"Jill's a girl. She's just my sister, but my father…"

"Your father asked me what I knew about you after two weeks. I told him I knew I loved you, and you loved me. He said he was satisfied with that for now."

"He's not." Katie said frowning. "He never liked anyone I brought home."

"How many guys have you brought home?"

Katie shifted uncomfortably. "Just two, but…Robert, you don't know him like I do."

"Which two?"

"Barry and Steven."

"Steven is the one I don't know. You went out with a guy named Steven?"

"That was in high school. He didn't like Steven at all. And then after bringing Barry home…things just didn't go well."

Robert began laughing. "What happened? You act like he tried to kill Barry or something!"

"It doesn't matter. I just don't want him treating you badly. I'm afraid of what he'll do."

"Barry's the one who slept with the bridesmaid at the wedding, right?"

She turned and frowned at him. "How is it you remember everything I tell you about every other man?"

"That's love, Sweetheart." He laughed.

Robert opened his eyes. He looked at the clock on the nightstand. It said 7:30. He climbed out of bed and walked quietly to the bathroom. He came out, put on some sweat pants and a t-shirt, and walked towards the kitchen. He found Jill sitting at the kitchen table drinking a cup of coffee.

"Good morning." Robert said, sitting down.

"Well. You're up early this morning! Is Katie up?"

"No, she's still asleep. She'll probably realize I didn't come back to bed after using the bathroom. She will show up sooner or later."

"She watches you that closely?" Jill laughed. "Would you like some breakfast?"

"Oh no, you don't have to cook for me! I'll just grab a glass of milk or something."

Jill smiled at him. "I don't have to leave for work for a little while. I can make you some eggs. How do you like them?"

"Really, you don't have to go to any trouble for me! I fed myself fine when I was single!" Robert laughed.

"Ok Mr. Independent. Just remember Katie can't cook!"

Robert found himself a glass and filled it with milk, "I hope I'm not going to be too much of a bother for you. I know Katie's all gung ho about us living together, but…"

"I've told you, you aren't a bother! So what are you going to do today; try to get to know your future bride better? Spend some time listening to her go on and on about clothes, maybe?" Jill asked with an evil smile.

"Actually, I thought about writing. I started my second book and really need to work on that. I guess the kitchen here would be the best place to set up my laptop and work, right?"

"What do you use, Word?" Jill asked.

"Yeah, I just plug in my little jump drive and type away."

"You can use the computer in my room if you want to!" Jill offered. "What a thrill to have a best selling author writing on my pc!"

Robert smiled at her. "You know, you actually sound a bit like Katie when you laugh."

She looked horrified. "Oh, don't even say that!"

"But you really don't mind if I use your computer? You're ok with that?"

"Of course I'm ok with that! You bought me that nice car. If you need a computer to write with; you're welcome to use mine!"

Robert downed the glass of milk. "Thanks Jill, I do appreciate it."

"Robert? Robert, where are you?" Came Katie's voice from the living room.

"We're in here, honey." He yelled. "I was just in the kitchen getting a drink."

Katie walked into the kitchen and sat down at the table. "Is Jill making breakfast?"

"No sweetie, she's just about ready to leave for work." Robert smiled.

"You know, I thought I might take a trip into work today, too. Just to see what's going on or talk about my trip to California?" Katie smiled shyly.

"That sounds great! I'd love to go with you, but I think I will stay here and write for a bit. You don't mind if I stay here, do you?" Robert asked.

Katie leaned over and kissed him on the cheek, "Not at all! You relax here, and I'll be back before you know it, ok?"

After the two women left the house, Robert walked into Jill's room and booted up her computer. He inserted his jump drive and opened the file for his second book. After a few minutes of staring at it, he began to write.

Five

Katie walked into the reception area and noticed her friend Julie sitting at her desk. Julie was on the phone but smiled widely as Katie walked in. Katie stood near the desk waiting for her to finish the call. She hung up, let out a shriek, and hugged her friend close.

"Oh Katie, you're back already? How was California?"

Katie broke out into a wide smile, "Oh Julie, I have so much to tell you. I'm so excited! Robert promised to marry me!"

Julie's face showed the appropriate shock. "Katie, he proposed to you? Oh honey, I'm so happy for you! Have you guys set a date yet?"

"Well, he didn't really propose. He just promised me he would in a couple of months. But he always keeps his promises; I'm not worried."

"Oh…I see." Julie said, looking less excited. "And now he's sent you back to work?"

"No, he actually wants to go down to Florida and meet my parents. I just wanted to come in today and see everyone."

"Well, we're certainly glad to have you back! So what happened when you got to California?"

"Well…I overslept and almost missed my flight. Then I drank a bit too much champagne on the plane…" Katie began.

Six

Robert didn't move from the chair in front of Jill's computer for a couple of hours. Inspiration struck him and he wrote more than he had for a long time. His mind whirled with the story he was writing. He heard the front door and heard Katie calling his name but paid no attention. He was too absorbed in the story he was writing.

She stuck her head in Jill's bedroom and saw him, "Hi sweetheart, I'm back! What are you doing, writing?"

"Yeah," he mumbled.

"I thought maybe we could get some lunch?" Katie asked brightly.

"Not really hungry, maybe later?" He mumbled again.

"Oh come on. You need to eat Robert!"

He didn't bother to answer this time. He kept typing and ignored her.

"Robert, are you even listening to me? You need to eat something. Can you stop for a minute? Please look at me when I'm talking to you."

He stopped typing and turned towards her. "What? What do you want? I'm busy here: Can't you see that? For God's sake Katie, can I have some privacy while I do this?"

He regretted everything he said as soon as the words had left his lips. Looking at Katie; he could see the hurt in her eyes. She turned and walked out of the room without another word. He dropped his head down onto the keyboard wishing he could turn back the clock for just a minute. He saved his file and shut down the computer.

He searched for Katie and found her in her room, changing into some sweats.

"Katie…I'm sorry. I didn't mean for things to come out like that."

"It's no problem, you need to write." She answered quietly.

"Honey...do you still want to have lunch?"

"You need your privacy. You need to write by yourself." She said as she pulled on a t-shirt. She walked past him out of the room. He followed her.

"Katie, can we please talk about this? I'm trying to apologize!"

"Your apology's accepted. Go back to your writing." She growled. She dropped herself into the living room chair and began flipping through a magazine.

He sat down beside her on the couch. "Are you sure you don't want to go somewhere for lunch? We can go any place you want! I'm ready! I'll even dress up if you want me to?"

"No. I'll just make myself a sandwich later." She said, not looking up.

Robert put his head in his hands for a minute and looked back up at her. "What can I do to make this up to you?"

"There's nothing for you to make up. You just need to write and I interrupted that. We're fine, Robert."

He got up from the couch and walked slowly back into Jill's bedroom. He booted her computer up and stared at the screen. He couldn't bring himself to write again. Instead, he just sat in front of the computer. After about an hour he heard the front door open again.

"Hi Katie, how was your trip into Manhattan?" He heard Jill ask.

"Fine."

"Just fine? No fabulous stories about how excited your friends were when they found out Robert promised to marry you?"

Robert couldn't hear Katie's response. He walked out of Jill's room, into the living room.

"Hi Jill, how was school?"

"What's going on? Are you two having problems already?" Jill asked, looking at Robert.

"Uh...well I was writing and..."

"No! We aren't having any problems!" Katie said angrily. "Mind your own business!"

Robert looked at Jill pleadingly.

"I see." Jill said, looking at Robert. "Can you get some bowls down for me in the kitchen?"

"Sure." Robert said, following her. He watched Katie as they neared the kitchen. As he got to the kitchen door she said, "Don't let her disturb your writing, *Robert*!"

"What do you need down?" He asked Jill.

"Take a seat."

"What? I thought you wanted some bowl off a shelf, or something?"

"She obviously won't let you talk to her, so talk to me. I keep all the bowls down where I can reach them."

"I yelled at her." Robert said simply.

"I see, and what did you yell at her for?"

"She came home. I was writing in your room when she came in and kept bothering me. I was just trying to write. I turned on her and yelled. I didn't mean it, and I told her I was sorry, but…"

"I see. The Little Princess didn't get what she wanted and now she's pouting?"

"I shouldn't have talked to her that way." Robert said looking at the table.

"Oh poo!" Jill rolled her eyes. "She didn't get her way and now she's all upset! If she really wants you as a husband, she'll need to learn to talk to you about how she's feeling! If she can't accept your apology, maybe she's not mature enough to get married."

"Oh, I'm not, huh?" Katie said angrily stomping into the kitchen. "You two figured you'd just come in here and discuss how immature little Katie is?"

"Katie, I don't want things to be like this between us!" Robert pleaded. "I wish there was something I could do…?"

She sat down at the table, across from him, "Oh we're fine. I still expect you to keep your promise and marry me. Even if you do think I'm just some immature, "*Little Princess*"! You won't get out of things with me just because you're an obnoxious asshole!"

"Go pout in the living room, Katie!" Jill pointed towards the doorway. "I'm going to make dinner! At least take Robert with you and talk things through with him!"

"Fine, let's go Robert! She doesn't want the *Little Princess* or the obnoxious asshole in her kitchen!" She grabbed his hand and led him back into the living room. She sat him down on the couch and went back to her chair.

"So, you at least want to talk about this?" Robert asked hopefully.

"There's nothing to talk about." Katie said, picking the magazine back up, "I told you, we're fine. Stay out of Jill's way!"

Robert sighed and turned on the TV. He sat there sadly, flipping through the channels.

Jill made them a nice tuna casserole and they all ate in silence. Katie didn't say another word to either Robert or Jill. After eating, they sat in the living room. Jill read a small book she had brought home from school while Katie and Robert silently watched the TV. Eventually, Katie got up from her chair.

"I'm going to bed now, are you coming?" She said flatly.

Robert nodded and got up from the couch. He followed Katie into the bedroom and watched quietly as she put on her pajamas. He stripped down to his underwear and climbed into the bed. She climbed in beside him, but lay with her back to him, close to her edge of the bed. He lay there silently beside her, afraid to speak or touch her.

After a while, he rolled out of bed and pulled on sweats. He walked out into the living room and turned on the TV. Ten minutes later Katie came into the living room, a concerned look on her face.

"Have I ruined things between us?" She asked as Robert looked up at her.

He patted the couch next to him, "Sit down, Katie."

She sat down next to him and looked at her hands. "I'm so sorry. I shouldn't have acted that way."

"I shouldn't have yelled at you Katie. You didn't deserve that, I should have been happy to see you when you came back from the office!"

"I just…when I was at the office, and told everyone…" She began to cry.

Robert put his arm around her and hugged her close, "Let it out honey, whatever happened, let it out."

She put her arms around his neck and hugged him back, "I *do* love you and *do* want to get married! But when I told people at work, some people would ask about my engagement ring, and…"

"And you don't have one yet." Robert finished for her. "I didn't mean to put this kind of burden on you."

"It's not really that…while I was there and was telling everyone what you promised me, one guy said…" She continued to cry, hugging him close.

"He said what?"

He said, "*Oh yeah, that's a great line!*"

"It's not a line. I meant what I promised. I just thought we needed to get to know each other a bit better before I proposed."

"I know! I trust you Robert! It's just…I…it just bothered me that someone would say that kind of thing!"

"Today is one reason I wanted us to wait a bit before I proposed. You understand I need to write, don't you?"

She leaned back from him and looked into his eyes, "Yes, of course I do! I just didn't expect you to…and I was still kind of upset about what that guy said…and…"

He smiled at her, "These are things we need to talk about, ok? When you're upset, you need to talk to me. I'm here for you, Katie. My writing's important, but if you need to talk, I mean *really* talk, just tell me. I thought you just wanted to go to lunch! I was so into my writing. I go off into these other worlds…"

"I know it's silly, but when you yelled at me, I felt like I was less important than your writing. That's silly, isn't it?"

He kissed her cheek, "Of course that's silly! You'll always be first in my life! We just need to talk about things once in a while, ok?"

She smiled at him, feeling better, "Ok. I'm sorry I acted the way I did. I just didn't know what to do! I was hurt and felt so bad and…"

"Don't I always make you feel better?" He asked, "Talk to me next time, ok? Scream at me if you have to but tell me how you feel!"

She reached for his hand, "Can we go back to bed now? It didn't feel right in there without you cuddled up next to me."

"Yes. I'm glad you feel better. Things didn't feel right without you cuddling up to me either."

Seven

Robert rolled out of bed early again. He walked into the kitchen and saw Jill with her morning cup of coffee.

"Good morning." He mumbled.

Jill looked at him with some concern. "Are things still rocky between you and Katie?"

"No, we talked last night, we're fine now. Our communication just needs a bit of work."

Jill took a sip of coffee. "I don't think she's used to a man she can actually talk to. You know? Someone she can actually trust and tell everything."

Robert sighed, "I'm not really used to having someone like that around either."

Katie bounced into the kitchen still wearing her pajamas and a robe. "Good morning Jill, good morning asshole!"

Robert pulled her down onto his lap and kissed her. "Good morning Little Princess! You seem all bouncy this morning!"

Katie giggled. "I'll have to go back to work soon. Will you be ok staying here by yourself all day?"

"Why do you have to go back to work?"

"I have rent and bills to pay, silly man! If I don't work, I don't get paid!"

Robert looked over at Jill. She tried to hide a smile and looked down at her coffee.

"How much do you make a month?" He asked.

"What difference does that make?"

"Tell me what you make and I'll write you a check for the rest of the year, ok? Then you won't have to work."

Katie wrinkled her brow. "You don't have to do that."

"Katie, we're planning on getting married, what's mine should be yours too. If you need some bills paid or want to go shopping, let me know!"

"I didn't want to pressure you. I didn't want you to think…well, that I liked you for your money."

Jill smiled and laughed, "She'll spend all your money on clothes, big shot! You shouldn't have said she could go shopping!"

"I will *not* spend all his money on clothes!" Katie said putting her nose in the air. "I'll save some for a house and some new furniture! And maybe..." She climbed off Robert's lap and leaned down to whisper to Jill. "A crib!"

Robert leaned over towards the two women. "Did you just say crib?"

"Do you like kids?" Katie asked.

"Yeah...I like kids. I'm guessing you'd like to be a mom someday?"

Jill stood up from the table. "I really need to be getting to work!"

"Is that so hard to imagine?" Katie asked. "Me as a Mom? I'd like to have some kids."

Robert smiled. "I'd love to have a family with you. Hey Jill, before you go, I have something for you to think about...?"

"For *me* to think about? I'm almost afraid to ask!"

"You said school will be out in about another week. Can we drive down to Florida and see your parents? We could either take your new car or I could rent one. I think it would be nice if you came with us though!"

Jill and Katie looked at each other. "Oh, I don't know. Katie and I in a car? Together? That's kind of a long drive."

"It'll be fun!"

"You're nuts, you know that? We'll probably just fight the whole way!"

A sad look crossed Katie's face. "We aren't children anymore! We can get along!"

"So that's a no, huh?" Robert asked.

"I didn't say no...I just want you to be sure. And that *is* quite a long way to drive, my baby."

"Yeah, that's why I said we could maybe rent one. I didn't want to put you on the spot to take your new car."

"Oh I'm fine with driving him. I'd really like to show my Dad the car! But the three of us cooped up in a car for that long of a drive? You'd better think about that."

"I have." Robert said looking at Katie again. "I haven't really talked to Katie about this yet. I think a drive down there would be good for us."

Katie looked shocked. Jill smiled at both Katie and Robert's expressions as she walked towards the kitchen door, "Ok, after you talk to her about it, let me know. I'd better get to work."

Eight

Katie gave Robert a worried look after Jill left. "Do you remember when you said if I really needed to talk to you…?"

"Of course," Robert answered. "Come on, let's go into the living room and sit on the couch. We'll be more comfortable." He took Katie by the hand and led her out of the kitchen. They sat on the couch and he took hold of her hands. "What's wrong honey? Don't you want to go to Florida?"

"No. I do want to go! But maybe…maybe we could go after we get married? We could go for our honeymoon!"

"You mean elope and then go down there? Not even meet your parents or have a big wedding?"

"I *do* want a big wedding. I *really* do, it's just that… Dad…" She tried not to cry.

"You're afraid your dad won't like me? Is that it? Oh honey, I don't think you need to worry about that!"

"You don't know him!" She sobbed. "He's always so… judgmental! He was a New York policeman and he'll do checks on you; things like that!"

Robert hugged her and began laughing. "That's ok, there's nothing in my past for him to find sweetheart! Let him look! Let him search, prod, and check! I'll still love you and we'll still get married, ok?"

"He'll threaten you!" Katie cried. "He'll be mean and tell you he'll do things to you!"

"You mean like when he told me he would kill me if I ever hurt you?" Robert chuckled. "He just loves you and wants the best for you, Katie."

"You see? When you talked to him on the phone he said he would *kill you*!"

"Oh Katie, don't be so dramatic! He also told me to call him Jim! I'm sure he's a great guy! How about you call him and we'll ask if he minds if we drive down to see him?"

"Right now?"

"Sure, right now. You call him and we'll say hello. And if he isn't nice or you don't think we'll be welcome, we won't go, ok?"

"You promise? When he starts yelling, can we stay here?"

"What if he takes things well? Do *you* promise to give him a chance and make the trip to Florida?"

Katie smiled. "He'll be mean, don't worry. Yes, if he's nice to you on the phone, I promise to give him a chance."

She found her cell phone and dialed her parent's number. After she dialed, Robert reached for her phone and pushed a button to put it on speaker.

"Hello?" answered a female voice.

"Hi Mom. It's Katie."

"Oh honey, I was hoping you'd call again! How've you been? How's Robert?"

"We're ok Mom, he's right here with me. We have the phone on speaker so he can hear you too."

"Oh good! I was hoping to eventually get a chance to talk to him! Hello Robert. Congratulations on your engagement!"

Robert looked over at Katie. "Uh…thanks. I really haven't proposed to Katie yet, I've just promised to. Soon though, I think we're headed in the right direction."

Katie smiled and reached out to hold Robert's hand. "Mom, we were thinking about driving down to Florida for a visit after school gets out. We are going to have Jill bring us in her new car."

"That sounds wonderful! I can't wait to see you all! And we'll finally get to meet Robert in person! That sounds great!"

"I can't wait to meet you either." Robert smiled. He looked at Katie and nodded.

"Uh Mom, is…is Daddy there?" Katie asked hesitantly.

"He's out in the yard puttering around. Just a minute and I'll go get him!"

"Oh Mom, you don't have to bother him!" Katie said quickly.

"Yeah, go and get him. I'd love to say hello." Robert said as he gave Katie's hand a quick squeeze.

"I'll be right back, hold on...!"

"Robert, do you really want to do this? Do we *have* to talk to him?"

"Oh Katie, he's your Father, not some monster! Stop worrying!"

"Hello?" Jim Benson's voice boomed over the speaker.

"Hi Jim. It's Robert. How've you been?"

"Robert? That guy who says he's going to marry my daughter?"

"Yes Sir. We thought we'd call and say hello. We were also thinking about driving down to Florida with Jill to see you, if that's ok?"

"We? We who? Where's my daughter?"

"I'm right here, Daddy." Katie said timidly. "We have you on speakerphone."

"Hi honey! How are things in New York?"

"Fine Daddy, you heard Robert, right? We were thinking about driving to Florida?"

"So you and Jill are going to drive down? That's great news. I can't wait to see you! When are you going to come?"

"Robert's coming too Daddy!"

"Yeah...him. Listen Katie, are you sure about this?"

"About coming down to see you? Well, Robert said..."

"About marrying this *guy*?" Jim interrupted her. "You just seem to be moving awfully quickly with this."

"I love him Daddy."

"I see...and you're going to bring him along with you, huh?"

"Yes." She looked up at Robert, concern showing on her face. "You might like him."

"You insist on doing this, huh? I can't talk you out of it?"

"Daddy; I'm a grown woman. I know it sounds like things

are moving fast but he hasn't even proposed to me yet! He just promised, he…"

"So he just said he *might* marry you?"

Katie looked at Robert, trying to plead for help with her eyes. "Daddy…"

"No, I promised I *would* marry her." Robert finally spoke up. "But you're absolutely right, things are moving fast. So I asked her to wait until we got to know each other better before I proposed to her. To make sure we *are* in love, and want to spend the rest of our lives together. So far, we still plan on getting married."

"You sound pretty sure of yourself, young man. Are you really willing to come down here and let me have a look at you?"

"Yes Sir, I'd love you to look me over! Would you mind if we drove down for a week or so, to visit?"

"How about you give me your social security number?"

"Daddy!" Katie screamed at the phone.

"How about my birthdate also?" Robert suggested. "I was born in Anaheim, California. You can also check my military records. I did four years in the United States Air Force."

"Robert, you don't have to tell him that stuff!" Katie pleaded.

"It's ok honey, if he wants to know about me, to check up on me; that's fine! He's worried about who his daughter wants to marry! I'm fine with him looking into everything!"

"You actually don't mind…?" Jim asked.

"No, I don't mind telling you anything you want to know. When I marry Katie, I'd like your blessing. If letting you look into my past gets me that; then I'm all for it!"

"Well, so far you've been very upfront and honest with me. I do appreciate that. Maybe…maybe my daughter did good to put some faith in you? I'll be happy to meet you in person and you're welcome to come down here. When did you and my girls plan on coming?"

"Probably next week after school ends. Jill will have some time off."

"I see, and Katie's job?"

"As far as I know, they're fine with her taking some time off."

"Katie, are they really fine with this? Or did you quit your job for this guy?"

"Yes, I quit my job for him!" Katie announced. "How about that? Are you happy now Daddy? I quit my job to marry this guy that I don't really know!"

"Oh you did *not*!" Robert said, glaring at her. "Why are you telling him that?"

"Don't worry, she gets like this." Jim said. "She gets defensive when I ask her questions about who she's running around with. Then she tries to say things to bother me. So she's still employed?"

"*Yes*, she's still employed!" Robert said, trying to pull his hand away from Katie. She refused to let go. "The publisher was happy to give her some time off to spend with me! I'll talk to her boss if you want to make sure!"

"Nope, I'm quitting!" Katie giggled. "One of you is going to have to support me for the rest of my life!"

"Are you sure you want to put up with this?" Jim asked. "She can be quite a huge pain in the ass, as you can hear!"

Katie leaned over and tried to kiss Robert. "Katie, stop it! Yes Sir, I fell in love with her, and believe me, I do realize what a pain in the…Katie, get off of me!"

Jim sighed. "Well ok. I can hear her giving you problems already. You're welcome to come and stay with us for as long as you'd like. Give me a call back either when you're alone, or when my daughter can behave, to let me know when you're coming."

"Not a problem Sir, I'll talk to you later. Goodbye!" Robert reached for the cell phone and hung it up just as Katie situated herself on top of him and began kissing him.

After letting her kiss him for a bit, Robert pushed her off of him, "So we're good to go to Florida, right?"

Katie looked at him dreamily. "I love you *so much*! You were so good talking to Daddy!"

"And now you expect either me, or him, to support you, huh?"

"You were going to write me a check!" She smiled.

"I'll tell you what." He smiled back. "How about we get ready and go shopping today? We can find some nice Florida clothes, stop at the grocery store, and buy some more food before I eat all of what Jill has, ok?"

"You're going to take me shopping?" Katie asked happily. "Oh that sounds like heaven to spend the day shopping with you!"

"Well, I didn't really mean…spend the day?" He asked.

Katie giggled as she walked towards her bedroom to shower and dress.

Nine

Robert picked up a bag of potato chips and walked towards the basket. Just as he was going to drop them in, Katie grabbed them. "No honey, you don't need those."

"What?" Robert wrinkled his brow. "What do you mean I don't need them? It's just something to munch on while I write!"

"We'll find you something healthier. Come on, I think they have rice cakes over here."

"Rice cakes? I don't want rice cakes! Come on Katie, I just want a few chips!"

"You told me you wanted to get back into shape, remember? I think if we change our diets just a bit and add some exercise, we'll be back in shape in no time!"

"We, huh?"

"Of course! I'll diet with you, we can be diet buddies!"

He walked over to another shelf and grabbed a bag of frosted cookies. "This buddy wants some cookies."

"*Honey*!" Katie scolded him. "Come on, we'll get some carrot sticks, or something! You don't need these kinds of snacks!"

Robert's face darkened. "Katie, I just want a few things to snack on, I don't see the problem with me…"

Katie leaned over and kissed him softly and sweetly. "I'm just taking care of you, Robert. I want you to be healthy, ok? Can you just try some healthy snacks? For me, please?"

He took a deep breath and sighed. "Ok, I'll try the healthy snacks. But if I don't like them, can I still maybe get some chips, or cookies later?"

"We'll see." Katie smiled.

They arrived home from shopping and noticed Jill's car was parked on the street. There was also a tow truck in the driveway. Robert climbed out of Katie's car, gathered the bags from the trunk, while looking at the truck carefully.

They walked into the house as a man was handing some paperwork to Jill.

"Robert, you're just in time! I donated my old car to the local high school for their auto shop classes. Help us push it out of the garage!"

"Ah, so that's what the tow truck is here for!" He said, walking into the kitchen to put down the bags he was carrying. He came back out as Katie was coming in the door, carrying a few more bags.

"Katie," Robert smiled. "Jill donated her old car to the school!"

"School, yes that's nice. There are a few more bags in the car, honey." Katie replied, disinterested.

Robert looked at Jill and sighed, "I'll help out with the car as soon as I get the rest of the bags unloaded, ok?"

"No problem." Jill smiled, as she led the driver out to the garage.

Robert unloaded the rest of the bags and then helped the driver push Jill's car out. He watched as the driver hooked it up and waved as he pulled away with Jill's old car.

"That was a nice thing you did." He smiled at Jill.

"Well, as a teacher, I always like to do what I can for the schools here. Since you were *so nice* buying me a new car, I figured I might as well be nice, too."

"Well, I'm proud of you!"

"Robert! Honey, come inside and try on your new clothes again, so I can see how they look!" Katie called out the door.

"Tell her no!" Jill smiled. "Let her get mad again, who cares?"

"Fortunately, I care." Robert smiled. He walked back to the house and Katie.

Robert walked into the living room wearing a pair of slacks and a t-shirt. He had the t-shirt tucked into the slacks and looked fairly neat.

"So how do I look?" He asked, holding his arms out and twirling around.

"Oh honey, I wanted you to try on the other shirt; the green one and the nice tie! You shouldn't wear a t-shirt with those slacks!"

Robert took a deep breath and then untucked his t-shirt. He walked over and sat down on the couch next to Katie. "Ok, time for a talk."

"Yes sweetie, we can talk. But can you try on the shirt first? I just want to make sure it looks good with the slacks."

He reached out and took Katie's hand. "Katie, are you listening to me? I need to talk about this, ok? I mean we *really* need to talk!"

She looked into his eyes, seemingly listening to him for the first time. "Of course, you know we can talk about whatever we need to!"

"Honey...I don't want to hurt your feelings...but I hate ties. I know you realize I usually only wear them for you! But once in a while, I'd really like to wear a t-shirt again! Does this shirt really look so bad with these pants?"

Katie looked him up and down again, and then sighed. "Stand up and let me see..."

He stood up. "I'm not wearing my worn out, old jeans. These pants are nice and the t-shirt is new. Do I really look so bad?"

She looked down at the floor. "No, you don't look bad at all. I'm sorry, I just really like clothes, you know? I always want to dress you up my way. And..."

He sat back down beside her again. "I know, sweetheart. And I know you just want me to look good. But for the drive to Florida, I want to wear comfortable stuff, ok? Just for the drive? When we're about to arrive at your parent's house, I'll wear whatever you want me to. Before that though, I want to be comfortable. Is that ok?"

Katie looked back up into his eyes. She smiled widely. "Of course that's ok! You see? We can communicate! All you had to do was talk to me! But can you still try on the green shirt?"

Robert sighed and kissed her. "Yes, I'll try on the green shirt. You're lucky I love you so much!"

Katie looked at Robert while she packed. "What's wrong?" She asked.

"Nothing."

"Honey, you look so sad. We're supposed to be communicating, remember?"

"Yeah, yeah, I know. I was just wondering what we have in common?"

"You're depressed about the clothes, aren't you?"

"No Katie, I just…"

She walked over and took him by the hand. She led him back towards the suitcase she was packing. "Take a look at what I've packed for you."

"Katie, you don't need to show me more clothes."

"Will you just look?"

He looked into the suitcase and found a pile of t-shirts, neatly folded. He reached in and looked through more of the suitcase. There were sweat pants, shorts, and even his old pair of jeans.

"You packed all this stuff? Where are all the new shirts and ties?"

She put her arms around his neck and looked into his eyes. "You hate ties."

"I know, but you always want me dressed up, you always like to…"

"I want you to be happy." She smiled. She leaned in to him and gave him a long, sensual kiss. "I'll pack your nice clothes in another suitcase, with my clothes. But I thought I'd maybe only pack a few of the nice things. If we need more, we can go shopping in Florida."

"But…?"

"But nothing, our life together means we take care of each other, Robert. It doesn't just mean I get what I want all of the time. I *did* listen to you when we had our clothes talk."

He smiled at her. "You did?"

"Are you happy now?"
"Yes, you've cheered me up quite a bit."

Ten

Robert put the last suitcase into the trunk of Jill's car. He shook his head as the trunk barely closed. He walked back into the house to see if the two women had finished filling the cooler.

"Katie!" He yelled, "After Jill pulls out of the driveway, I want you to pull your car into the garage."

"We're in the kitchen, Robert!" Katie replied.

He walked into the kitchen, "Did you hear me? When Jill pulls out, put your car into the garage."

"Oh, my car will be ok where it is, I don't need to do that!"

"Katie, listen to what I'm saying, ok? Park in the garage, it'll be safer in there!"

"We live in a pretty good neighborhood honey. I'm sure my car will be fine."

He put a hand to his forehead, "Don't argue with me, ok? Will you just do what I'm telling you to do?"

"I don't see what the big deal is. What's the difference where my car is parked?"

"Oh for God's sake, just give me the keys and I'll move it myself! Just...just go back to whatever it is you're doing!"

Jill looked over at Katie. "He's right. It'll probably be safer in the garage while we're gone."

Robert looked at the cooler sitting on the kitchen table. "Is this packed up yet? What *are* you guys doing?"

"No, it's not *packed up* yet!" Katie said, as she put her hands on her hips. "Would you like to drag it off anyway? I mean you don't seem to want us to finish anything!"

His look softened as he noticed the look Katie was giving him. "Look...I just...I just want everything to be ready for tomorrow, ok? I don't mean to push you girls around, but it's going to be a long drive. I just want us to be ready for it."

"Keep working Katie," Jill said, patting her shoulder. "I'll move my car and Robert can put yours into the garage."

"Be careful Robert, it's a long drive into the garage!" Katie said nastily.

Robert sighed as he followed Jill into the living room. She found Katie's car keys and handed them to Robert.

"I just can't win with her, can I?" He asked.

Jill smiled at him. "She's under just as much stress as you are Sex Fiend, maybe even a little bit more. She's really nervous about this trip. Don't take what she says personally, ok?"

"Why is she so nervous about seeing your father?"

"I said she's nervous about the trip. Daddy is a part of it but there are more things she's worried about."

Robert followed Jill over to her car. "What else is there to be nervous about?"

"Why don't you ask her? She's told me you guys are working on your communication. Talk to her Robert, it'll be worth your time."

He stood watching while she pulled the car out of the driveway. He walked towards the curb and climbed into Katie's car. He started it, pulled into the garage, and walked back into the house. He came into the kitchen to find Katie standing over a counter, making some sandwiches. He came up behind her, put his arms around her waist. After a quick hug he kissed her cheek.

"I'm sorry I came in here demanding things. I do love you, you know? Can we talk?"

"It's ok Robert, we're fine. I know you're just anxious about the trip."

"How about you Katie? Are you really ok with this? Are you really ok with driving to see your parents?"

She turned towards him just as Jill came back into the kitchen. "Yes…I do want to do this with you, it's just…"

"If this really bothers you, we can put off the trip."

"No, it's not that! I do want to go, I'm just…there are a lot of things on my mind."

Jill sat down at the kitchen table. "Tell him, Katie."

"Tell me what?" Robert asked.

"Jill…can you please stay out of this!"

"Just *tell him*!" Jill scowled. "He deserves to know what's bothering you!"

"Fine." Katie said, turning around to face Robert. "You want to know what I'm worried about? I'm worried about money, ok? I haven't been back to work since I flew to California!"

"You don't have to worry about that! I told you, what's mine is yours! We have plenty of money sweetheart!"

"You see?" Katie said looking at Jill. "I told you he wouldn't understand! That's why I didn't bother talking to him about it!"

"Try explaining it to him, Katie. He wants to listen to you! He's trying to communicate from his side!"

"He won't like it! I didn't tell him because I didn't want him all upset before the trip. Do you have to force things?"

Robert looked confused. "I won't like what?"

"Sweetheart, it's nothing. Don't worry about it!" Katie said, putting her arms around his neck. She hugged him close. "Just know that I love you. It's not important right now."

"Are you sure? You know we can talk about anything! If something's bothering you…?"

Katie sighed. "I'm fine. I can't wait to show you off to my parents when we get there. Let's just make the trip and we'll go from there."

Robert took a deep breath and looked into her eyes. "I remember telling you everything was fine, but it really wasn't."

Katie kissed him. "It's fine Honey. It's nothing you really need to worry about."

He looked over at Jill. "Are you're sure?" Jill shrugged back at him.

Katie climbed into bed and snuggled up to Robert. He was lying on his back, staring at the ceiling.

"Are you excited about tomorrow?" She asked him.

"Yeah, I guess so." He answered quietly.

Katie caressed his cheek. "What's wrong?"

"I'm fine. I'm just thinking."

"You're still worried about what Jill said today, aren't you?"

"You said it was something I wouldn't like and you can't even talk to me about it?"

"I just didn't want you worrying about me on the trip! I didn't mean it like that! I *do* want to tell you everything!"

Robert sighed and kissed her, "Katie, if you aren't comfortable talking to me about whatever it is, then that's fine. I just really want us to be able to talk about anything."

She rolled over onto her side and gave him a serious look for a few seconds. She looked into his eyes. "I want to work. Robert, I know you're a famous author and you have a lot of money and can take care of everything...but I miss my office! I love you more than anything. If you really want me to be a stay at home wife after we get married, I can live with that, but..."

"But that's not what you really want?" He finished for her. "Katie, why would I not like that?"

"You...you said you wanted to travel! You wanted to go places and do things together! How can we travel when I have a job to go to every day?"

"You really didn't quit, did you? When you went in to your office the other day, please tell me you didn't go in there to quit!"

"No, of course I didn't quit! But I know you don't want me working anymore. And..."

"Katie, if working makes you happy, then you should work. Why wouldn't I want you to do that? Were you really afraid I wouldn't like that?"

"But you said..."

"Yes, I asked you if you wanted to travel with me! If you wanted to go places and see things while I wrote! I didn't mean you had to change your life around for me! We can always go places over a weekend! You'll get vacation time and we can take trips then! If you want to work Katie, then you should work!"

She gave him a worried look. "Are you sure? You aren't just telling me this because you know it's what I want to hear. Are you?"

"Of course I am!" He laughed. "Katie, why did you pack all those t-shirts, sweat pants, and jeans for me?"

"Because you don't like to dress up, but this is different!"

"You packed all that stuff because you knew it would make me happy to have those clothes to put on, right?"

"But Robert, if you don't want me to work…if you want to travel…?"

"Katie, what I want is for us to be together and to be happy! If working makes you happy, then I want you to work! You're right, with the money I've made from writing, neither one of us has to work. But if that's what you want to do, I'm all for it!"

Katie sighed as she looked at him. "I think I fall more in love with you every day."

Robert began laughing. "Well, assholes need all the love they can get! Good night, Little Princess."

Eleven

The alarm began to beep. Robert reached over and turned it off. He began to gently shake Katie, "Honey, it's time to get up. We need to get moving."

Katie kept her eyes closed and let out a small whine. "Five more minutes, ok?"

Robert sighed and climbed out of the bed. "I'm going to take a shower. After I get out, you have to get up!"

He walked into the bathroom yawning. He took a quick shower, dressed, and came back into the room to find Katie still in bed. He shook his head looking at her and walked down the hall to Jill's room. Jill's door was closed but he could see light coming from under the door. He knocked. "Are you up, Jill?"

"Yes, I'm up! I'll be out in a minute, ok?"

He walked back down the hall to Katie's room. Robert watched her for a minute. He leaned down, kissed her on the cheek, and tried to wake her again. She whined again. "Five more minutes please!"

He pulled her covers off. She curled up in the fetal position but still didn't get up. Finally, Robert put his arms under her legs and back and lifted her out of the bed.

"Honey, what are you doing?" She asked sleepily.

"We've got to get going, Katie. So where am I taking you to; the kitchen for coffee or the bathroom for a shower?"

She opened her eyes and gave him a sleep filled look. "I'm an adult, Robert. I can get up on my own!"

"I see, coffee. Ok, here we go." He carried her out of the room and to the kitchen. On the she put her arms around his neck and pressed her lips to his, sliding her tongue gently into his mouth. He stopped momentarily as he entered the living room, kissing her back. He seemed to forget what he was doing. A minute later he came to his senses and began moving towards the kitchen again.

Robert sat at the table while Katie made coffee. He yawned as Jill walked into the kitchen.

"Good morning, you sound like you're still as tired as I am!" Jill said with a smile.

He returned her smile, "I'll be ok. Are you going to be ok to drive?"

"Yes, I'll be fine once I get some coffee in me. Good morning, Katie."

"Morning." Katie mumbled.

"Give me your keys while you're waiting for the coffee and I'll go and check the oil and water, ok?" Robert said, holding out his hand.

"You'll…" Jill asked, cringing. "The dealership does that, right?"

"The dealership won't be in Florida when I check it again. Come on, I won't hurt anything. I'm just checking to make sure everything's fine before we leave!"

"I know you won't hurt anything, I just…" Jill looked over at Katie. "I know you bought me the car. I really appreciate it. I *do*, it's just…"

"You're just really worried, aren't you?" He asked.

"I've always struggled with cars! I've spent so much time hitching rides to work from other teachers. I now have this beautiful car, and…"

Robert reached over and took Jill by the hand. "Come on, get your keys and I'll teach you how to do this yourself."

Jill gave him a worried look but allowed him to lead her to her room to get the keys. They walked out towards the driveway and her new car.

"Ok, open the hood."

"How do I…?"

"It's just a little lever near your feet, on the driver's side." Robert said as he opened the door for Jill to get inside. She climbed in slowly and he pointed out where the hood release was. She pulled it and jumped as she heard a click. She looked up at Robert, half expecting him to laugh at her. He didn't.

"Ok, now we go around to the hood. Come on, back out of the car." He said. They walked over to the hood and Robert lifted it open.

"Don't ever touch anything here after you've been driving the car, ok? If the engine's hot and you have trouble, call me, a tow truck, or someone else. Don't touch the engine."

Jill nodded. "Ok, it's not hot now, is it?"

"No, no one's been driving it. You see? Feel the engine right here, its cool." He placed his hand on the engine. "If the car had been driven recently, I'd probably burn my hand doing this. It gets pretty hot. Ok, now you see that ring right there? Go ahead and pull it out. You won't have to pull hard, it slides right out."

Jill reached carefully for the ring Robert had pointed at and slowly pulled out the dipstick. As it came out, Robert carefully took hold of it and leaned close to her.

"You see the line that says full? The oil is on that line. That means the oil's good and we don't need to put any in. Do you also see how the oil is transparent? That means all the oil in the car is in good condition. When the oil starts to look dark, it's time to be changed."

Jill looked closely at the dipstick. "That's all there is to this?"

"Yeah, we're almost done." He slid the dipstick back into the car and pointed at a plastic container near the side of the engine. It was full of some kind of yellowish liquid.

"That's what we look at to see if there is enough water and anti-freeze. See how the liquid is near the line that says full? We're good there, too."

"Ok," Jill said, looking at him expectantly.

"And that's it!" Robert said closing the hood. "We've checked the fluids and everything's good to go! We'll check them again after we've driven for a while."

Jill put her hands on her hips. "That was it, that's all you wanted to do?"

Robert nodded. "Yeah. If it needed oil or water, we could have put some in, but being a new car, I didn't really think it would. It's always prudent to check, though."

"No one's ever bothered to show me that kind of stuff before." Jill smiled. "They've always just…done it for me. I had no idea it was so simple! You need to teach me more about cars!"

Robert laughed as they walked back towards the house. "Maybe on the trip I can show you some things. Cars aren't always as complicated as people want you to think they are."

Katie had set out napkins, coffee for her and Jill, and a glass of milk for Robert. There was also a poptart in front of each spot at the table.

She smiled as Robert and Jill came back into the kitchen. "Did we have a fun car lesson?"

"Yes we did!" Jill smiled, as she sat down and started to eat her poptart.

Robert looked pleased. "You remembered I don't like coffee!"

"Of course I did, silly!" Katie said, as she leaned over to kiss him. "We need to finish off the milk before we leave. There's a little bit left after you finish what's in your glass, ok?"

He smiled at her. "For you Katie? Anything!"

Katie sipped her coffee. "It'll be good to see mom and dad again."

"I can't wait until he sees my car!" Jill smiled. "And I also can't wait to see the look on Dad's face when I show him I can check my own oil now!"

"Yeah…" Katie looked back down at the table.

"Are you still worried about what your Father will think of me?" Robert asked.

"Kind of," Katie said, still looking down at the table. "I do want you to meet them, but…I'm just nervous, you know?"

"Everything will be fine, trust me."

"Have you told *your* family about me?" Katie asked, looking up at him.

"Yeah. I called them the other day while you were in the shower. They're anxious to meet you."

"Are they?" Katie asked smiling. "And they just accepted you telling them you were going to marry me…just like that?"

"Just like that!" Robert laughed. "Yes, but…well…my sister seemed a bit upset. It's the same, old, story. She thinks you want to marry me because of my money. My brother said he'd love to talk to you. Feel free to give him a call if you want the third degree."

They finished breakfast. Robert loaded the cooler full of sandwiches and drinks and put it in the backseat of the car. Katie climbed into the backseat with the cooler and Robert sat up front with Jill to help with directions.

"How far do you want to go today?" Jill asked, as she backed out of the driveway.

"I figured we could make it to at least Baltimore. We can find a hotel there and spend the night. We can continue on in the morning."

"Do we have reservations somewhere?" Katie asked from the backseat.

"No," Robert answered. "We can just find a place. It shouldn't be a problem."

"Oh honey, we should have reservations somewhere! What if we get there and there isn't anyplace with vacancies?"

Robert turned around with a smile. "It's Baltimore Katie, not some tiny town with only one motel. We'll be fine!"

She sat back in her seat scowling. "We need reservations! You aren't used to the city, Robert! You need to listen to me once in a while!"

Robert smiled over at Jill and reached behind him into the back seat. He felt around until he found Katie's leg, and then patted it. "There, there, honey. We'll be there before you know it!"

"Don't touch me from up there!" Katie yelled. "Communication, remember asshole?"

This only made Robert laugh harder.

They had been driving for what seemed a long time. Robert turned and looked into the back seat. "Hey Katie, grab me one of those sandwiches in the cooler please."

"I can give you a healthy snack, if you want." Katie answered, digging in the cooler. "We're starting a diet, remember? You need to eat healthy!"

She handed him a small bottle of apple juice and a rice cake. Robert took the apple juice but just looked at the rice cake.

"What the hell is that? It looks like a coaster."

"It's a rice cake, it's good for you!"

"Give me a sandwich. Those are good for me, too."

"You need to wait until lunch time for a sandwich. Just eat the rice cake."

Robert finally took the rice cake from her and looked at it. He turned it this way and that, staring at it. "I feel like I should be setting my drink on this. Here, take it back. I don't want to eat this."

"It's good for you! Just eat it, how do you know you don't like it if you won't even try it?"

"I'm not eating this! Get it out of here; it's creeping me out!"

"Just keep it up there with you. Maybe you'll change your mind later."

Robert rolled down his window and flung the rice cake out of the car. He rolled the window back up. "There, and that's that! I'll bet the birds won't even touch that thing!"

Both women reacted at the same time, screaming.

"Oh my God, you did *not* just throw something out of my car!" Jill yelled. "Are you trying to get me a ticket?"

"What is wrong with you?" Katie yelled at the same time. "How could you do something like that?"

"I told you I wasn't going to eat it!" Robert said with a shrug.

"Katie, you need to get him under control!" Jill yelled. "I'm pulling over at the next rest stop and he's riding in the back seat!"

"What?" Robert cried. "The back seat? Oh come on, I won't throw anything else out the window!"

"That's a good idea," Katie agreed, "If he wants to behave like a child, he can ride in the back seat like a child! I'll move up front!"

"I'm sorry, ok? Can we just keep going and I'll stay up here?"

Jill got off the freeway at the next exit. She pulled into a gas station and parked near the pump. "We need gas anyway. Can you be trusted to put in gas without screwing around?"

"I thought we'd try to make it to Baltimore and then gas up there?" Robert smiled.

Jill crossed her arms and continued to glare at him.

"Fine, fine, I'm putting in gas!" He sighed and climbed out of the car. He inserted a credit card and began to pump. Katie climbed into the front seat while he was out of the car. He could see the two sisters leaning close and whispering. Every few seconds they would glance in his direction.

He finished filling the car and opened the passenger door. "Ok Katie, climb back into the back seat."

"We told *you* to ride in the back because you can't behave!" Katie said with a stern look. Both women crossed their arms and stared at him. He sighed and climbed into the back seat next to the cooler. Jill pulled out of the gas station and back onto the freeway.

As they drove, Katie leaned over and began whispering to Jill. Both women began to giggle.

"What's so funny?" Robert asked. "So you're just going to sit up there and make fun of me now?"

"Don't be so paranoid!" Katie said with a smile. "Who says we're making fun of you?"

"Yeah, whatever, I'll just take a nap then." He said, leaning against the window and closing his eyes. "Wake me when we're in Baltimore."

Twelve

The car stopped and Katie was shaking him. "Robert honey, you need to wake up!"

He opened his eyes groggily. "Huh? What's going on. Are we in Baltimore?"

"Almost, we stopped in a little town on the outskirts."

He sat up and rubbed his eyes. "On the outskirts? Why didn't we go all the way into Baltimore?"

"We're not sure where to go." Katie said, looking worried.

Robert climbed out of the car and stretched. He saw Jill standing nearby.

"Good morning sleepy head. Nice to have you back with us." Jill said with a smile.

"You didn't need to stop here; just drive into the city and pull over at whatever hotel looks nice."

"I'm...I'm not really comfortable with driving in a city." Jill said, the smile falling from her lips. "I know that probably sounds stupid."

"Would you like me to drive?" Robert asked.

"Well..." Jill started. She looked over at Katie.

Robert sighed. "I'll behave. I won't throw anything out the window and I won't..." He glanced over at Katie, "I won't drive like an idiot, ok?"

"I know all about what you did in my car!" Katie said, putting her hands on her hips. "You don't need to try and hide it!"

Robert looked at Jill. "I thought you said you weren't going to tell her?"

"We're sisters stupid. Can we trust you to drive, or not?"

"Yes, you can trust me." Robert said holding out his hand. Jill handed them to him and they all climbed back in the car. Robert adjusted the seat and pulled back onto the freeway.

As they drove through the city, Jill spoke up. "You know, a bath would really feel good after this drive! Can you get us a place with a bathtub?"

"That *does* sound good! Yes honey, get us a place with a bathtub!"

Robert began laughing. "Most hotels have bathtubs, girls. I'm sure where ever we stay will have a bathroom!"

"But they don't all have tubs, do they?" Jill asked. "Some places just have showers."

Robert pointed to a building off in the distance, "Look at that, a Marriott Hotel in Baltimore! I love those, are you ladies good with staying there?"

Jill and Katie looked at each other and then nodded. He pulled off the freeway and into Baltimore. After weaving a couple of streets, he arrived at the hotel. He pulled up at the main entrance and stopped the car.

"Ok, you two stay here and watch the car. I'll go and get us a room, ok?"

"We should come with you!" Katie said eagerly.

"No, we're in a strange city. I want you two to stay in the car. It won't take me long. Just hang out and watch things. I'll be right back." He climbed out of the car and headed inside.

He walked up to the front desk and was greeted by a smiling clerk, "Good evening Sir, how can I help you tonight?"

"Do you have any vacancies?"

"Yes Sir, we have rooms available. Will it be just you staying with us tonight?"

He glanced back towards the entrance. "Uh no...there's three of us, myself and two women. Do your rooms by chance have bathtubs in them?"

"The standard rooms have a shower with a small tub. We do have a suite available that has an extra large bathtub. It's one of our larger rooms though and it has a Jacuzzi. It's $1,625 a night."

"How many beds does it have?"

"There is one king sized bed in the master bedroom and queen bed in a separate bedroom."

"Ok, that sounds good. I'll take that for tonight." He handed the clerk a credit card from his wallet.

"Mr. Wacaster?" The clerk smiled. "Any relation to the author?"

Robert looked up in surprise, "Yeah, I am the author. You've read my book?"

"You're the guy who wrote *The Treaty*, right? Oh, I can't wait for the movie!"

Robert smiled warmly. "Thanks, I appreciate talking to people who like my book. I've started the sequel."

He made small talk with the clerk as she checked him in. She handed him the keys and he walked towards the entrance. He glanced in a nearby shop and saw little pink bottles. He walked in to take a closer look. They were bottles of bubble bath. He bought two and had the clerk put them in separate bags. He went back to the car.

He climbed in the driver's side. "Ok, the parking garage is right around the corner. I bought you each something." He handed Jill and Katie the bags.

"What's this?" Jill asked, opening the bag.

Katie gasped. "It's bubble bath! So you got us a room with a bathtub in it?"

"Bathtub *and* Jacuzzi." Robert mumbled.

He parked the car and climbed out. Katie climbed out and walked over to him.

"Are we taking all the luggage up with us?" She asked.

"Just take what you need, ok?" Robert answered. "We're only here overnight. Bathing suits, pajamas, whatever you need for when we get up in the morning."

"Oh, most of my stuff is in our big bag." Katie said with a smile.

"I need the stuff in my suitcase, too." Jill said. Both women stood smiling at Robert. After a large sigh, he pulled the two large suitcases out of the trunk. He led them into the hotel and to the elevators. Their room was on the top floor.

Katie gave Robert a worried look as the elevator went up. "How much was this room?"

"Oh, don't worry about that! If it helps us relax after that long drive, it's worth it."

"But how much was it?" Katie persisted. "We need to save our money. You shouldn't be just throwing money around, Robert!"

"Trust me, I have plenty of money."

"New York is expensive, Robert! I'm going to have to set a budget for you!"

The elevator doors opened and they walked to end of the hall. Robert opened the door and hauled the luggage inside. Both women gasped.

"Oh my God, is this really our room?" Katie asked.

Jill walked into the bathroom and came back out saying, "Dibs on the bathtub first, Katie!"

"Well that's not fair. It's my fiancé who paid for the room! I should get the first bath, right Robert?"

Robert walked over to a large window and looked down at a Jacuzzi. "I don't care who does what, I'm climbing into this hot tub and relaxing! Sit in the hot tub with me Katie. After Jill's done, you can take yours."

She walked over and took a hold of his hands. "Honey, we really do need to start saving money, ok? We're going to be married. Can you please ask me next time before you spend a lot of money like this?"

"It's only $1,625 a night, Katie. For one night, it's fine."

"But can we just talk about things? Please?"

He hugged her close. "Of course; I didn't realize it would bother you when I spent money. I'll be happy to talk to you before I do anything like this again, ok?"

She hugged him back and held him close. After she released him, she looked into his eyes, "I shouldn't do that to you, should I?"

"Do what?"

"Nag you about money? You know how to handle your own money. You always know what to do."

"You just worry about things, don't you?" He asked, kissing her.

"Of course I do! I just want us to be happy."

He began to take off his shirt. "We are happy, aren't we? I know I am! Why don't you run into the bathroom and look at the bathtub Jill's so excited about?"

She gave him a worried look and then kissed him again. "I really do love you. You really are going to marry me, right?"

"Of course I am! Don't you worry about that!"

She smiled and walked towards the bathroom where Jill had already begun to fill the bathtub.

Katie came back out of the bathroom to see Robert climbing into the Jacuzzi.

"You've put your suit on already?" She asked with a shy smile.

"No, no suit." Robert smiled back at her.

"Then what are you wearing? You didn't just get in there in your underwear, did you?"

He continued to smile widely at her.

"Oh my God! You mean…you…?" Katie gasped.

"I've got a seat right here next to me for you, sweetheart!"

"*Robert*, Jill's here in the room with us! You should at least put on your bathing suit!"

He stood up in the tub and held out his arms. "She's in the bathtub Katie, we have the Jacuzzi all to ourselves! At least for now!"

Someone knocked on the hotel room door and Katie jumped. Robert stepped out of the Jacuzzi and wrapped a nearby towel around him. He found his wallet and pulled out some cash and then walked over to the door. He opened the door and let in a room service clerk with a cart.

"Just park it anywhere." Robert smiled. Katie covered her mouth with both hands, a shocked look on her face. Robert handed the clerk the cash and walked him out of the room. He walked over and pulled a large, silver, cover off the cart. There was a large plate with strawberries, whipped cream, and a bottle of sparkling cider.

"There we go. A tub, some strawberries, and something to drink!" He smiled.

"Oh my God, how much did that cost?" Katie asked, still looking shocked.

"Want me to wheel the cart into the bathroom and throw some strawberries into Jill's bath water?"

Katie still looked upset. "Oh Robert..."

He walked over and hugged her. "Katie, stop worrying about money, ok? I called for this while you were in the bathroom. When we get to Florida, I'll call my accountant. You can talk to her and put together any kind of budget you want for me, ok?"

Katie hugged him back. "I'm sorry I worry so much. I'm just not used to having a lot of money. We weren't really ever poor, but we just...we just never had a lot of money to just spend like this."

"I really never did either. I'll let you talk to the accountant and you'll feel better after that, ok?"

She smiled up at him. "I trust you, Robert. You don't need to prove anything to me. I know it's silly for me to worry and you should probably just ignore me..."

"I'll never ignore you." He smiled back. "You're a smart woman Katie. Don't think that you can let me do whatever I want. Sometimes you might need to take charge. Worry all you like!"

She looked down at the towel he was wearing. "Can you *please* put something on?"

Jill walked out of the bathroom wearing a robe with the Marriott logo on it. Robert was sitting on a small couch in the living room and watching TV. He had put on a pair of pajamas and was munching on the strawberries.

"Katie! Jill's done with the bathtub. Do you still want a bath?" He yelled. Katie walked out of the smaller bedroom.

"You're done already?" She asked, smiling at Jill.

"I could have stayed in there forever!" Jill smiled back. "But I know you wanted a turn. We do need some sleep if we want to get an early start tomorrow."

Robert began to get up from the couch. "Do you want me to run the bath for you?"

Katie walked over and kissed him. "I can run my own bath sweetheart but thank you." She walked into the main bedroom and the large bathtub.

"Don't take all night, Jill wants to go to bed!" Robert yelled.

"I'm in the smaller bedroom, right?" Jill asked, looking confused.

"Nope, you get the big one with the tub." Robert said, as he sat back down and returned to eating the strawberries.

"Oh, I don't need the big room. You and Katie should be in there!"

"She's already turned down the bed in the smaller room for us. The big one's yours, no big deal."

"You don't need to do that. I'll be fine in the smaller one."

"You didn't need to drive us to Florida either. I'll roust her out of the tub in a bit and you enjoy the big room, ok? Want some strawberries?"

Jill sat down on the small couch next to him. "You didn't have to spend this kind of money. A regular room would have been fine. You don't need to keep trying to impress us."

He handed her a strawberry. "You wanted a tub, this room has a tub. Don't worry about things. You and Katie are so worried about how much I spend. It's not that big of a deal, I promise you!"

She looked at him for a minute and then ate the strawberry. "Fine, if you say so! I still think a regular room would have been fine, though."

Thirteen

Robert opened his eyes sleepily as the phone began to ring. He was lying on his side with Katie's arm around him. He reached over and picked up the receiver.

"Uh…yeah?"

"Good morning Sir. This is your six o'clock wake up call."

Robert sighed and hung up. He rolled over onto his back and Katie snuggled up against his chest. He kissed her.

"It's time to get up honey. We have to get back on the road."

Katie kissed his cheek and then relaxed back onto his chest.

"Come on Katie, we need to get up."

"No," she whined. "Can't we just stay here another night? I don't want to get up. It's so nice here!"

He tossed the covers away and pulled out of her arms. "Sorry baby, we need to go." He sat up, yawned, and walked into the smaller bathroom. By the time he came out, she was sitting on the edge of the bed watching him.

"Are you sure we have to leave? I'm sure Jill would be willing to spend another night here?"

"That would be another $1,625. You're good with that? Spending that kind of money and putting off your parents?"

Katie sighed and looked at the floor. "No, I guess not."

"Are you still worried about your father?"

"You just don't understand what he's like!" Katie said looking up at him. "He once told me I shouldn't date until I was forty!"

"Would you like to wait eight more years before we get married?" He asked with amusement.

"That's not funny!" Katie said, glaring at him. She got off the bed and walked past him to the bathroom.

Robert pulled on some sweat pants, walked to the larger room, and peeked inside. Jill was already up and dressed.

"Come on in. I'm decent." She said as she caught sight of him.

"You're up already and almost ready to go? I'm proud of you!" Robert said with a smile.

"I'm excited about getting to Florida. I was up before the wake up call. I heard the phone ring just as I was getting out of the shower. I figured it would help if I was ready early so you can deal with Katie."

"She really is worried about your father." Robert said, looking at the ground. "Do you really think he'll be that hard on me?"

"Well, Katie's always been his little princess. I guess I was too, but Katie was always…really close with Dad. He's just… picky about who he wants around his daughters. I don't even know if I'm saying this right?"

"Well, all we can do is show up and see what happens."

"So far, I think he'll be fine with you. You've been taking such good care of his babies, how could he not like *you*?" Jill giggled.

"Yeah." Robert mumbled. He walked back to his room and heard the shower running. At least Katie was up and moving.

They checked out of the hotel and were back on the road. Robert sat in the back seat as the two sisters, once again, sat up front. They continued along the highway and Robert's phone began to ring.

"Hello?"

"Hello Robert! Are you still in New York?" It was Paul.

"Pauly!" Robert said happily. "I've been meaning to call you! You got the first two chapters, right?"

"Yeah, I've got them. I'm still working them through. You didn't answer my question, are you still in New York?"

"Kind of…"

"Kind of? What's kind of?"

"Well…I…ah…Katie and I decided we wanted to get married, and…"

"You got *married*? And you didn't invite Kelly and me?"

"No, we didn't get married *yet*! But I promised I'd propose eventually and now we're on the way to meet her parents in Florida."

"Oh thank God! You scared me there for a minute! You're flying down to meet her parents now?"

"Well, we're driving. I think we just left Maryland."

Katie leaned around to look into the backseat. "Who are you talking to?"

"It's Paul," he said, glancing up at her. "She seems a bit afraid her father won't like me. I talked to him on the phone and I think things will be ok."

"I see. Well say hi to Katie for me! I wondered what was going on, I haven't heard from you since you left California! Well, except for the pages you've emailed me."

"Yeah, well…we've been learning to be a couple."

"I remember those days." Paul laughed. "Have you had a fight yet?"

"Yeah, but we worked things out. It's taking getting used to."

"I'll bet it is! Kelly will be really excited when she hears you're getting married! Have you set a date yet?"

"No, I haven't even proposed yet! Soon, though. I'll let you know as soon as we figure it out, ok?"

"Ok. Well, I'd better let you go. I can hear Kelly calling for me. Give me a call when you get more time!"

"I will, I'll probably call you from Florida. Take care, Paul."

"You, too! Bye."

"So how is he?" Katie asked, leaning back towards Robert.

"He's ok. I forgot to tell him we were planning on getting married."

"But you've told him now that he's called you, right?"

"Of course, don't worry honey, it's not a secret!" Robert laughed.

"You can keep it a secret if you want. Just keep your promise and ask me."

He leaned up and kissed her cheek. "I'll ask you. Just give me a bit more time, ok?"

She turned back around in her seat smiling. Robert could only guess what was going through her mind.

They drove all day. The sun was setting below the horizon as they arrived at a small two story house in Tampa. All three of them were exhausted from the ride. Their parents came out and waited for them by the front door.

Katie climbed out and helped Robert out. She took his hand and walked up to her parents. She neared them, let go of his hand, and ran to hug her father. She hugged him tightly and then hugged her mother. Jill hugged them both too. Katie turned around, grabbed Robert's hand, and led him up to her parents. She suddenly felt like she was sixteen again, bringing home her first boyfriend.

"Mom, Dad, this is Robert!"

Robert held out his hand politely and Katie's mother shook it. After a few seconds of staring at him, her father finally reached out and shook his hand too.

"Well, let's go inside, we can get the luggage later. We will get you settled in first." Her father said quietly. He led them into the house and sat himself down in his chair in the living room. He gestured for Katie and Robert to sit on a nearby couch. Katie held Robert's hand tightly. Jill and Katie's mother sat nearby in a couple other chairs.

"So...you're the guy who thinks he's going to marry my daughter?" He asked, looking at Robert.

"Well..." Robert started.

"Yes! We've decided we're going to get married, Daddy! I told you that!" Katie answered.

"And you can support my daughter, correct?"

"He's a best selling author, Daddy! Of course he can support me!"

Robert glanced up at her. "Katie..."

"And how long have you two been going out?"

"Daddy, we've been together more than a month, if you must know! And Robert says that…"

"Can Robert answer for himself?"

Robert gave Katie's hand a squeeze and smiled up at her. "Relax Katie. He just wants to ask me some questions."

"He wants to make you out to be a bad guy!" Katie said turning to him. "He's always so…over protective! I'm a grown woman now!"

Jim looked at his daughter and sighed. "Katherine, can you, Jill, and your mother go upstairs and get settled in."

"Come on Robert." Katie said, getting up.

"I need to stay here." He answered, looking up at her. "You go ahead, I'll be fine."

Katie looked at him and seemed almost close to tears. Robert nodded at her, and as she passed her father, she whispered, "Please be nice to him?"

After the women walked upstairs and out of the room, Jim looked back at Robert. "Sometimes I *am* over protective when it comes to my daughters. But so far, when we've talked on the phone, you seem like you have a good head on your shoulders. Do you mind having a frank talk with me?"

"Not at all," Robert answered. "I don't have anything to hide."

"Fine. I was a cop for 25 years. I'd like to think I'll know if you aren't being truthful with me. Katie seems to think your writing can support the two of you, is this true?"

"Yes, I'm financially stable. I made enough on my first book to just stay home and write professionally now. I don't need to work anymore."

"I see, and how much did you make, if you don't mind my asking?"

"I receive a royalty check each month. The more my books sell, the more I make. My first book sold over three hundred thousand copies. I sold the film rights. I'll be able to support her."

"Forgive me if I sound naive, but how much is that? How much do you actually have from your book?"

"Right now from the movie deal and the books that were sold is somewhere around eight million in the bank."

"And so that's how you were comfortable with buying Jill a new car, huh?"

"Well...that just happened. Her starter went out and...I just thought it was the right thing to do."

"Ok, have you ever hit Katie?"

"*No I haven't ever hit Katie*! Why would you even ask me that? I love her!"

"Ok, ok, don't get all riled up! I'm just a worried father! I don't want her around someone who hits her!"

"I don't hit her! Sheesh, is this going to be our entire conversation? I can support her, I love her, I don't cheat, I'm not some maniac, and yes I promised to marry your daughter!"

"Have you slept with her?"

"Yes, I've slept with her."

"Sex, I meant have you had sex with her?"

Robert sighed. "Yes, we've had sex. We use protection, but we have had sex, ok?"

"I wanted you in separate rooms, but my wife convinced me you could be trusted if I let you stay in the same room together. I have three separate beds, though. I expect you and Katie to sleep in separate beds under my roof. No sex here until you're married. Am I clear on that?"

"Separate beds, Katie won't like that." Robert said, scratching his head.

"I'll have a talk with my daughter about it, but *you* understand me, right?"

"I'll talk to her. She won't like it, but it's something we'll work out. I'll respect the rules of your house."

"I'll make sure she understands." Jim said again.

"No need, I can talk to her. I'll get the message across."

Jim began to laugh. "You think you can just tell her no and she'll listen, huh?"

"I think she'll listen to me, yes."

"She's a stubborn girl. I don't think you know who you're dealing with. When she doesn't listen to you, let me know. I'll make up the couch for you!"

Jill came walking down the stairs. "And how's our little chat going? Did you get the *no sex under my roof talk* yet?"

"You be quiet!" Jim yelled. "What are you doing down here so soon?"

"I need my bag. I have a few things to show Mom."

"We can help you with the bags." Jim said standing up. "Come on Writer, let's go." Robert stood up and followed him outside to the car. As her father approached her new car, Jill smiled widely.

"What do you think? I designed it on a computer and then it was delivered to the dealership for me to pick up!" Jill said proudly. "I named him Bennie!"

Jim looked the car up and down. "It's very nice sweetheart! I'll check your oil and water later for you."

"I know how to check the oil and water *myself*, Daddy!" Jill smiled. "Robert taught me!"

He glared at Robert. "Did he now?" Jill opened the trunk. Robert and Jim began to pull out the luggage. Katie and her mother met them at the door. Katie followed Robert closely as they went upstairs. Robert glanced around the small room and saw three small beds. He put the bags down and Katie took hold of his hand. Robert looked at her and could see how nervous she still was. He smiled and kissed her.

"Everything's fine." He whispered.

"Well, I'll leave you two to get settled. When you're done and if you aren't too tired, come back downstairs. We can visit some more before bedtime!" Jim said with a smile.

"Thanks, I'd like that." Robert said, returning his smile. "Once Katie and I are settled in, we'll be back down."

Jill watched Robert and Katie and let out a small giggle. She found several books in her suitcase and followed her parents downstairs, leaving them alone.

"He's crazy if he thinks we're going to sleep in separate beds!" Katie said when they were finally alone.

Robert took a deep breath and lay back against a pillow on one of the small beds. He didn't say a word.

"I mean, if he thinks he can tell *us*…we'll just go to a hotel! I mean, we *are getting married*! A husband and wife shouldn't be sleeping in separate beds!"

Robert took another deep breath and then quietly said, "No."

"Excuse me?" Katie asked, moving to lie down next to him.

"No, Katie. We won't go to a hotel, and we can't sleep together here; separate beds."

"You're going to let him tell you what we can, and can't do together? Robert…"

He sat up on the bed and pulled her up to sit next to him. "Katie, listen to me, ok?"

"No, you need to listen to *me*; you shouldn't be letting him…"

Robert put one finger up to Katie's lips. She instantly stopped talking.

"*Listen to me*, ok? For right now, your father accepts me. He accepts that I love you and that we plan to get married. We are staying in *his* house. He has asked me for us to sleep in separate beds and to not have sex under his roof until we're married. I've agreed to that, ok?"

"But I didn't agree…" Katie said, sounding near tears. Robert held up one finger again and she stopped.

"I'll be right here in the bed next to you. It'll be fine. I know you're used to sleeping next to me and you like to cuddle. On this trip we will respect his wishes, ok? When we go downstairs, we can sit on the couch and cuddle while we talk to your mom and dad. But up here, we do things *his* way. When we're married, I'll insist we get to sleep together, but for now, we can't."

"What if I can't sleep without you?"

"I'll be right here, honey."

"Maybe if we just wait until…"

"No." Robert said simply.

Katie gave him a sour look. "You aren't going to let me talk you out of this, are you?"

"When I marry you, I'd like your dad to be at the wedding, and happy. Is that too much to ask?"

"Would you settle for him at the wedding; but cranky?" Katie smiled.

Robert laughed and took her by the hand. "Come on, it's time to visit!"

They walked downstairs to the living room to find Jill, Jim, and Emily, his wife sitting around the coffee table chatting. Robert and Katie sat down in two empty chairs next to each other.

"Well, well," Jim said with a smile. "You decided to come down and visit with us after all, huh? I'm glad to see the two of you!"

"Hi Mom, hi Daddy." Katie said quietly.

"We were just wondering what this wedding of the century was going to cost me?" Jim asked.

"Oh, I have plenty of money. I don't think you really need to…" Robert started.

"Nonsense," Jim interrupted him. "If my daughter's getting married, I'm paying for the wedding! No discussion about that, I don't care how much you have! I take care of my girls!"

"Jim…" Emily said quietly, putting a hand on his arm.

He turned to her with a serious look. "I'm paying Em, that's the end of it!" He looked back at Katie. "How about you give me a head start and tell me where you plan to have it?"

"Oh…ah…we really haven't discussed any of the details yet. I just promised. I haven't even gotten to the proposal yet." Robert said, leaning back in his chair.

"Oh, is that right? I guess you don't know my daughter as well as you thought you did then, huh?"

Jill began to giggle and Katie shot her a nasty look.

"We just haven't talked about it yet, Daddy! We have plenty of time!"

"But you know where you want to have the wedding, don't you?"

"Well…" Katie said, looking nervously at Robert.

"You already know where you want to get married?" Robert asked

"You're kidding, right?" Jim laughed. "Probably from the time you first met she's known! I'll bet she even has the napkin colors for the reception planned out already!"

"Don't exaggerate!" Katie frowned. "You make it sound like I pushed myself on Robert just for a wedding!"

Jim leaned back in his seat just as Robert was doing. "Ok, ok, I'll let it go for now. I was just asking! You know how hard it is to reserve places in New York, sometimes?"

"And the napkins need to match the bride's maid's dresses!" Katie said quietly.

Jill began to giggle again and Jim turned back to her. "I'm sorry sweetheart. I didn't mean to interrupt you. What was it you were saying about your kids?"

"That they all made me cards for the last day of school. It was during art time and I didn't even tell them to! It was so sweet! But Katie's the one getting married. Go ahead and embarrass her more if you want to, Dad."

"I don't embarrass her!" He looked over at Katie. "Do I?"

"Well…I don't know what you said to Robert earlier, but…"

"But what?"

Robert turned towards her. "Yes Katie, but what?"

After a quick look in Robert's eyes, Katie crossed her arms, "But nothing. I still don't like it, though!"

Robert began to laugh. "Yeah, well it was a long drive here from Baltimore. I hope no one thinks I'm being rude, but I think I'm going to hit the hay."

As he stood up, Katie jumped up and grabbed his hand. "Yes, *both* of us will hit the hay!"

Jim stood up and held out his hand. "Well, I'm glad we had our chat. It was nice to meet you. Do you need me to talk to her?"

Robert shook his hand. "No, we had a chat already. She's not happy, but she'll follow the rules." He looked over at Katie, "*Won't you?*"

"Maybe; maybe not!" She smiled. As they went upstairs, Jill followed.

Robert walked to the bathroom and put on his pajamas. He walked back into the bedroom and sat down on his bed. Jill sat down next to him as Katie stepped out to use the bathroom.

"So I guess you and our dad are getting along ok, huh?"

"Yeah, so far he's been pretty cool about me marrying Katie."

"Just no sleeping together under *his roof*? How did you get Katie to go along with that?"

"We just talked it out. She can be reasonable when she has to!"

Jill began to giggle. "Sure she can!"

Katie came back into the room and sat down on the other side of Robert, "How about I just lay here with you and we talk for a bit?"

"Go over to your bed, Katie!" Robert scowled. "Rules are rules! You can talk to me from over there if you want."

She kissed him on the lips. "You *are* marrying me!"

Robert laughed as she walked back over to her bed. "Yes honey, I *am* marrying you! Get some sleep. Things will look better in the morning!"

Fourteen

Robert opened his eyes as daylight streamed through the window. Katie and Jill were still asleep. He quietly got up, pulled on some sweat pants and a t-shirt, and walked to the bathroom. He decided not to go back to bed so he picked up his shoes and went downstairs. He heard some noise in the kitchen and found Jim and Emily sitting at a small dining room table.

"Good morning!" Emily smiled. "Would you like some coffee?"

"Oh, no thank you. I'm not much of a coffee person."

"Are Katie and Jill up?"

"No ma'am, they're still asleep. I woke up and came downstairs. I thought I might take a quiet walk outside, if you don't mind?"

"If the girls get up soon, we can all have breakfast together!" Jim said happily.

"Yeah, that sounds good. I won't be long outside. I'll get them up when I am finished." Robert answered. He walked through the living room and out the front door.

Robert took in a deep breath. It was a humid and foggy morning. He noticed several dark clouds on the horizon and wondered if it would rain. He looked at the house next door and saw man staring at a Mercedes. The front tire was flat. Robert walked towards him.

"Got a flat this morning, huh?"

"Good morning!" The man smiled. "I don't suppose you know how to change a tire?"

"Yeah, don't you?"

"Well…I've just…you see, I'm a psychologist and well…?"

"Would you like some help changing it?" Robert grinned, seeing how upset the man looked.

"Would you mind? I feel so embarrassed about this! I really don't have much experience with cars!"

"Not a problem," Robert smiled and walked over to the Mercedes trunk. "Let's see if you have a lug wrench and jack in your trunk?"

The man opened the trunk and held out his hand. "I'm Dr. Ben Richards, clinical psychologist. Are you my new neighbor?"

Robert shook Ben's hand. "No, I'm here visiting my fiancé's parents. Did you just move in?"

"Yes. I've started a family therapy practice and got my office set up. I was about to go in. I came out and found the flat tire!"

Robert pulled the jack, lug wrench, and a tiny tire out of the trunk. He began to loosen the lug nuts on the flat tire.

"Looks like you've only got a doughnut, Doc. After I put it on, you'll need to head to a tire shop and get your flat fixed."

"A...doughnut?" Ben asked.

Robert began jacking up the car. "Yeah...you shouldn't really be driving very far on one of these. A tire shop can fix your flat rather quickly."

"Oh...ah...do...do you know where a tire shop is?"

Robert pulled the flat off the car and pushed the doughnut in place. "No, but I'm sure I can find out where one is for you. Did you want me to ride down there with you?"

"Oh, I was hoping you'd offer to do that!" Ben smiled, sounding relieved. "I'm usually good with people but cars just confound me!"

Robert let the jack back down and began laughing. "I see. You sound like my fiancé. I'll go ask my future father-in-law where a tire place is, get my wallet, and I'll be right back, ok?"

He walked back into the house and found Jim. "Hey, where's the nearest tire shop? You neighbor has a flat and I'm going to help him get it fixed."

"You've met the neighbor? We've been wondering who moved in next door! How about I come along and show you were the tire place is?" Jim asked.

"Sure, I don't think he'll have any problem with that!"

The two men walked out the door and back to where Ben was waiting.

Fifteen

"Good morning Mom, where's Daddy?" Jill asked.

"Oh, you just missed him! I guess Robert met the new neighbor and he had a flat tire on his car. Your dad and Robert went with him to a tire shop."

"You have a new neighbor?" Jill asked. "Are they still out there?"

"They might be," Emily smiled. "I think you missed them!"

Jill walked out the front door and looked across to the other house. She could see Robert and her father talking with a handsome man in a suit. She watched the three men but her attention was focused on the neighbor. She just couldn't seem to take her eyes off of him. Robert looked over, saw her, and waved. He signaled for her to come over. Jill was so nervous she ran back into the house.

"Are they still out there, honey?" Emily asked.

"Uh…yeah, they're…is Katie up? I need to see Katie!" She turned and ran up the stairs.

Katie was sitting up on her bed yawning as Jill hurried into the bedroom. "Katie, Katie, you have to help me!"

"Help you with what? Where's Robert?"

"You brought a bunch of make up with you, right?"

"Make up? You need make up?" Katie asked curiously. "You hardly use any at all. Why do you want some of mine now?"

"I just…well, maybe you could help me out with a few things? Maybe help fix my hair and do my make up? You always look so good!"

"Why do you want me to do your make up and hair? Where's Robert? Something's going on, isn't it?"

"No, nothing's going on! I just…I just want to look really good, and thought maybe…will you help me?"

Katie rubbed her eyes and walked towards the bathroom, "Yes Jill, let me take a shower and I'll do your make up and hair."

"And maybe loan me a dress?"

Katie stopped in front of the bathroom door. "A dress? What is going on? You never want to borrow clothes from me!"

"I just want to look good!" Jill said again.

Katie crossed her arms and looked at Jill.

"Ok, fine! Robert and Daddy were out talking to the neighbor. He's really handsome! They were trying to wave me over but I wanted to look good before I met him! Are you happy now? Go ahead and make fun of me!"

Katie broke out into a huge smile. "You like the neighbor? Oh Jill, that's so great! Of course I can loan you a dress! We'll have you all fixed up in no time! I'll make sure Robert takes you over there and introduces you properly! I'm so happy for you! He's not married, is he?"

"Oh, I didn't think about that! Oh no, I hope he isn't!"

Katie hugged her. "Don't worry, we'll just ask Robert. He'll find out everything for us! Just a minute and we'll start on your hair!"

Sixteen

Robert and Jim walked in the front door chatting away. "I hate those things," Robert was saying. "I know people want to make money, but geez! Cars should come with spare tires, not doughnuts like that!"

"Have you checked Jill's car?" Jim asked. "We should see if she has a full sized spare. If not, we need to make sure she gets one."

Katie and Jill came down the stairs. Katie was first and was wearing a blue dress. Jill was behind her wearing a bright red sun dress. Both women had feathered their hair out and seemed to be dressed up.

"Wow, you guys look great!" Robert said, as he caught sight of them. "Are we going out for breakfast, or something?"

"Where is he?" Katie asked.

"Where's who?" Robert asked, looking around.

"The new neighbor. Mom said you guys were helping him with his car! Didn't you invite him back for breakfast?"

"We just showed him where the tire place was," Jim answered. "Then he dropped us off and had to go."

"Oh…we thought…" Jill said sadly.

"Well, is he coming back soon? Could we maybe invite him over for lunch? Welcome him to the neighborhood?" Katie asked.

Robert walked over and kissed her. "Don't worry about him, he's gone. I'm sure he'll be back though, he's not very good with cars."

"Are we ready to eat?" Jim asked.

"Yes, breakfast is ready." Emily smiled. "If everyone wouldn't mind coming into the dining room. We put the leaf into the table so it should be big enough."

Jim sat down at the table and looked at Robert. "I'm proud of you for helping him like that, it showed me a lot."

Robert smiled. "Thanks. I really appreciated you coming along and helping too!"

Jim smiled up at Emily. "This one's not too bad. He just might work out."

"What are we having?" Robert asked, ignoring the comment. He sat down next to Katie. "I'm starving!"

"Oh…uh…well, I made some bacon and eggs. Katie said you were on a diet and she has something special for you."

"Special, I like special." Robert smiled.

"So, is he single?" Katie asked.

"Is who single?"

"The new neighbor. Did you ask if he's married?"

Robert turned and glared at her. "Are you dumping me already? You want to know if the neighbor is *single*? What the hell?"

Emily set a small fruit cup in front of both Robert and Katie.

"No, I'm not dumping you!" Katie smiled innocently. "It was just a question! You don't need to get all bent out of shape over it!"

Robert picked up a spoon and wolfed down his fruit. "Ok, that was good, what's next?"

"You may have a glass of milk next, unless you want to eat the *cup*?" Katie scowled at him. "Did you have to wolf it down like that? That was your breakfast! We're on a diet, remember? Besides, you didn't answer my question; is he single?"

Jim smiled and let out a small laugh.

"If you aren't dumping me, why do you care if someone else is single? And what do you mean that was my breakfast? Don't I get any bacon and eggs?"

Emily set a plate of bacon and eggs down in front of both Jim and Jill. They began to eat quietly, watching Robert and Katie.

"I just wanted to know! Maybe he has a wife we need to invite over, too?"

"Actually, I think he has four wives, doesn't he Jim?" Robert said, looking over at Katie's father.

Jim quickly shoveled a fork full of eggs into his mouth and shrugged.

"You just think you're so clever, don't you?" Katie scowled. "Daddy, is he married, or not?"

Jim looked at Robert, and then back over at Katie. "We just went with him to get his tire fixed, honey. We didn't really…well…"

Robert looked hungrily at Jim's plate. "Can I maybe have a piece of bacon?"

"No, you may *not* have bacon!" Katie shouted.

"You'd better tell her what she wants to know," Jim smiled. "Or you'll pay for it. She doesn't let go of things easily."

Robert looked over at Katie as she folded her arms and glared at him. "Ok, yes. If it matters, he's single. Are you happy now?"

"Single with a girlfriend, single and engaged, what kind of single?"

Robert looked over at Jim, who began laughing. "Don't look at me, Writer! You're the one marrying her! The easiest solution is to just tell her whatever she wants to know!"

"He's single. Single, as in no girlfriend, no wife, and no pets. I'm not even sure he has any plants, ok? He's a psychologist. After I helped with his tire he said he'd be happy to give us a free session of marriage counseling. I told him I'd have to ask you first! We helped him get his tire fixed and he went to work, ok? That's all I know about him!"

"He's a psychologist?" Jill asked dreamily.

"A head shrinker. He shrinks people's heads to the size of oranges." Robert joked.

"That's all you know?" Katie asked, sounding a little less upset.

Robert sighed. "Can I change the subject for a minute? While we were going to the tire place, your dad showed me this huge mall nearby. He suggested you might want to go shopping today? There are a few jewelry stores. Maybe we can look at engagement rings?"

At the mention of rings, Katie's face instantly changed. "Really? You want to ring shop today?"

"Yeah, I thought we could drive over there. Would you like to come along with us, Jill? Maybe drive us over?"

Jill still seemed to be off in a fog. "A psychologist..."

Katie leaned over and began to whisper to Jill. After a few seconds, Jill began whispering back. They both glanced at Jim and Robert.

Jim gave Robert a suspicious look. "They're whispering, good luck today!"

"Is that bad? What do you mean good luck?"

Jim turned to Emily, who smiled back at him. "They've been fighting since they were little. When they get together on something; when you find them whispering together, it's always trouble!"

Robert watched the two women whisper for a few more moments and then spoke up. "Hey Katie, are you sure I can't maybe have one piece of bacon? Just one? I'm taking you shopping!"

Katie stopped whispering. "No, no bacon! It's not good for you! Daddy shouldn't even be eating it!"

"Look, since we're going shopping, how about I give you a hundred bucks for one piece?"

As he pulled out his wallet, Katie held out her hand. "May I see that, please?"

"What, my wallet?"

"Yes."

"Uh...why do you want to see my wallet?"

She kept her hand held out and just glared at him. After a few seconds, he handed the wallet over to her.

As she began searching through it, her eyes widened, "Oh my God, Robert! What are you doing with all this money?"

"It is for the trip. I didn't know if we would need any cash during the trip here! I told you I was using the ATM when we were at the grocery store before we left!"

"And you think you can just waste money on bacon, huh?" Katie scowled. "Just pay some money and ruin the diet?"

"I don't want to ruin anything, I just wanted…"

"Fine, fine, you take your bacon!" Katie interrupted him. "And of course you'll want to buy me a piece, right?"

"Uh…"

"And Jill, and Mom and Dad, right? I need some new shoes anyway! Here, take this back!" She shoved Robert's wallet back at him after pulling out a handful of cash. She got quickly up from the table, walked over to Jim's plate and picked up a single piece of bacon and tossed it in front of Robert.

"Bon appetite!"

Robert looked over at Jim. "You're coming to the mall with us, right?"

Jim smiled and shook his head. "No, I have a few things I need to get to around the house, but you have fun!"

Seventeen

After breakfast, they walked out to Jill's car to head to the mall. Robert opened the door for Katie and helped her into the back seat. Once she was in he climbed into the front seat.

"Hey, aren't you going to sit back here with me?" Katie asked.

"Maybe you'll find some single guy who wants the seat." Robert replied nastily.

Jill started the car and Robert began giving her directions the mall.

"Oh, come on! We just wanted to know about the neighbor!" Katie smiled, reaching up to touch Robert's arm.

"Katie, *don't*!" Robert said, turning angrily around and glaring at her. She pulled her hand quickly back, looking hurt. Robert turned back around and looked out his window.

"You're really upset, aren't you?" Katie asked quietly.

"What do you think?" He growled back. "You asked me if another guy was single in front of your parents and sister! How did you think that would make me feel?"

"But I didn't mean for me! I just…I wanted…" she stopped in mid-sentence and thought about what she was saying. "Oh, oh *no*! I didn't mean to make you feel like *that*! I was just…I was asking…" her emotions began to run wild again.

"Katie, how would you feel if I asked some of the women clerks at the mall if they're single in front of *you*?"

"But I didn't mean…" she sniffed and opened up her purse, taking out a tissue.

"Don't be mad at her, ok?" Jill said looking over at him. "We got all excited and Katie helped me get all fixed up. I kept pushing her to ask you if he was single; Ok? If you have to be mad at someone, be mad at me!"

He ignored her and looked back out the window. They drove along in uncomfortable silence and were soon in the mall parking lot. Jill parked and Robert climbed out of the car. He held the door open for Katie who got out and stood looking sadly at the ground. Robert watched her for a few seconds and then put a hand on her back.

"Are you ok, Katie?"

"I didn't mean…please don't ask any other girls if they're single!"

Robert put his arms around her waist and pulled her into a hug. "It's ok Katie. I won't ask any other girls that."

She hugged him back tightly. "I didn't realize how that would make you feel, but thinking about how I'd feel if you asked someone else…"

He hugged her against himself, holding her close. "Oh Katie, what am I going to do with you?" He looked into her eyes, reached up, and brushed a tear off her cheek. "Don't cry, I'll get over being mad. I know you didn't mean you wanted someone else."

"You have every right to be mad at me! I'm just awful sometimes, aren't I? I didn't even let you eat what you wanted for breakfast!"

He smiled at her. "Come on Princess! People are inside waiting for you to spend my money! He took her by the hand and began leading her towards an entrance to the mall. "Come on Teacher!" He yelled at Jill. "Don't just watch us fight and make up, come on into the mall!"

Jill took Robert's other hand and smiled at him. "I figured things would be ok eventually. Everything's just a fairy tale with you two, isn't it?"

Robert snorted, "Too bad you didn't realize that when you were chasing me off your porch the day we met!"

Eighteen

They entered the mall and a nearby jewelry store caught Robert's eye. He guided Katie in that direction. She was looking into all the stores they passed and at first didn't seem to realize where he was leading her. Finally, they entered the store and she realized where they were. Jill parted from them and went into the store next door.

Katie gasped. "Oh Robert…are we where I think we are?"

"Yup, we're in Florida." He replied with a chuckle. They walked over to a counter and were met by a male clerk in a nice suit.

"Good morning. How my I help you today?"

"We'd like to look at some engagement rings, please." Robert smiled. Beside him, Katie began to smile widely, and blush.

"Of course, did we have a specific price range in mind?" The clerk asked.

"No, just show us what you have, and we'll see what she thinks."

"I see." The clerk pulled out a small rack of rings and began to show them to Katie. She tried a few on, and after a few minutes, her gaze went to a diamond studded ring still under one of the glass counters. She breathed in and looked up at Robert, who had been watching her closely.

"May we please see that one down there?" He asked, pointing at the ring.

"Of course!" The clerk smiled. He put the other rings back and pulled out the single golden one. He showed it to Katie, who removed it carefully from the case and tried it on her finger. Her face lit up, she smiled at Robert, her eyes near tears again.

"This is the one. Oh Robert, this is the one I want! Can we get this one?"

"We're just looking, remember?" Robert chuckled. "And besides, it's supposed to be a surprise. You're just supposed to show me rings you like and then I pick one out and give it to you when I propose!"

She looked down at the ring on her finger. "But this is the one. Can't we just get it and then I can pretend it's a surprise when you give it to me?"

He grinned. "We'll see. Let's look around a bit more and maybe we'll come back, ok?"

The smile left Katie's face. "Ok, I guess…but this is the one I want. I just thought…well, that maybe we could get it and…"

"Don't worry. I'm sure you'll get what you want."

Katie slowly took off the ring and handed it back to the clerk. He put it back in the case. Robert and Katie began walking out of the store.

"Oh shoot! I think I left my wallet in there!" Robert said at the last second. "You go ahead and tell Jill about the ring you found. I'll catch up in a second, ok?"

Katie stopped and looked at him closely, a half knowing smile on her face. "Why did you have your wallet out in there?"

"Just go ahead, I'll catch up!"

He walked back up to the clerk and could feel Katie watching him from outside the store. "Hey, I want that ring. Can you put it aside for me?"

"Of course, did you want to put some money down, or…?"

"It's supposed to be a surprise, so I can't right now. But can you give me an hour or so to come back? I need to get rid of her."

"Certainly, I'll put it behind the counter for now. I can only hold it for today, though."

"Oh, don't worry. I'll be back for it!" He walked back out to Katie, who was still just outside the store, watching him carefully.

"I didn't see you get your wallet." She said quietly.

"Silly me, it was in my pocket the whole time!"

"Did you tell him to put my ring away somewhere?"

"Your ring?" He asked innocently. "Put it out of your mind Katie, don't worry all day about that, ok?"

They walked in front of the store Jill was in. She came out to meet them. "So, did we look at some rings?"

"Yes, we did!" Katie replied. "But Robert didn't buy me the one I liked. He said we might go back later. I hope it's still there!"

"Really, there was something you wanted and Robert *didn't buy it*? Are you feeling ok, Sex Fiend?" Jill laughed. She reached up and touched his cheek with the back of her hand. "You don't have a fever, do you? You didn't give the princess what she wanted?"

Robert gave her an annoyed look. "Wow Jill, you *really* look nice in that dress, is it new? And your hair looks so good today! Did you go to a salon or something?"

Jill's smile faded to a disgusted look. "Ok, ok, truce! I really hadn't planned to come to a mall in a fancy dress like this!"

"It's not that fancy," Katie smiled. "Ignore him, you look really nice today!"

They walked along the mall and Katie found a small shoe store. She was trying on many different pairs of shoes. Robert decided to escape to go and buy the ring.

"Katie, you know I'm not much for shoes. How about I just take a walk and I'll meet you back here in a bit, after you've tried on a few more pairs?"

"You're leaving? I can forget the shoes, I'll come!" Katie said with a huge smile. "Where do you want to look, I want to go, too!"

"Uh…I thought you wanted to try on shoes? You don't need to follow me!"

"We're going to be married, honey! I want to go where ever you're going! I can forget the shoes for now!"

He realized she somehow sensed what he wanted to do. "No, no." He sighed, "Go ahead and try on the shoes, I can wait."

"Are you sure?" She asked smiling brightly. "We can go where ever you want!"

"Yes, I'm sure. Go ahead and try on the shoes."

A short while and a few stores later, Robert was carrying several bags and spotted a small bar.

"Hey look," he said excitedly. "I haven't seen a bar inside a mall since I was in the military! This is great! We should go have a drink!"

Katie gave him a sour look. "You don't drink."

"Well, I didn't mean me! I can have some cranberry juice or something. But you girls can have a drink if you want? Would you maybe like some champagne, Katie?"

She scowled at him. "Oh, you'd just love that, wouldn't you?"

"I wouldn't mind a drink." Jill said with a smile. "A glass of wine sounds nice right now! We are on vacation Katie, come on!"

"Well, it at least looks like they serve food, too. Maybe we can have some lunch?" Katie answered, as she allowed the other two to lead her inside the small bar.

They sat down at a small table near the entrance. Robert set down the bags as a smiling waitress came to their table. "Good afternoon, can I get you folks a drink, or maybe something to eat?"

"I'd love some cranberry juice." Robert spoke up.

"Some of your house red wine, please?" Jill asked.

Katie looked at Robert for a minute and then asked for some cranberry juice and a menu.

The waitress walked away and Robert reached for Katie's hand. "You can have a drink Katie. Just because I don't' drink doesn't mean you can't either!"

She smiled back lovingly. "No, I'm happy with cranberry juice."

A few seconds later he replied. "I really do love you."

Katie began to blush. "I love you, too."

Robert turned and looked at Jill. He watched her for a few seconds. She noticed him looking at her and gave him a funny look. He spoke up. "You know, all joking aside, you really *do* look very nice today. The dress even looks fantastic on you!"

Jill smiled. "Thank you." Jill's smile suddenly fell from her face and her eyes widened.

"What's wrong?" Robert asked. "It was a *real* compliment! What's wrong with…me…" He suddenly realized she was looking behind him. He turned around and saw Ben standing nearby, watching him.

"Robert? Is that you?"

Robert stood up and began waving him over. "Ben! What are you doing here?"

"I finished with my appointments a bit early today and thought I'd just take a walk through the mall! It's a great place to people watch. I never thought I'd run into *you* here!"

"Would you like to sit down, maybe join us for lunch? We'd love to have you!"

"That would be wonderful, yes I'd like that! Who are these two lovely, young ladies?"

"This is my future fiancé Katie, the one I went on and on about earlier, and this is her sister, and my future sister-in-law, Jill. Ladies, this is Dr. Ben Richards."

Ben shook both women's hands and sat down. Jill watched him carefully; her eyes still open wide and a frightened look on her face.

"Would you like something to drink?" Robert asked. "The waitress should be bringing our drinks over pretty soon, we just ordered."

"Oh, I'd love some red wine." Ben smiled.

"I'll get it, I can get it!" Jill screamed. "I'll be right back with it! Katie, can you come and help me?"

Katie smiled in a knowing way. "Of course, will you gentlemen please excuse us? We'll be right back with the drinks."

"Of course, and thank you!" Ben said. Both he and Robert stood up as the women got up from the table. Jill walked quickly towards the bar with Katie right on her heels. The waitress was on her way back with the drinks but Jill stopped her. After a few words the waitress handed the drinks to her.

Ben looked over at Robert. "Very pretty girls, you're very lucky!"

"Yeah, lucky is right," Robert replied with a smile. "I'm not even very good with women, but I guess I'm pretty good with those two. One of them is even still single!"

"Is that a hint you're tossing in my direction?" Ben smiled . "I've never been very good with women either. I always seem to have my nose buried in some book."

Robert watched Katie and Jill having some kind of discussion at the bar. A few seconds later they brought the drinks over to the table.

"We'll be right back," Katie said politely. "We just need to use the little girl's room."

"Not a problem!" Robert laughed.

As the two women left, Robert turned to Ben. "Hey, as it happens, you can do me a huge favor while you're here!"

"After you helped me with the flat tire? Of course, I'll do what ever I can for you!"

"I need to run a quick errand. Can you keep the girls occupied for me for just a few minutes?"

"Uh…yeah, I guess I could do that. What did you need to do?"

"Don't worry about that. When they come back, just tell Katie I went to take a shit or something, ok? Just keep her busy and don't let her leave the bar. You can do that, right? Shrink her head, or something!"

Ben scowled at him. "Lovely metaphor. Yes, I can keep them busy."

"Thanks," Robert said with a huge smile. He jumped up from his chair and moved quickly towards the jewelry store.

Nineteen

"Jill? Jill honey, take it easy, you're hyperventilating!"

"Katie," Jill said, taking several deep breaths. "What do I do? How do I even talk to him?"

"Just relax! Pretend he's Robert! He's right here. We can ask him anything we want to know now!" Katie smiled.

"Oh my God, I don't even know if I can go back out there! Did you *see him*? He's *gorgeous* and a *doctor*! Katie, he's got to have a million girlfriends!"

"Yeah…I can see now why Robert was so upset about me asking if he was single." Katie said thoughtfully. "I'd better go apologize again." She began to walk out of the bathroom but Jill grabbed her arm.

"Katie, *please don't leave me here all alone*!"

"Come on Jill. Let's go back to the table. If he really makes you that nervous, just talk to Robert. He doesn't make you nervous, does he? Just concentrate on him and maybe, little by little, you'll feel more comfortable around Ben?"

"Oh Katie, I don't know. Maybe we should just stay in here?"

"Remember how nervous you were picking up your new car?" Katie laughed. "Come on honey. Let's go back to the table. I'll be with you the whole time!"

Jill allowed Katie to lead her out of the bathroom and back to the table. They sat down and Ben smiled at them.

"Ah…Robert had to run to the restroom. He said he'd be right back."

Katie sat up in her chair and began to look out into the mall. "The restroom, he went to the restroom, really?"

"We were just in the restroom…and we didn't even see him in there!" Jill said nervously.

"He doesn't go into the women's restroom!" Katie said and gave Jill a confused look.

"That's right, we're women! We go into the women's and he goes into the men's, isn't that funny!" Jill smiled and let out a nervous laugh. The smile suddenly dropped from her face. "I'm sorry, I'm being an idiot, aren't I?"

"Not at all," Ben smiled warmly. "You just seem a little nervous. It's not uncommon to be nervous around new people. Robert's gone and here you are with some guy you don't even know."

"And he went to the restroom?" Katie asked. "Are you sure?"

Ben ignored her and looked over at Jill. "Your father mentioned you're a teacher, or was that Katie? I'm sorry. I didn't have the best of mornings."

"Yes, I'm a teacher." Jill answered nervously. "I teach kindergarten back in New York."

"Kindergarten, really? That's a very interesting developmental time! I have a friend who's a very good child psychologist!"

Robert walked back into the jewelry store and smiled at the clerk, "Hi, remember me? I'm back but I really don't have a lot of time. You put the ring aside for me, right?"

The clerk returned his smile, "Yes, I did! I didn't think you'd be back so soon though! Just a second and I'll get it for you."

The clerk walked away and Robert looked into the case in front of him. It was filled with different bracelets. The clerk returned with the engagement ring in a small box.

"Hey ah…these bracelets are pretty nice! Can I see that diamond one over there, please?"

"Certainly," the clerk smiled. He pulled the bracelet Robert was pointing at out of the case and Robert looked at it carefully.

"I think I'll take the bracelet, too. Hopefully it'll take her mind off the ring if she gets a little antsy about it!"

"I…see." The clerk said with an uncertain smile. "For the ring, if you'd like, we can send it out to be cleaned and have the stones and setting checked? That normally takes less than 24 hours. The ring would be back and ready to be picked up tomorrow afternoon."

"That sounds good," Robert smiled as he handed a credit card to the clerk. "If I can't get over here myself, can I have someone else pick up the ring for me?"

"Of course, no problem! Just have whoever comes for the ring to have the receipt. It should be ready after 3pm."

"And I can have the bracelet now, right?"

"Of course."

The clerk carefully placed the bracelet in a small velvet case and handed it to Robert. He reached down and inserted it into his sock and covered his ankle with his pant leg. The clerk looked at him curiously.

"Oh…ah…when I go back, she'll probably feel my pockets to try and find the ring. She can be pretty tenacious when she wants to find something. It should be safe in my sock, though!"

"Oh…of course…" The clerk smiled, handing Robert his credit card back along with a receipt. "Don't lose this receipt. You'll need it to pick up the ring!"

"Gotcha," Robert said, shoving the receipt and card back into his wallet. "Thanks!" He left the store and hurried back towards the bar.

Robert could see Katie looking around out towards the mall. He ducked behind a nearby pillar and watched her for a bit. After a minute, Jill said something to her and she turned away from the entrance to listen to her sister. He quickly moved back into the bar behind her. He then walked back to the table as if he had been in the restroom in the back of the bar.

Robert sat back down at the table next to Katie. "Sorry sweetheart, but when you've got to go, you've got to go!"

She smiled widely at him. "You went to the bathroom?"

"Yeah, the fruit you gave me for breakfast just ran right through me!" He looked over at Ben. "So, did they give you the third degree while I was gone?"

"Oh, we've just been chatting." Ben smiled.

"Talking about baseball or something?" Robert joked.

"No. Speaking of that, the Yankees will be in town Friday! I love baseball but the games have been sold out, I guess!" Ben laughed.

"Oh, there's got to be some tickets somewhere! I'll bet I can get some!" Robert boasted.

Katie reached over and patted his leg up near the pocket. "You just went to the bathroom, nowhere else?"

"Do you know someone who could get you tickets?" Ben asked. "Really? I would love to see the game in person!"

"I don't know," Robert said, looking curiously over at Katie. "But I can talk to my publisher, he might know someone. Katie, what are you doing? That's my cell phone!"

Katie began to giggle. "I just felt that lump in your pocket and didn't know what it was! I didn't know if…"

"You didn't know if *what*?"

"I like baseball!" Jill said with a huge smile. "I *love* the Yankees!"

"I didn't know if…"Katie started out nervously. "If…Jill, you know you don't like sports! When did you start liking baseball?"

"I like baseball!" Jill glared at Katie.

Robert took a hold of Katie's hand and began to gently caress it. "I'll give him a call and let you know! He knows a lot of people. He might be able to help us out. Do you have a number I can reach you?"

"Oh, of course! I'm glad I've met you, Robert! I've only know you a day, and already you've done so much for me!" He reached into his pocket and pulled out several business cards. He handed one to Robert, and one to each woman. "I've had a very nice time meeting all of you. Feel free to call me anytime! We'll have to get together again, sometime!"

Robert looked at the card. "Which one should I call? The office number and just leave you a message?"

"Oh no, those are special cards." Ben smiled. "They have my cell phone number written on the back. If I'm busy, just leave a message and I'll call back as soon as I can."

Robert turned the card over and saw the number. "Ah, I see! Ok, I'll give you a call as soon as I find out anything."

"His *personal* number..." Jill said quietly, almost reverently.

"I'll look forward to that! I'd actually better get going. I still have a few things to do at the office before I go home." He stood up and reached out to shake everyone's hand again. Robert shook his hand and Ben quietly walked out of the bar.

Robert turned in his chair and put Katie's hand on his other pocket. "Did you want to feel this one, too?"

She felt his pocket for a few seconds and yanked her hand back. "Why would I want to feel your pockets?"

"I don't know, because it's not even in there."

"What's not in there?" Katie asked curiously. "Are you hiding something from me?"

Robert smiled at her and put his hand on her shoulder, rubbing it gently. "We don't hide anything from each other, do we sweetheart? We tell each other everything."

Katie smiled, but her smile quickly faded. "Do we? If I ask you something, will you tell me the truth?"

"I'll always be truthful with you, Katie."

"Did you really go to the bathroom?"

Robert smiled, and leaned close to her ear as he whispered. "No."

"Where did you go?"

"Out."

"Out *where*?"

"I just took a walk. You're worried about something, aren't you?"

"I just don't like not knowing something." She said quietly.

Robert looked over at Jill, realizing she hadn't said a word since Ben had left. "Are you ok? Why are you so quiet?"

Jill had a huge smile on her face and was looking off into space.

"Jill, I asked if you were ok!" Robert said a bit louder.

"Huh, what? Yes I'm fine! Do you have to be so loud? Katie, can you please put a leash on him, or something?"

After paying the bill, they got up from the table to leave. Robert picked up all of Katie's bags and they headed for the mall exit.

Katie took a hold of Robert's arm as they walked. "Robert, can we please maybe...?"

"Maybe, what?"

"Oh...maybe...go and look at the ring again on the way out? Please?"

He walked a little bit as she watched him expectantly. "Katie, do I disappoint you?"

She looked hurt. "Of course not!"

"Have I ever disappointed you? Since we've been together, haven't I always given you everything you wanted?"

Katie thought for a minute. "Well, yes. But I just wanted to maybe see it again. Did you go and buy it when you left the bar?"

Robert smiled. "If I did, it's supposed to be a surprise."

"I can still be surprised!"

Robert began to laugh. "Let's go back to your parent's house, Little Princess."

Twenty

Robert hung up his cell phone and dialed another number. He had been calling people since they got back to the house. Katie watched him with a dull look on her face.

Jim stood beside his daughter. "Who's he calling all this time? I thought he was a writer, not a salesman!"

"He wants tickets to some stupid baseball game!" Katie said, shaking her head. "The neighbor mentioned some team would be in town and they got all worked up over it!"

"Is he trying to get tickets to the Yankee game this weekend?" Jim asked.

"Yes, I think it was the stupid Yankees."

"That's been sold out for weeks, honey!" Jim laughed. "He'll *never* get tickets!"

Robert stood up and began to yell. "Yes, *yes*! I've got em'!"

Katie walked over and sat down next to him. "You finally found someone with tickets to the stupid game?"

"Yes," Robert said, as he hugged her happily. "There is a bookstore owner here in Tampa who has two tickets right behind home plate! He said he'd be happy to trade them to me if I didn't mind signing some of my books that he has in stock!"

"And do I have to go to this…game?"

"If you want to come, sure! He said there were two tickets. I can tell Ben I'm sorry, maybe next time, if you want to go?"

"What do *you* think?" Katie asked, crossing her arms.

"That…you don't like sports and…and uh…don't want to go?"

Katie smiled and kissed him. "Well, you really are starting to know me pretty well, aren't you?"

"Do you mind if I go to the game with Ben?"

"Not at all, you go and have fun!"

"You actually found tickets?" Jim asked.

"Yeah, I did!" Robert smiled. "Did you want to go instead of Ben? I'd be happy to take you along!"

"No, that won't be necessary. You go to the game with the neighbor, and I'll stay here and visit with my daughters."

Emily came out of the kitchen just then, and called them all to dinner. Robert pushed his cell phone into his pocket and followed Katie and Jim into the kitchen.

After dinner was finished, Robert looked over at Emily. "That was really good! I really appreciate the meal, I'd be happy to do the dishes for you!"

"Oh, you don't have to do that!" Emily returned his smile. "It won't take me very long, but thank you anyway."

"Oh, it's no problem at all! Maybe Katie can help me?"

"Let him do the dishes, Em!" Jim smiled. "And while he's in there doing that, we can visit with the girls!"

Emily scowled at him. "You would actually do that, wouldn't you? How about Robert helps *me* with the dishes, and you visit with *your girls*?"

"That sounds ok," Robert smiled. "I don't mind helping out." He began helping Emily clear the plates and glasses from the table.

"Thank you very much!" Emily said when they were in the kitchen together. "I did want a chance to get to know my future son-in-law!"

"Yeah, I haven't really had much of a chance to talk to you, have I? I'm sorry about that. I know how worried Katie was about what her father would think about me. I didn't mean to ignore *you*!"

Emily began to laugh. "You don't need to apologize. I know what both Jim and Katie are like. Here, you rinse off the dishes in the sink and hand them to me. I'll put them in the dish washer."

Robert began rinsing the dishes and handing them to her. "Jill said you were a teacher?"

"A retired teacher, yes."

"And I guess Jim was a cop, huh? How do a teacher and a cop end up getting together?"

Emily laughed. "How do a writer and an executive assistant get together?"

"I guess you've got a point there. Katie was so worried about bringing me to meet Jim, but so far he's been really nice!"

"Well, you have to understand him. Since the girls were first born, he's always been so protective of them. He and Katie were *very* close when she was little. But as she got older, discovered clothes, boys, and girl things, she just kind of drifted away from him. When she brought that first boy home, he got a little upset. And ever since then…well…"

"What happened?"

"Well…"

"Oh come on, did he really go nuts, or something?"

Emily began to laugh. "He didn't like the boy at all, and Katie got all upset and they had this big fight."

"Was that the first one, the high school kid…let's see, Katie said his name was…Steven, I think?"

"You actually listen to her, huh? I'm proud of you, Robert! Yes, his name was Steven."

"And then she brought Barry home?"

Emily sighed. "I guess she's told you everything, huh?"

"Well, she told me he cheated on her. She's said she wanted me to know everything about her."

"Jim…well, he was a police officer and he saw a lot of things while he was working. And he was always so worried about our daughters. He'd do anything to protect them. But Katie was always so…carefree. She…well, he was always so worried about how she flirted with everyone while she was in high school. She was just being young, of course, but…"

"And so she was afraid that when she brought me to meet him, he would see me as some kind of a threat?"

"That's possible. But I can tell you right now, he likes you, and so do I!"

"You think he likes me, really?"

"Honey, I know he does. While you guys were at the mall, he even said, *Em, maybe this guy isn't so bad after all?*"

"And that means he likes me, huh?" Robert laughed.

"Sweetheart, coming from Jim that means you're wonderful!" Emily said, laughing with him.

Jim sat down in the middle of the couch and waved for his daughters to come and sit next to him. Both Katie and Jill sat down on the couch on either side of him. He reached out and hugged them both. Sitting next to him, Katie again felt sixteen again.

"Maybe I should have stayed in New York? I miss you both, so much!"

"We miss you too, Daddy." Jill said with a smile.

"How about you?" Jim asked Katie. "I guess you don't miss me?"

"Of course I miss you!" She said hugging him again.

"How have you girls been? I know we really haven't talked in so long. Especially you, Katie! Ever since…well, you just don't call and talk to me very much. I miss you guys!"

Katie sighed. "I didn't want you to chase Robert off! I know how you can be, and I really love him!"

Jim rubbed his chin. "I know. I can see that. I can see how he is with you, honey. I'm sorry about that last one, Larry, or whatever his name was."

"Barry," Jill corrected him.

Jim began laughing. "You stay out of my apology! I'll get to you in a minute, Ms. Teacher!"

"Robert isn't like Barry." Katie said looking down. "Please don't treat him the same way."

He sighed. "How did you guys grow up so fast? It seems like only yesterday I was watching a Jets game, with Katie on my knee and Jill in her crib! Where did the time go?"

Katie smiled. "I remember watching football with you! It was always so fun. But I just don't…I just don't like sports anymore."

"I know," Jim said pulling both her and Jill close. "I know honey, times change. You've grown into a woman right in front of me! But just because we don't watch football together anymore doesn't mean I love you any less. So, how about you tell me a bit more about your writer? You fell in love with him pretty quickly!"

Katie began to smile. "Oh Daddy, he's just…he's wonderful! I knew he was the one from when I first met him!"

He sighed again. "Is that so?"

"I actually like him a lot too, Dad!" Jill smiled. "And not just because he bought me a new car! You'd be proud. I tried to run him off on Katie's first date with him!"

Jim laughed. "You did? You didn't like him at first?"

"Well, I thought he was going out with her for the wrong reasons. I thought…"

"She thought he just wanted to sleep with me!" Katie said scowling. "She didn't understand how sweet he had really been!"

"And now that you've slept together, he still treats you right?" Jim asked.

"Daddy, that's none of your business whether or not we've slept together!"

"Relax honey, I already asked him, and he's admitted that he's slept with you!" Jim chuckled. "He's been pretty honest and up front with me."

Uh huh, now that you know what's happened between us, you think he's just…just some guy, and that you need to…" She pulled away from him, near tears.

Jim put his arm around her shoulders again and pulled her back next to him. "And now that I know that, I think I really like him. I think you did good finding him."

"You…you *what*?" Katie asked, looking up at him.

"I like him. He's been honest about everything I asked him. He said he loves you very much and only wants the best for you. He's asked for my blessing to marry you, and I'm going to give it to him."

Katie felt her eyes filling with tears. "Really? You really like him?"

"How could I not like someone both my girls really like? Now then..." He turned back to Jill. "It's your turn! Let's hear about all those little boys and girls you teach now!"

Robert and Emily finished the dishes. Before they walked back out into the living room, Robert stopped her, "Hey, would you mind doing me a favor?"

"Certainly, what did you need?"

"Well...while we were at the mall today, Katie and I looked at a few engagement rings. She found the one she wanted, and I bought it. But it's supposed to be a surprise. It's still at the jewelry store and I need to pick it up, but she won't let me go anywhere by myself! Could you pick it up for me and hide it until I need it?"

"You've already bought her a ring?" Emily asked with a smile.

"Well, she said it was the perfect one, and it was what she really wanted. I can't say no to her for something like that. Can you pick it up for me?"

"Of course, but don't get too carried away with spoiling Katie, ok? Just because she wants something doesn't mean she should automatically get it!"

"I know...but...well, this is the ring she said she wanted. And I do love her." He handed Emily the receipt. "They said it should be ready sometime after three tomorrow. They're just cleaning it and checking the setting."

"You really are good to her, aren't you? No wonder Jim likes you so much. You don't mind if I take him along to pick it up, do you?"

"Not at all, I really appreciate this!"

They walked back out into the living room and sat down. They both smiled as they watched Jim hug his daughters.

"Dishes are all done!" Robert beamed. "Hey Jill, could I ask for a ride tomorrow?"

"A ride to where?"

"Well, I need to go to this bookstore in town to sign a few books. The guy is going to trade me some baseball tickets to the Rays-Yankees game on Friday."

"Hmm, let me think about that."

"I can take a cab, I guess. I was just hoping…?"

"Don't be stupid! I was just joking! You bought me that wonderful car, of course I'll give you a ride anywhere you want!"

"I want to come, too!" Katie spoke up. "I want to go with you while you sign books!"

"There's not much to do in a bookstore besides look at books until I'm done, honey."

"I like books!" She pouted.

Robert began laughing. "No you don't! I don't think I've ever seen you with a book in your hand! What's the last book you read?"

"She likes magazines," Jim smiled. "You can find her a copy of some fashion magazine or…" he smiled at Katie. "Maybe Bride Monthly or whatever bride magazines are out there?"

Katie kissed him on the cheek. "I do like magazines… thank you, Daddy."

"Ok then! Anyone who wants to come along is welcome, I don't mind. Jim, Emily?"

"No thank you, we have an errand that we just have to get to tomorrow." Emily smiled.

"We do?" Jim asked.

"Yes, we do."

Jim looked at Robert. "Are your books really that popular? That people want you to sign them?"

"Well, book. I've only had one published so far. But yeah, people went nuts over it. When Katie and I were in California, I was working with the guy who's directing the movie version."

"I'll have to call some guys at my old precinct and see if anyone's read it. I know a few guys who read a lot. What's it called?"

"*The Treaty.*" Jill spoke up for Robert. "I'll bet someone you know has read it!"

Jim looked over at Katie. "You don't mind if I call about him, if I'm just asking about his book?"

"Would it matter if I cared?" Katie asked. "You'd just call anyway!"

"If it bothers you, I won't call anyone. I don't want things to be so…distant between us." Jim said looking down at the floor.

"You call anyone you'd like." Robert smiled. "It doesn't bother me a bit for the whole world to know that I'm marrying Katie!"

Katie smiled at him.

"Well," Emily smiled. "We have some cake, if anyone's interested?"

Twenty One

Katie was lying on her bed looking at the ceiling. She had been quiet for a long time. Jill was lying on her bed, reading a book. Robert sat on his bed watching Katie.

"You didn't sleep well last night, did you?" He finally asked.

"I'm fine, honey."

"I could hear you tossing and turning. The longer we're together, the closer we're becoming, Katie. Are you sure you're ok?"

She sighed. "I had a little trouble sleeping, but I'm ok."

"It's not that bad sleeping without me next to you; is it? I'm still in the same room."

"It's not that, I know you're right next to me. I just… well…I was so worried about how Daddy would react when I brought you to meet him."

"He's taken things pretty well so far though, hasn't he?"

"He has, yes. I was just thinking about…about when I was younger."

A knock came at the door and Jim stuck his head inside. "I saw the light and heard you guys talking. Is everything ok?"

Robert got up off his bed and walked over to the door. "Yeah, we're all fine. We were just having a chat. Would you like to come in and join us?"

"Oh, I don't want to intrude! I know you and Katie would probably like some privacy…" He glanced over at Jill. "I just thought…well…I…"

"You might as well come in and sit down, since you're so nosy!" Katie frowned.

Jim looked at Robert, who waved him inside. He was wearing pajamas and sat down on Robert's bed, carefully watching Katie and Jill. Robert sat down on Katie's bed, next to her. He brushed a strand of hair away from her eyes. "Go ahead, you were thinking about when you were younger?"

"Like when you tried to sneak out?" Jim asked, with a small smile.

Katie sat forward and looked at him. "Maybe. We had that huge fight."

Jim turned his gaze to Robert. "She brought this kid home from school. He had long blonde hair and I didn't like him. After he left, we had this big fight and I grounded her."

"Don't tell him this story!" Katie said, looking at Robert. "It's *awful*!"

"I remember that," Jill said sitting up now, too. "It was right before that big school dance, right?"

"Yes, right before some dance. She stayed in her room all day after school and wouldn't talk to anyone. Later on that night, I hear all this screaming coming from her room…"

"Daddy, this isn't funny! I felt so bad, I cried for weeks… *weeks*!"

Jim looked at her for a few seconds, and then down at the floor. "I hear Katie calling for help. As a cop the first thing I think of is that someone is in her room hurting her. I ran in there to find her trying to climb out the window. But while she was climbing out, she got her pants stuck on a…" a small chuckle escaped him. "On a nail. And she was so afraid to rip her pants that she panicked and started screaming!"

"Those were my best *Jordache Jeans*! I love…I really…" Robert could see tears forming in her eyes.

"I unhooked her pants from the nail and pulled her back inside. I remember being so afraid after that…"

"Afraid, right!" Katie yelled. "Tell him the rest!"

"Well…you have to understand the things I've seen…I didn't want…I was just trying to protect…" He covered his eyes with one hand.

"He nailed boards across my window!" Katie said angrily to Robert.

"Her mother made me take the boards back down when she found out. Less than a year after that, she went to college and I started having nightmares about her getting hurt. I know how you are…how…trusting you can be. I just worried about you! And then…you just…you just stopped talking to me! I just wanted you safe!"

Robert looked over at Katie. Her face had softened quite a bit. "You were having nightmares?" She asked. "Why didn't you tell me?"

He wiped his eyes and looked over at Jill. "I had them after you left, too. I couldn't sleep after you girls left. But I'm the big, bad, tough, cop! That's not supposed to happen!"

Robert pushed Katie off her bed and towards the bed Jim was sitting on. She sat down next to him and put her arm around him. "I never knew that. Daddy, you should have told someone about these things!"

"And you brought that other one home. That…stuck up guy in the suit!"

"And you thought he would hurt me? Why didn't you just tell me?"

"Would you have even understood? I just worried about you! I didn't like the way he looked at you! I didn't like the way he acted, or treated anybody else! But you didn't see the things I did! You don't know the things I've seen people do to each other!"

Now Jill got up and walked over to sit on the other side of Jim. "Dad, have you ever talked to a professional about these things?"

"How could I? How could I tell some *stranger* that one of my daughters didn't want to talk to me anymore because I just wanted her safe?"

"I always wanted to talk to you!" Katie said, tears running down her face. "But you were always so…nosy, so protective! Sometimes it was like you were smothering me! Always wanting to know where I was, who I was with and…" She stopped and thought for a second. "You were just worried, weren't you? You were having nightmares about me?"

"I'm *so sorry*, Katie! I just wanted you safe! I never meant to push you away! When you called and said you were going to come and visit…I was so happy! Part of me didn't want to like Robert when you got here, but…but he's promised me he'd protect you! He doesn't look at you like the others you ran around with! He…"

"He looks at me like the sun rises and sets on me." Katie said quietly.

Jim began laughing through his tears. "Yes, just like the sun rises and sets on you! I'm sorry you had to see your old man all sobbing like this!"

Both Katie and Jill hugged him tightly. "Don't you worry about us!" Katie smiled. "Robert will take care of us now, *both* of us, until Jill finds her special guy, right Robert?"

"You betcha!" Robert smiled back. "Hell, I'll even hire security to follow them around, if you want!"

Both Katie and Jill glared at him with angry looks. "No you won't!" Jill laughed. "You feel free to watch out for us, but I don't need some thug following *me* around!"

Jim laughed and looked up at Robert. "Thank you. Thank you for bringing my daughters here…for bringing Katie back to me…thank you for caring."

Twenty Two

Robert opened his eyes to the sun streaming through the window. He yawned, stretched, and sat up on his little bed. He walked over to Katie's bed and kissed her on the cheek. She let out a soft moan and rolled over onto her side. He turned towards the door and began to walk quietly out of the room.

"I hope you don't think you're going somewhere without me?" He heard her say softly. He turned back around and walked back to sit on the edge of her bed.

"No, I guess not." He smiled and kissed her again. "Are you ready to get up?"

"I'd rather lay here and cuddle with you!"

Robert let out a quiet laugh. "I'll bet you would! I'm going to go downstairs and see if I can sneak a bit of breakfast."

Katie sat up and yawned. "I'll come, just give me a sec to wake up, ok?"

He looked over at Jill. She was still sleeping peacefully. "Jill! Are you awake yet?" He screamed. "I think she's still sleeping, Katie!"

"Katie, muzzle your asshole pet, ok?" Jill mumbled and rolled over so her back was facing Robert.

He walked over and kissed her cheek. "Good morning to you, too!"

Jill opened her eyes. "Oh, that's just gross! Can you please keep your lips off of me? Go fuck your girlfriend, or something!"

"Yes, come and fuck your girlfriend!" Katie laughed. "She'd like that!"

Robert began laughing too and pulled Katie out of bed and to her feet. "Come on, breakfast time."

"I'm still in my pajamas!" Katie protested. "Can I please get dressed first?"

"No," Robert laughed. "Time for breakfast in our pajamas!" He grabbed her by the hand and pulled her out of the room.

They walked into the kitchen. Jim was seated in his normal spot at the table with a plate of bacon and eggs in front of him. He smiled at Robert and Katie. Robert sat down next to him.

"Just a minute and I'll get your breakfast, honey." Katie said, kissing Robert on the cheek.

As she turned towards the refrigerator, Jim quickly tossed a piece of his bacon in front of Robert, and winked. Robert smiled and quickly gulped it down.

"So, how'd you sleep last night?" Robert asked.

"Honestly? I think that's the best I've slept since I can't remember when!" Jim smiled. "Thanks." He tossed another piece of bacon in front of Robert. Robert gulped it down and Katie slammed a fruit cup down in front of him.

"I saw that! Knock it off, that's not good for you!"

Robert and Jim smiled at each other. Emily smiled at the both of them and then looked over at Katie. "They seem to be getting along pretty well this morning!"

"They aren't behaving! Robert's on a diet and Daddy shouldn't be sneaking him bacon! It's not good for his diet!"

While she was talking to her mother, Jim nudged one more piece of bacon off his plate, and Robert snatched it up. Katie quickly reached over and grabbed his arm, "Should I just get his gun and let you two play Russian Roulette? Neither of you thinks you have to listen to me, do you?"

Robert dropped the bacon piece. "Oh come on Katie, it's just some bacon! A couple pieces won't hurt me!"

"Fine, eat it! Do anything you want, it's not like I care about you or anything, is it? It's not like I want you healthy, or like I'm trying to diet with you, is it?"

Robert looked down at the table. "Sorry, Katie. He just knows I like bacon."

"She thinks if she makes you diet, you'll live forever!" Jim smiled. "Go ahead and eat the bacon, she'll get over it!"

Katie glared at him. "I'm going to have Mom put you on a diet, too! If you two can't behave, I'll just get rid of the bacon all together while we're staying with you! Get used to fruit for breakfast, Daddy!"

Jim leaned over towards Robert. "She's really fussy, are you sure you want to keep her?"

Robert smiled up at Katie as she glared back at him. "Yes, fussy or not, I do love her. She's a keeper."

"A keeper until when?" Katie growled. "One of you has a heart attack?"

"She's so grumpy today!" Robert smiled at Jim. "Just a second and I'll see if I can cheer her up." He got up from the table and walked out of the kitchen. He walked upstairs and found the small velvet case with the bracelet he had bought, and came back downstairs. He walked into the kitchen and sat back down next to Jim again.

"Well," Katie asked. "Are you going to tell us why you just walked out of here? Was your leaving supposed to cheer me up?"

"Come here." Robert smiled.

"I can stand over here while you tell me whatever it is!"

"Fine, then close your eyes."

"Why?" A small smile crept onto her face. "If you're going to propose, I need my eyes open to see it!"

"Oh sorry, that's coming, but not today. Close your eyes, or come over here."

Katie walked over next to him and crossed her arms. "Ok, I'm here, now what?"

"Close your eyes anyway." Robert laughed.

"You just want to be difficult, don't you?" Katie smiled at him.

"Yes, I just want to be difficult."

Katie closed her eyes and he gently took her right hand in his. He turned it palm up, just as he had done when they had first met. He opened the small velvet case, pulled out the bracelet, and fastened it on her wrist.

"Ok, open your eyes."

Katie opened her eyes and gasped at the bracelet. She grabbed him around the neck and hugged him tightly. "Fine, you can have a little bacon! I just worry about you!"

Robert hugged her back. "Are you in a bit better mood now?"

"What do you think?" She smiled, a tear running down her cheek.

Jim smiled up at Emily. "I don't think I could have found a better guy for her myself! That was very nice of you, Writer!"

"Don't let him fool you Dad. He's a sex fiend pig." Jill said as she walked into the kitchen. She sat down at the table next to Robert. "Still can't keep your hands off her, can you?"

"You hush!" Katie smiled. "See what he got for me?" She held out her arm so Jill could see the bracelet.

"Very nice, is there anything to eat for breakfast?"

"Just a minute sweetie, and I'll make you some eggs." Emily smiled.

"Maybe the headshrinker will buy you something like that someday?" Robert smiled.

Jill avoided his gaze. "I don't know *what* you're talking about!"

Jim looked over at Robert. "The neighbor? She likes the neighbor?"

"We ran into him at this little bar in the mall," Robert smiled. "You should have seen the way she was looking at him!"

"Ah," Jim nodded. "So that's why you girls wanted to know if he was single! Jill likes the neighbor! I'll have to check him out."

"That's nice, that's just great!" Jill glared at Robert. "Now he'll be running warrant and back round checks on Ben just because you said that! You need to mind your own business!"

"Once I sign the books and get the tickets, I need to call him anyway. Are you sure you don't want to go to the ballgame with me?" Robert asked.

"Oh, no! You go on ahead, I'll be fine! When you call him though, see if you can get his social security number, or at least his birth date. Birth date works fine."

"Don't you *dare* tell my father Ben's birthday!" Jill said angrily. "You two just mind your own business!"

Robert smiled and winked at Jim. "We'll check him out."

Twenty Three

Jim gave Jill directions to the bookstore It was a fairly short drive, close to Jim and Emily's house. Jill parked and they climbed out of the car.

"So what do you do, just sit somewhere and sign your name?" Jill asked.

"Well, it's not an *official* signing," Robert explained. "Those are supposed to go through my agent. I'll probably just go in the back somewhere and scribble in all his books. Then they end up putting stickers on the books saying that they've been signed by the author. He can help advertise the bookstore using that. Maybe he'll take my picture signing them, I don't know."

"So we shouldn't be in here that long?"

"I don't know, hopefully not."

They entered the large store and looked around. Robert walked up to the front counter and asked to see the manager.

"Can I tell him what you need him for?" A young, cute girl in a ponytail asked.

"Tell him it's Robert Wacaster, and I'm here to sign a few books for him." Robert smiled.

A wide smile crossed the girl's face. "You're…oh my *God,* I should have recognized you! I *love* your book! I…I can't believe you're here to sign for us! This is *wonderful*!" She beamed at him and sighed.

"You were going to call the manager?" Robert asked, after a minute.

"Oh, oh yes! I'm so sorry!" She giggled. She walked quickly to a nearby phone.

"Well, I can't say I like *her* very much!" Katie scowled. "Not very efficient at all! And did you see the way she was *looking* at you?" She took a hold of Robert's hand and moved closer to him.

"I get that once in a while at the book signings, honey. Sometimes girls just…well, I get a few looks."

"And you probably enjoy that, don't you?"

He turned towards her and smiled. "I like when I get looks from *you*!" He leaned over and kissed her. She smiled back at him.

"Oh no, here comes Miss Flirty!" Katie said, her face frowning again.

"Mr. Schultz is in the back, if you'd like to follow me?" The young girl beamed.

"I really don't want to see the back," Jill smiled. "I'll just wait for you out here and look at the books, ok?"

"Ok, would you like to come along, Katie?"

"I think I'd *better*!" She continued scowling. "If Miss Flirty will be there!"

The girl led then into a back room and over to a grey haired man who was sitting near a pile of Robert's books. "Mr. Schultz, here he is!"

The older man stood up and held out his hand. "Ah, Mr. Wacaster! We spoke on the phone! I was thrilled to hear from you!"

"Oh, please call me Robert!" Robert smiled as they shook hands. "I was happy to just sign books for baseball tickets! I mean, I feel like I'm getting the best part of the deal!"

"Robert…" The young girl said dreamily.

"He's *engaged*!" Katie growled, glaring at her.

"And please call me Sherman!" Sherman said, as he offered both Robert and Katie seats nearby. "Thank you for bringing him back here Becky, but you'd probably better get back out to the counter."

"If you have a book you'd like me to sign, please catch me before I leave!" Robert smiled. Katie frowned at him. "Oh, this is my fiancé; Katie." He said quickly, catching the look from her. Sherman reached out and shook her hand.

"I didn't want to trouble you for too long, but here are the tickets. I managed to round up all of your books that we had on the floor. They actually sell pretty well. We had 15 of them in stock. I know that's a lot, so if you didn't want to sign them all…?"

"Oh, of course I'll sign them all!" Robert smiled. "I really appreciate the tickets! Did you want to take a picture of me signing, to help with advertising?"

"No, just signing the books for us is fantastic! I'll have Becky put up a display of the signed books near the front door. I'm sure they'll sell pretty well!"

Robert found a pen and began to sign the books piled near him. Katie watched him for a minute and then leaned close to whisper to him. "I'm sorry about when I asked if Ben was single."

He stopped signing and looked at her. "I know, you've already apologized honey. I'm not mad anymore, we're good."

"You didn't think that girl was cute, did you?"

"What girl?"

"The young one: Miss Flirty?"

"Yeah, she was ok, why? It's always fun to see someone who gets all excited over something I wrote."

"Is that what you want?"

"Is…Katie, are you jealous of that *kid*? I was just being polite to her."

"You told her to catch you on the way out."

He kissed her and smiled. "It helps sell books, Katie! I didn't ask for her number, I didn't ask if she was single, I just told her I would sign a book for her. I want to marry *you*, ok?"

"So even if some younger model comes along…?"

"I want to grow old with you. I don't want someone younger. Besides Katie, you're ten years younger than I am. *You're* the younger model!" He began to laugh. "No one will ever take your place in my heart, ok? Hand me those books, please?"

A nearby phone rang and Sherman answered it. He excused himself and walked back out to the front of the store. After a few minutes, he came back into the back.

"Uh...Mr. Wacaster...Robert? I have someone asking to see you out front. Would you mind stepping out there?"

Robert looked at Katie. "Who is it?"

"I don't know...but he seemed to know you were here. He also wanted one of the books you're signing."

Robert quickly scribbled his name in a book and then looked at Katie. "Who would know I'm here besides you and Jill?"

"I don't know, but you said being polite sells books, right? Let's go and see who it is! Do you want me to go out first and see if it's someone crazy?"

"Yeah, your Dad would love me sending you out first to confront some crazy person. Come on, let's see who it is."

They walked out to the front counter to find Jim and Emily standing there.

"Daddy, what are you doing here?" Katie asked happily. She came out from behind the counter and hugged him.

"I gave you directions to the bookstore, remember? I wanted one of your writer's books! And since he's here signing them, we thought we'd come and get one!"

"Katie could probably get you one for free from the publisher." Robert said, shaking Jim's hand.

"Oh no, I want to buy one! Don't you get money every time someone buys one of your books? It helps support my daughters, right?"

"Yes, I do get paid for every book that gets sold, thanks." He smiled, handing a signed book across to Jim.

"I talked to a friend back in New York. He's read it and told me it was pretty good! He seemed quite impressed that I knew you!"

Robert looked over at Katie. "Well, eventually you'll be related to me!"

Katie hugged Jim again, and Emily walked over near Robert. "We picked it up for you. It's in my purse, I can see why she loved it, it's beautiful!"

"You can hide it for me, right?" Robert whispered.

"Oh, of course! You just let me know when you need it. I'll have it somewhere safe!"

"Thanks," Robert said as he walked out from behind the counter and gave her a quick hug. "Did you guys have any plans right now? It'll only take me a few more minutes to sign the rest of the books. We can go someplace nice for lunch."

"That sounds lovely!" Emily said, looking at Jim. "We'd love to have lunch with you kids!"

"Yeah," Jim smiled. "I think that would be fine! Where's Jill?"

"Oh, she's around somewhere looking at books. Katie, please go find Jill. I'll finish with signing the books and then we can be on our way, ok?"

"I can trust you, right?" Katie asked.

"Trust him, what do you mean?" Jim asked, glaring at Robert.

"Yes, you can trust me! And feel free to introduce your Dad to Becky, if you want?" He began laughing and walked back into the back as Katie scowled at him.

"Who's Becky?" Jim asked.

Twenty Four

Robert finished signing the books and they drove to a nearby restaurant. Once they were seated, Robert watched Jim flipping through his book. Katie sat next to him and was flipping through a magazine. She held it out to him, showing him a picture of a young girl wearing a wedding dress.

"I kind of like this one. What do you think? I like all the lace, but I'm not sure about the neckline."

Robert took the magazine and looked at the picture. "Uh… you…ah…you like this? Uh yeah, you'd look beautiful… planning ahead already, huh?"

"Oh, weddings take a lot of planning, honey. I'll have to have the perfect dress, and you'll need the right tuxedo. We'll have to find the right place and the right person to do the wedding. Sometimes you need reservations way in advance. I'll have to find dresses for the bride's maids. There are a thousand details I'll have to plan for!"

Jim put down his book and looked across the table at Robert. He smiled and let out a small laugh. "Any second thoughts, Writer?"

"No, none at all," Robert glared back. "It sounds pretty complicated but I still want to marry her."

Katie put an arm around his neck and pulled him close for a kiss. "You're so perfect and we'll have the perfect wedding!"

Jill leaned over to Jim and whispered something. They both burst out laughing. Robert watched them while Katie reached out to touch his leg and said. "Ignore them. They won't think it's so funny when I involve them in all the planning!" She took the magazine back from Robert and began to flip through it again.

Robert pulled out his cell phone and dialed Ben's number. The phone didn't ring but went right to voice mail.

"Hi Ben, it's Robert. I managed to actually get two tickets to the Rays game on Friday night! I just wondered if you want to go? They're great seats, right behind home plate! Give me a call back when you get time, ok? Thanks." He glanced over at Jill who was watching him carefully. "Oh, and Jill says to tell you hi! She had a great time at lunch with you the other day."

"Who was that?" Jill asked, sounding panicked. "Who did you just tell hi for me!"

"I don't know. Just some guy." Robert smiled.

"You did *not* just call Ben and mention my name, did you?"

Jim looked at her. "What's the big deal about him saying hi for you?"

"The *big deal* is that it sounds like I'm throwing myself at him! I don't just throw myself at men!"

"How is saying hi throwing yourself at someone?" Jim asked.

"It…it's just…he shouldn't have done that without my telling him to!" Jill said, visibly upset now.

"I thought you liked him?" Robert asked. "Should I call him back and tell him you didn't say hi?"

"You are *such* an *asshole*!" Jill shouted angrily. "Excuse me, I need to go to the bathroom!" She got quickly up from the table and walked back towards the bathrooms.

Robert looked over at Katie. "What did I do? I was just trying to be nice!" He looked over towards Jim. "I…I didn't mean anything, I was just trying to tell him hi for her!"

Katie put a hand on his shoulder. "It's ok, I'll go talk to her. I don't think this is about you, honey."

Katie got up to follow Jill and Robert looked over at Jim. "Why did she get so mad?"

Jim sighed and looked down at the table. "I don't know, I don't think I've ever understood either of my daughters." He turned towards Emily. "Did you understand any of that?"

"It sounds like she really does like this Ben. But it also sounds like she's having a hard time sorting out her feelings about everything that's going on right now. I think the way things are moving so quickly between you and Katie might be bothering her a bit, too."

"Huh," Jim snorted. "You'd think it would be *me* running to the bathroom to cry about things moving too quickly! I accept you, why doesn't she?"

Katie walked into the women's restroom and found Jill standing near a back stall. She had her hands covering her face.

"Hi Katie, I knew it would be you who would come after me. Can you tell Robert I'm sorry? I really didn't mean to yell at him!"

Katie walked over and hugged her. "What's really wrong? Is it Ben, do you really like him that much?"

"It's...it's everything, really. I mean...you've found the perfect guy, you're planning your wedding...your life is always so...perfect! I mean, Robert just walked into your life, right? And now...now someone who is cute and charming walks into my life. I don't know how to handle it!"

"He's single; maybe we could get you a date?"

"Katie...I don't know if you can understand! You've always been so good with men! I never know what to say, or how to act! I've always been the bookworm, the teacher, the...I don't know, the...spinster, like you always call me when you get mad."

"How do you talk to the little boys when you're teaching?" Katie asked.

"That's completely different!" Jill yelled. "You see? You don't understand! It's always so easy for you! Everything always just falls into your lap! I was so nervous when we were in that bar with him, I couldn't even talk to him!"

"I've been nervous before." Katie said hugging her again. "Sometimes I'm just good at hiding it. I've also made mistakes, Jill. Remember Stewart? Remember Barry? Everything hasn't been so easy for me. Yes, I have Robert now, but..."

"Were you ever really nervous with him?" Jill asked.

Katie sighed. "Do you promise not to ever tell him? Not to repeat this?"

Jill just looked at her sadly.

"Well, when he gave me that beautiful watch, at first I thought he was some married guy who just wanted to have sex with me. I thought he just wanted to use me, just like Stewart. Remember how mad you seemed at him?" She let out a little chuckle. "He called me from outside when he came to pick me up for our first date and said some crazy lady had chased him off the porch!"

Jill now let out a small laugh, too. "Yes, I took some flowers away from him and kept hitting him with them, telling him I'd call the police!"

"I think he was always more nervous than I was. When he took me to dinner that first time, he confessed that he was scared to death of me. I suppose he was probably really scared to meet Daddy, too. But he did what he had to do for me."

"I don't know if I could ever get over being nervous around Ben."

"Let's go visit him tonight!" Katie suggested. "You and I can take a walk over to his house and we'll say we're there to talk about the free marriage counseling he offered for Robert and me! I'll be with you the whole time!"

"I…I don't know." Jill answered sadly. "Why would I be going with you to talk about that? Katie, what if he realizes…?"

"Realizes what?" Katie said, smiling. "If you get nervous, I'll just do all the talking! You just tag along, ok? You can pretend to be there for moral support for me!"

"I…I guess we could do that. I suppose we should go back out there so I can finish ruining lunch."

"Oh poo! You haven't ruined anything!" Katie smiled. "After lunch we can get you all fixed up. We should go shopping for clothes and then we'll go over and see him!

Now let's go before Daddy starts doing checks on the waitresses!"

Jill giggled and followed her back out to the table.

They came back to the table and Jill walked over and hugged Robert. "I'm sorry about that, I shouldn't have yelled at you."

He hugged her back. "Uh…what was that all about? I mean…I just…"

"Its ok sweetheart," Katie said to him as she sat down. "Nothing you have to worry about."

Jill sat back down next to Jim. "Sorry, Dad. Sorry, Mom."

Jim looked closely at her. "Are you ok?"

"Yes Dad, I'm fine! I just…I just needed a talk with my sister, is all. I'll be ok."

He looked at Katie and then back at Jill. "Maybe we should move back to New York? I don't want to be so far away if you girls need help sometime."

"Oh Daddy, don't be so melodramatic!" Katie scowled. "You don't need to move back to New York!"

"The Writer says you guys will be calling me at least once a week from now on, just so I know you're safe!"

"He said *what*?" Katie asked, looking at Robert.

"I don't see once a week as unreasonable," Robert smiled. "Besides, you'll need to keep him up on all your wedding plans, right?"

Katie crossed her arms. "Well…I guess I do need to keep you informed if you insist on paying for things!"

"There, you see?" Jim smiled. "Everything's settled!"

"Sweetheart?" Katie cooed at Robert. "If Jill and I wanted to go shopping today, would you mind?"

"You want to shop more?" Robert asked, his eyes wide.

"Well, we just wanted to look at a few things. You can ride home with Mom and Dad. We could take the car shopping, just us girls?"

"Uh…I guess if Jim and Emily don't mind…I can give you some money, if you need it?"

"We'll just need a little bit," Katie smiled, as Robert handed her his wallet. "Thank you!"

"I'll leave you twenty five dollars in here, ok? You don't mind?"

"Uh…yeah, I guess that's all I need?" Robert said quietly looking over at Jim.

"How much did you have in there?" Jim asked. "How much did she take?"

Robert mumbled something Jim couldn't hear.

"I'm sorry, how much?" Jim asked again.

"I took three hundred dollars, if it's any of your business!" Katie snarled.

Jim looked back at Emily. "Maybe we'd better go back and buy a few more of his books before she puts him in the poorhouse?"

Twenty Five

Robert sat in the back of Jim and Emily's car. They drove along quietly until Jim finally stopped at a red light and turned to look into the back seat.

"How'd you make them stop fighting?"

"What?" Robert asked.

"Katie and Jill don't seem to fight as much around you. They seem closer than I've ever seen them. What did you do to stop them from fighting?"

"I...I don't know. They fought a bit when I first met Katie, but...?"

"Oh Jim, is it too much to believe that your daughters might be maturing a bit?" Emily wrinkled her nose.

"Yes, yes it is! I watched them fight for years! How many times have they called about some argument since we moved to Florida?"

"Well...maybe he just makes them feel safe?"

"And I don't?"

"Just be happy your girls are getting along, ok?" Emily laughed.

"What do you think she's going to buy with three hundred dollars?"

"Probably clothes," Robert mused. "She always wants to buy me clothes when we go to some store. She'll probably end up buying Jill some new dress, or something."

"They never want to share anything!" Jim growled. "They even fight over the house I left them with back in Queens! And now here *you* are in Florida with my two daughters and they're getting along better than I've ever seen them!"

"Well, I...uh...?" Robert stammered.

"Oh Jim, leave him alone and just enjoy the fact that they're finally getting along!"

"Yeah, I guess you're right: I shouldn't look a gift horse in the mouth!"

A couple hours after Robert, Jim, and Emily arrived home, Katie and Jill showed up. Robert was sitting in the living room watching TV with Jim when the two women walked past them and upstairs carrying several bags.

"Hi Katie, I'm glad you're back!" Robert yelled as she walked past him.

"Uh huh, that's nice!" Katie yelled back.

Jim looked over at him. "I told you when they were whispering it was trouble. She's found enough stuff shopping to forget all about you!" He began to laugh.

Robert got up and followed the girls upstairs. He got to their room and tried to open the door. Katie screamed and pushed it back closed. "We're in here dressing!"

"You were dressed when you walked past me downstairs!" Robert yelled back. "What the hell's going on, you can't even be bothered to say hello to me when you walk past me now?"

Katie opened the door and stepped out into the hallway, closing the door behind her, "I'm sorry, you're right. Hello!" She put her arms around his neck and pressed her lips to his, kissing him gently.

"What is going on?"

"Nothing...we're just having a little...sister time! I didn't mean to ignore you!"

"Sister time? And you can't be bothered to tell me anything about it, huh?"

Katie glanced at the closed door. "Well...we were just... trying on some clothes we bought. We just got carried away having fun. I didn't mean to ignore you!"

"We're supposed to be working on our communication, Katie. You can't tell me what's really going on?"

She looked down at the floor, her face changing to show a bit of worry. "I...I can, but...we didn't really want you to... well, to get involved."

"Involved in *what*? Never mind, I don't even care! I'm going back downstairs! If you ever decide to trust me...?"

Katie kept her arms around his neck and stopped him. "I *do* trust you, you know that! She's just nervous, ok? Come here and I'll tell you everything!"

Katie took him by the hand and led him into the nearby bathroom. She closed and locked the door behind them once they were inside.

"You couldn't just tell me in the hallway? You don't think I'll go downstairs and tell your Dad what's going on? What's with all the secrecy?"

Katie took a hold of his hands and gazed into his eyes. "She really likes Ben. But she's scared to death to say anything to him!"

"And that's supposed to be a big secret?" Robert scowled.

"No," Katie said, still looking dreamily into his eyes. "But we bought her a new dress and some new shoes. I was going to do her hair and make up. We were going to go over there tonight and pretend I was there to talk about the free marriage counseling he offered you and me."

"You were going to go over there without me?"

"We just wanted to go over by ourselves! And that seemed like a great reason to be over there talking to him, ok?"

"How do you suppose it'll look when you go over there and ask about counseling without me? It'll look like we don't even communicate, like we aren't even together on things, Katie!"

"Oh it will not! I'll just tell him you're busy with Daddy, and sent us over!"

Robert sighed. "All this trouble because Jill's scared of this guy? Remember when I told you how scared I was of you?"

Katie put her arms around his neck and kissed him gently again. "You aren't scared anymore. We just need to get her used to talking to him! I've always been the one good with men. She's always been so…shy, I guess? So if we went over together and I started us all talking…maybe she'll open up with him?"

"Well, don't go over there and ask him about the counseling. Go over there and tell him you're there to ask about the ballgame in person. He likes baseball; that'll put him in a good mood. Tell him the tickets are right behind home plate. You came because I'm an impolite pig and you girls thought he should be invited to the game in person."

"You aren't impolite, though!" She sighed.

"And you won't be over there just to invite him to the game either."

"Katie?" Jill called, knocking on the bathroom door. "Are you in there, Katie?"

Robert quickly kissed Katie, opened the bathroom door, and walked out. "Hi Jill, how was shopping?"

"Oh, uh…hi Robert." Jill said, avoiding his gaze as he walked past her. She was wearing a short, flowery dress.

He stopped a bit down the hallway and looked at her. He was about to open his mouth and say something but Katie caught his eye and began shaking her head. He closed his mouth and walked back downstairs.

"Ok, what is the hubbub about?" Jim asked as Robert sat back down on the couch.

"They're going to get all dressed up and go bug your neighbor."

"I'm going then, too!" Jim said, standing up.

"You want your daughters all upset again?" Robert asked. "They don't even want *me* over there with them, and I'm the one who invited him to the baseball game!"

"I don't know if I trust that guy, though! I don't think…"

"Let em' go." Robert said, rubbing his chin. "I think it's something they need to do. They'll be fine. If they aren't back within a reasonable amount of time, we'll kick in his door, ok?"

"They'll be ok, Jim. You have to learn to trust your daughters!" Emily said from a nearby chair.

"I trust my daughters!" Jim pouted as he sat back down. "I don't trust the rest of the world!"

An hour later, Katie was calling Robert back upstairs. He got up from the couch and walked up the stairs. Katie met him at the top landing. "Can you distract Daddy for us and get him out of the living room?"

"Why?"

"She's..." Katie looked back at the bedroom door. "Well, she's a bit self conscious and afraid of what he might say if he knew she was going next door all dressed up. Just distract him until we get out of the house, ok?"

"He already knows what's going on. I told you I was going to go downstairs and tell him." Robert said, sounding bored.

"You *told him*?" Katie asked angrily. She put her hands on her hips and glared at him. "And now I suppose he'll want to follow us over there? Or maybe stand outside and stare at the house while we're inside?"

"No, he'll stay here with me. He just worries about you girls, remember? He'll be ok. He agreed to stay here unless you guys were gone for too long. How long did you think you might be over there?"

"I don't know, but you shouldn't have told him!"

Robert began to laugh. "I don't know what the hell all this secrecy is about, Katie. Just take her over there and get this over with, ok? I'll stay here and keep him calm. We can talk about my book, or something. He's actually been reading it!"

Well...don't you be making any cracks about Jill when she comes down! She's already nervous enough!"

"No cracks, got it." Robert smiled. "By the way, you look beautiful! Come back and spend some time with me so I don't get all jealous, ok?" He gave her a quick kiss on the lips and headed back downstairs.

"Jim," he said, as he sat back down. "They're heading over to see Ben now. We're not supposed to make any cracks about Jill, ok?"

Jim glared at him. "I don't make *cracks* about my daughters!"

"Ok, ok," Robert held his hands up in front of him. "I'm just saying…!"

Katie and Jill came down the stairs. Jill was still wearing the short, flowery dress, and Katie was dressed in a longer, white one. Both women looked stunning. They came into the living room. Robert and Jim stood up.

Jim walked over to Jill and put his hands on her shoulders. "You look absolutely beautiful! Good luck!" He leaned over and kissed her cheek.

Jill Glanced over at Robert, and then back to Jim. "Thank you, Daddy. We won't be long, ok?"

Jim also looked over at Robert, and then at Katie. "You… you take all the time you want, I think Katie will keep you safe for me."

Jill hugged him. "Thank you!"

The two women walked out the front door and towards Ben's house.

Jim looked over at Robert as they left. "He'd have to be pretty stupid not to like her…right?"

"Right." Robert agreed.

They neared Ben's front door and Jill began to slow down. "Katie, I'm not sure I can do this!"

"Sure you can, we're just here to invite him to the baseball game, remember? He likes baseball!"

Katie rang the doorbell; after a few seconds Ben opened the door. "Well, hello Katie, hello Jill! What a nice surprise, to what do I owe the pleasure?"

"Well, I know Robert called you on your cell phone about that stupid baseball game, but we thought you should be invited in person! So we thought we'd come over and let you know he did get tickets for Friday."

"Oh the game," he frowned. "Yes, I had meant to call Robert back about that! It sounds like a lot of fun and I was looking forward to going, but it slipped my mind to return his call! I'm glad you came over to remind me! Did he come with you?"

"Uh, no, he's still trying to get to know our Dad." Katie beamed. "Sometimes he's not as polite as I want him to be!"

"Would you ladies like to come in?"

"Oh, thank you! We can come in for a bit, can't we Jill?"

Jill had been staring at Ben with a frightened look on her face. "Uh…uh yes, I think…?" She mumbled.

Katie stepped into the nice house and pulled Jill along behind her. They followed Ben into the nicely furnished living room.

"Please, have a seat. Have you given any thought to the free marriage counseling I offered Robert? I hope he's at least talked with you about it?"

"I do think we'll be taking you up on that." Katie said, finding a seat on the nearby couch. "We love each other, but we do have a lot of things to work out before we get married."

"You really like baseball?" Jill managed to ask quietly. She sat huddled next to Katie.

"Oh, I *love it*! I was always watching it on TV since I was a child. Collecting cards has been a big part of my life! I'm thrilled that Robert was actually able to get tickets!"

"They're…they're behind the home plate." Jill began to blush a deep shade of red.

"Really? Right behind home? Oh, I can't wait for Friday now!" Ben said, his face showing his excitement.

"This is really nice," Jill remarked quietly, looking around. "Did you have someone design everything in here for you?"

"Oh, you mean my house? No, I did everything myself! You really like it? I was hoping all this expensive furniture wasn't too…ostentatious?"

Jill, still blushing, managed to look him in the eyes. "You know, it's really nice to be around someone who can use large words like that and actually know what they mean!"

Ben let out a small chuckle. "You're a teacher, right? You don't know any teachers who use big words?"

"I teach kindergarten," Jill smiled. "I deal with children. Big words are usually hard for them to understand. I'm still taking classes to get my masters degree, though. Every time I go to a class, I have to adjust from *The wheels on the bus go round and round*, to psychological learning curves and how to implement teaching strategies."

"That's interesting," Ben leaned forward in his chair. His blue eyes seemed to sparkle. "We should maybe get together and discuss school sometime. I'd really enjoy talking to someone who doesn't want to tell me all about their problems and nightmares!"

Katie watched as Jill slowly warmed up to him. She smiled and leaned back against the couch. She couldn't wait to run back and tell Robert how well Jill had done talking to Ben.

Robert sat watching Jim. Every so often, he would look towards the front door, and then glance at his watch.

"How did you and Emily meet?" Robert finally asked.

"Oh, uh…I took her out and she married me later on." Jim said quickly.

"We met in high school." Emily laughed. She shot Jim an exasperated look. "He was the big jock and would always tease me when he would see me! He always called me *Book Worm*, and would make fun of me in the hallways between classes whenever he saw me."

"I did not! I wasn't always making fun of you! I'm not that bad of a guy!"

Emily got up from her seat and walked over behind Jim's chair to put her arms around his neck. "One day while I was in college, I was late for a class. I had overslept and was driving a bit fast, trying to make it to campus on time. I still lived at home back then. And this stupid cop pulled me over!"

"She was doing 55 in a 25 mile an hour zone!" Jim scowled. "She could have killed someone!"

"He looked in the window at me, he was so handsome! Of course, this was a few years after we had graduated high school. I remembered him, and still remembered how he used to tease me."

"Believe it or not, this woman actually says to me, '*Can you please not give me a ticket? I'll do anything, even go out with you!*'"

Robert smiled, clearly enjoying the story. "Wow, and then you two went out and fell in love, huh?"

"No, the prick still wrote me a speeding ticket." Emily laughed.

"About a month later I was thinking about her. I felt bad about writing the ticket," Jim continued the story, stroking Emily's arm. "And so I looked up where she lived, went over to her parent's house, and knocked on the door. I asked to see her, apologized about teasing her, and writing her the ticket. She still wasn't very happy with me, but I ended up asking her out."

"And then she went out with you, right?"

"No, he was still a prick for writing me the ticket and teasing me!" Emily laughed. "I told him to get lost!"

"About a month later, she was late again. Someone else pulled her over. I was driving past and saw her on the side of the road next to the police cruiser. I pulled over next to them and told the cop writing her the ticket that I would take care of it. I let her go."

"And she still didn't like you?" Robert asked, laughing.

"Well…about a week later I saw him at a Dairy Queen one night and he bought me an ice cream cone. We started talking and that's when I started going out with him."

"I guess it was just meant to be." Jim said, smiling up at his wife. "So how did you and my daughter meet?"

"Oh…uh…" Robert started out uncomfortably. "Well, I came into her office. She looked pretty sad and her watch was broken…"

Just as he began the story, the front door opened and Katie and Jill came back into the house. Jim jumped up from his chair, looking them over carefully. "Well, how did things go? Is everybody happy now?"

Jill walked over to where Robert was sitting, leaned down, and kissed him on the cheek. "Thank you for getting him baseball tickets."

"No problem, I guess he's going to the game with me then?"

Jill just sighed and walked up the stairs towards their room.

Robert looked over at Katie. "So what happened? What the hell was that kiss for?"

Katie sat down next to Robert on the couch and kissed him on the cheek herself. "That kiss was because you're *wonderful*!" She sighed and put her head on his shoulder.

Robert looked over at Jim. "Do you have any more speeding tickets left?"

Twenty Six

Robert returned from the bathroom wearing his pajamas and plopped down on his bed. He took a deep breath and closed his eyes.

"Robert…?" Came Jill's voice.

"Yes, Jill?"

"Do you think I'll ever have a relationship as good as yours and Katie's?"

He began to laugh.

Katie returned from the bathroom next and sat down on her bed. "What's so funny?"

"She wants a relationship as good as ours."

"And you think that's funny? We have a great relationship, what's so funny about that, *Robert*?" Katie scowled.

"She makes it sound like we don't have to work at it! Like things just come naturally for us! We fight all the time, Jill! We struggle with communication! Don't get me wrong, I'm head over heals in love with your sister, but sometimes things are a struggle for us!"

"Oh they are not!" Katie said, moving over to sit down on Robert's bed.

"What are you doing? Get off my bed!" Robert said opening his eyes. Instead of moving, Katie lay down beside him and pulled him close for a kiss. "Ok *one kiss*, but then you need to get back to your bed before your dad comes in here and sees this!"

She kissed him and cuddled up next to him, closing her eyes with a relaxed sigh.

"I've only seen you guys fight that one time after you said you yelled at her." Jill said, sitting up on her bed. "You guys always seem so…connected now."

"She yells at me every night when I throw clothes on the floor," Robert laughed. He pulled Katie close and kissed the top of her head. "Or if she catches me trying to put on the same clothes I wore the day before."

"Clothes are to be changed *every day*," Katie said with her eyes still closed. "You know that, Robert! Why do you think we have a hamper? I don't even make you wash them! All I ask is that you change your clothes in the morning!"

"I wear the same pajamas every night."

"That's different! And we do wash them every couple of days, you don't even notice, do you?" She opened her eyes and glared at him.

"You see?" Robert said, sitting up and pulling Katie up with him. "She gets all shook up about clothes! God forbid I should wear the same pair of socks twice!"

"But…that's just a small thing, you guys work that out. I meant…well…you guys just…go together perfectly. I know it hasn't really been that long, but I can't imagine Katie without you anymore."

"I can't imagine my life without him anymore, either." Katie said, kissing him again.

"Katie…*please*!" Robert said with a worried look on his face. "It's hard enough for me to keep my hands off you at night. Your dad's going to come in here and see this!"

"Let him see!" Katie giggled, pressing her lips to his again for a long, passionate kiss. "We *are* going to get married, aren't we? Let him throw his fit! I thought you two were getting along?"

"We *are*!" He said as he moved Katie back over to her own bed. He sat down beside her. "I just don't want that to change, ok? I do love you, and you know I want you with me at night, but I want him to keep liking me, ok?"

"Do you think he likes Ben?" Jill asked.

He doesn't really know him." Robert answered. "Maybe we'll go over and visit him tomorrow? We can go to his office address and pretend to be crazy. He can just fit us in."

"I told him we had a lot of things to work out and would love his counseling." Katie put her arms around Robert and hugged him close, kissing his cheek.

Robert let her hug him for another minute and then walked back to his own bed. "I'll just *bet* you did! And what do we need to work out, Katie? Am I supposed to be sexually dysfunctional, we don't get along, what did you tell him?"

"That's between me and our therapist!" Katie giggled. "That's private!"

"Our relationship is private, right." Robert sighed. "You be sure and let me know if things work out between us, ok?" He closed his eyes again.

"Do *you* like Ben, Robert?" Jill asked.

"I don't know, why?"

"I just…wanted to know. I like him."

He opened his eyes again and glanced back over at Katie. "What really went on over there tonight?"

"We just had a nice visit." Katie smiled.

He watched Katie for a few minutes and then closed his eyes again. Katie moved over to sit on Jill's bed and they began to whisper.

Twenty Seven

"Good morning, Sunshine!" Katie said, kissing Robert's forehead.

He opened his eyes groggily as she was caressing his cheek and running a hand through his hair. "Wha…is it morning already?"

"Yes Darling, it's time for breakfast."

"Oh…uh…yeah. Ok, I'll be up in a minute." He rolled over to his side. Katie still sat on his bed and began to rub his back.

"Oh, that feels so good," Robert purred. "Thanks, Katie." After a few minutes, he sat up and she smiled at him. "Don't think I don't appreciate it, but why are you rubbing my back for me?"

"Can't I pamper my sweetheart?" She said as she kissed him. "You know how much I always like touching you!"

He looked at her suspiciously. "Yeah…yeah, I do know. Ok, I'm up. Let me just jump in the shower really quick."

"I'll be here when you get out!" She said happily.

Robert took a quick shower and then returned to the bedroom to dress. Katie had his faded jeans and favorite, black t-shirt laid out on the bed for him. He dressed quietly, occasionally giving her a suspicious look. He finished and she kissed him again, took his hand, and they walked downstairs for breakfast.

He sat down at the table in his usual spot, near Jim. Katie brought him over a plate of eggs and bacon and set it in front of him.

He looked up at her curiously. "What's this?"

"That's your breakfast, silly!" Katie beamed. "You keep asking why you don't get bacon and eggs! There you go! Can I get you anything else? Do you want a glass of milk?"

Robert looked over at Jim. "Did you do something to her? Why's she being so nice to me?"

"I was just going to ask you the same thing." Jim said, as they both looked curiously at Katie.

"I can't be nice to the man I love?" Katie said, pretending to feel hurt. "I just want to make you happy!"

He looked down at his plate. "What happened to the diet? To just eating fruit? Yesterday you got mad and said bacon would kill us."

"Oh, you were right, honey! You need a good breakfast in the morning! I thought about it, and it won't ruin your diet to have a few eggs and a bit of bacon."

"If I were you, I'd enjoy this until you find out what's really going on!" Jim grinned. "Because something's up, I can smell it!"

"Yeah, I think you're right." Robert said, as he began to eat his eggs. Katie just smiled at him and gave him a hug.

After breakfast Robert looked over at Jim. "Did you have any plans for us today?"

"Oh, not really. I was going to mow the grass or something. You guys shouldn't worry about bothering with us all the time! If there's somewhere you want to do, or see, head out! I trust you with my girls!"

"Wow, I haven't mowed grass since I was a kid!" Robert sighed. "I always loved the smell. Do you have a grass catcher or do you need someone to rake afterwards?"

"You can rake the grass for me if you really want to. It would be nice to have the company out there while I work."

Robert looked up at Katie. "You don't mind if I help with the yard work, do you?"

She hugged him again and kissed his cheek. "You can do anything you want!"

"How about we take a walk first?" He replied, giving her a suspicious look.

"A…walk?" Katie stuttered. She began to sound unsure of herself. "Yes, I guess that would be nice."

Robert finished eating and took her by the hand. They walked out the front door. He led her slowly down the sidewalk. At first, he just walked along, holding her hand, looking peacefully around. Finally, after they had walked a few blocks, he spoke up:

"Ok, what's going on?"

"What do you mean? We're just taking a nice walk."

Robert stopped walking and turned her towards him. He put his hands around her waist and pulled her into a hug. "What is it that you're afraid to tell me this time?"

"Why would I be afraid to tell you something?" She asked, hugging him back. "Just because I love you and showed you some attention this morning?"

He looked into her eyes. "Katie...*please*?"

She sighed and looked down at his chest. "I want something."

"What? You know all you have to do is ask me for anything, and if I can, it's yours! Are you still worried about that ring?"

"No, no...I...I want..." She looked back up and into his eyes again. "Oh Robert, I want something from you and I know you won't want to give it to me!"

"What do you want? Just tell me, Katie! Why can't you just trust me?"

She pulled him back into another hug. "Oh, you know I trust you! I do! But I just don't like taking something away from you!"

"Taking something away from me? What were you going to take from me?"

She pulled back from the hug and Robert could see tears forming in her eyes. "I want...well, I wanted your..." She sniffed and covered her mouth with her hand.

He caressed her cheek and brushed away a tear. "Why are you so shook up about whatever this is? Did you change your mind about marrying me?"

"Oh my God, *no*! Don't ever think that! I love you and really want to marry you! I really do, but..."

"But what, sweetheart? You know whenever you feel bad I can always make you feel better! Just tell me what you want, ok?"

She sighed. He could feel her shaking in his arms. "Can I please…I want your baseball tickets."

"My…tickets?" He asked. "Why would you want my baseball tickets? Katie, you don't even like sports!"

"I know, and I feel so awful asking for them! You worked *so hard* calling everyone and then signing all those books!"

"Why would you want my tickets?"

"I was going to give them to Jill. She likes Ben *so much*! She's so afraid to try and get a date with him."

"And so you wanted to send her to the ballgame with him? She doesn't even like sports, does she?"

"No, but if they went together…if she spent the night with him doing something he loved…?"

"When did you come up with this little plan?"

"I was thinking about it last night."

"And so you figured if you were really nice to me…?"

"I just felt…honestly sweetheart, I just felt so *guilty*! I want to help out my sister. I know how much you wanted to go to that game and how hard it would be for you to give up your ticket!"

Robert hugged her again. "Katie, there's only one you, and one Jill. There's plenty of baseball. I'll get other tickets, these are yours."

She hugged him back tightly, "Are you sure? I know you really wanted to go!"

"Katie, how could you think I wouldn't give you my tickets if you asked for them?"

"Well…I…I thought you probably would, but…but I didn't want to take something like that away from you."

He smiled at her and caressed her hand as they began to walk back towards the house. "I'm *giving* you the tickets. You aren't taking anything away from me!"

She put her arm around him and leaned her head against his shoulder as they walked, "You're so special, Robert, do you know that?"

"Yeah, special and gullible. Would you like a tiny bit of advice?"

"I know I should just talk to you when I need something, right?"

"Well, yes," he grinned. "But if she'd really like to make an impression, she should wear some jeans and a baseball jersey when they go. Maybe a hat, too? If he really likes baseball, he'll appreciate her dressing all up like that."

"I was going to do her hair and find her a nice dress. She should dress up for her first date with him!" Katie said looking up at him confused.

"What team does he like?" Robert asked. "Trust me honey, a jersey and a hat will be something he'll remember."

"What team, how would we know that? Can't you go over and…I don't know, talk sports with him or something?"

"Sure," Robert laughed. "And after we discuss sports, I'll just say *By the way Ben, I won't be going to the ball game tomorrow!*"

They arrived back at the house to see Jim already out mowing the front lawn. Robert watched him for a minute still holding Katie's hand.

"Did you want to go and tell her I said yes and take her shopping for a jersey?"

"Um…I'd like to, but…" Katie gave him a worried look. "She doesn't know I was going to ask you for the tickets."

"What do you mean she doesn't know?" Robert asked, confused. "You didn't talk this over with her first?"

"She would have probably said no!" Katie snapped, concern coming across her face. "But she really deserves a night out! And I thought…well…"

"You just figured you'd set things up for her without telling her, huh?"

"We've been so close the last couple of days!" Katie whined. "She let me do her hair and she wanted to try on my clothes! She was never like that with me before!"

"Well, let's go tell her." Robert said, leading Katie back into the house. They found her wearing some old jeans and a t-shirt and chatting with Emily. She smiled as they walked into the living room.

"I thought I'd help you rake the yard after he's done mowing!" Jill said, holding out her arms, showing off her work clothes.

"Uh…" Robert looked over at Katie. "Jill, we kind of have something to ask you."

"Something to ask *me*? This doesn't sound good!" She said, looking from Robert to Katie.

"Well, uh…" Robert started, glancing in Katie's direction. "My agent called and wants me to do a few things on Friday while I'm here. I can't make it to the ballgame. Katie hates sports, so I was wondering if you might like to use my ticket?"

Jill just looked at him for a minute. Then she crossed her arms. "You aren't a very good liar. That's the best you could come up with, your agent called you? No thank you, I hate baseball."

Robert shot Katie another look. "Ok, yes I'm lying. But we really did want you to use the ticket and go to the ballgame."

"Katie was so nice to you this morning so she could get you to give me your baseball ticket. Then she could push me into a date with Ben?" Jill asked, scowling at them.

"I love him! What does my being nice to my fiancé have to do with him giving you his ticket?" Katie asked angrily.

"Oh, poor Jill can't get herself a date! We'll just get one for her!" Jill mocked.

"Girls, please!" Emily said, stepping in between the two women. "You don't need to fight over this!"

"Just take the ticket!" Katie yelled. "Why do you always have to make such a big deal about everything?"

"And why do you have to always poke your nose into my business?"

"Katie, she said no, it's ok." Robert said, trying to pull her away from Jill.

"She's just being stubborn! She figures if she never has a date, she never has to deal with any emotions!"

Robert stepped in front of Katie and looked her in the eyes. "Katie, she said no. She doesn't have to go if she doesn't want to. Leave her alone, ok?"

"Yes, leave me alone, *Katie*!" Jill mocked. Katie tried to push past Robert. He pulled her out of the living room out onto the front porch.

"Oh, I can't believe I went through all that to talk you into giving her your baseball ticket, and then she acts like that!" She fumed.

Robert turned her to face him and looked into her eyes. "You've never been shy in your life, have you?"

"Oh yeah, let's go there!" She yelled. "All we tried to do was help her out, and she just threw it back in your face!"

"Has there ever been a time in your life when a cute guy walked by you and you didn't say hi to him, or smile at him, or something like that?" Robert asked.

"What does my saying hi to cute guys have to do with this?"

"You were never afraid of talking to a guy, were you?"

"I've been nervous before." Katie said, starting to pout. "But she just…"

"Did you know that sometimes people can be so shy that it affects them physically? Katie, sometimes people can't even talk to anyone else!"

"She's a *teacher*, Robert! How can you be a teacher and be so shy that you can't talk to people?"

He rubbed his chin. "She teaches little kids, honey. That's completely different."

"That's what she said, too! But it just sounds like an excuse to me!"

"Well, like it or not, she said no to the tickets. Just like your Dad's rule about not sleeping together until we're married, we need to respect what she wants, ok?"

Katie looked at the ground. "I just wanted to help her…she seemed to like him so much!"

"Well, I know it's hard, but the best way you can probably help her, is to leave her alone."

Jim had just finished mowing the grass and walked up onto the porch. "So Writer, did you figure out why she was being so nice this morning?"

"She wanted to give my baseball ticket to Jill, but Jill said no."

"Your baseball ticket," Jim asked, confused. "Why would she want that? She hates sports, just like Katie does."

"I wanted her to be able to go somewhere with Ben! I was just trying to help her get a date!" Katie said, putting her hands on her hips and glaring at him.

"And she said no, huh? Go ahead and start raking. Katie, you help him out."

"I am *not* raking your yard in these shoes!" She fussed. "Besides, it was Robert who wanted to get his hands dirty, not me!"

"Ok, then stay out here and watch." Jim said, as if he was giving an order. "I'll have a chat with Jill."

Jim walked into the house and got himself two beers from the refrigerator. He returned to the living room and sat down next to Jill. He opened a can and held it out to her.

"I don't drink beer Dad, you know that."

"I'll just set it over here for you, in case you want it in a bit, ok?" He set the beer down on a nearby table. He opened the other can and took a deep drink.

Jill sighed, and then turned towards her father. "So they sent you in to try and make me go to the baseball game?"

"What game? Who's trying to make you go to a game?" Jim asked, pretending innocence.

"Dad, I just don't want to force myself on the poor man! And I know Robert went to a lot of trouble to get those tickets, he should be the one to go to the game!"

"Ok," he said simply. He took another drink from his can of beer.

"Mom, will you tell him I don't want to go to the stupid game!"

"Don't go then." Jim said hugging her. "No one's going to make you do anything if you don't want to. I just finished with the lawn and thought I'd come in and have a beer with my daughter."

"What abut your *other* daughter?"

"What about her?"

"You don't want to have a beer with her, too?"

"She's out playing with the writer. You don't mind sharing a drink with the old man, do you?"

Jill sighed again and looked at him. "It's not that I don't want to go, part of me really would like to! I'm just…so confused!"

Jim took another drink of his beer. "You live in New York, he lives here. He's the big, handsome, doctor, and you're just a teacher, right?"

"Maybe, I don't know!" Jill said shaking her head.

"How many times have I told you how proud your Mother and I are of you? How many times have I told you how important teaching really can be?"

"A lot, but…"

"Then you aren't *just* a teacher, are you? You aren't less important than some doctor! Please don't look at things that way."

"I don't know what to think anymore. I wish…I wish someone would look at me the way Robert looks at Katie! I wish…that some important writer would bring *me* jewelry! I'm so happy for Katie and Robert, but some days…
sometimes I just get so *jealous*! She was always the pretty

one, the popular one, and then she ends up with this perfect guy!"

"Is that what this is all about? Why you've been letting her dress you up while you're here? So you can attract some perfect guy?"

Jill picked up the can of beer on the table and took a drink. "Yes, no, maybe, I don't know! When I met Ben, he was so… handsome, and so nice, and…"

"And after meeting him, you suddenly got really worried about what happens if he doesn't like you, right?"

"I don't want to go to the game, alright?"

"Then don't go. No one will say another word to you about it, I promise! But just think about this: Maybe this Ben guy has been waiting for the perfect woman to walk into *his* life. Maybe he's been waiting for you?"

"And so you're telling me to start a long distance relationship with him?"

"No, that's not what I meant. Do you really like the writer? Do you really think he's a good match for your sister? Or do you suppose they'll get divorced after she dresses him up for a few years?"

"He's nice. He keeps her spoiled, so they'll probably stay together. She told me he had a long talk with her about dressing him up. That's probably why you don't see him in a tie everyday now."

Jim smiled in a knowing way. "I was wondering about that."

Jill finished off the beer in her hand and handed the can back to Jim. She moved over and put her head on his shoulder. "Dad, what happens if I go to the game and…and think I really like him?"

"Do you really like him now?"

"Maybe."

"But what if he doesn't share your feelings? Then the world ends, right?"

"This isn't funny, Dad!"

Emily sat down on the other side of Jill, "Honey, I think what your dad means is that all you can do is try. You know how shook up Katie has been after she had broken up with someone? It hurts sometimes, but all you can do is try! But if you don't want to, if you don't want us saying another word about the neighbor, we won't. We just want you to be happy!"

Jill gave her mother a sad look. "He *is* handsome. And he can actually speak intelligently!"

"Well then, maybe I should go over and invite him to dinner tonight?" Emily asked, putting a hand on Jill's leg.

"We've already went over and harassed him last night!"

"Well, if he thinks its harassment, then he doesn't need to come to dinner! But I think it would be nice for him to come; you and I can cook something special!"

"You really wouldn't mind that?" Jill asked.

"I think that's a good idea, too!" Jim beamed. "Then I can check him out for myself."

Jim walked out onto the front porch. Robert was raking the front yard, while Katie stood on the sidewalk giving him directions.

"You've missed a spot!"

"I'll get to it, just give me a chance."

"Over here! I said *over here*, you're raking in the wrong direction!"

"Isn't there another rake? I told you if you think I'm doing this wrong, get a rake and help me out!"

"I'm *not* raking grass in these shoes! Now do it the way I told you to!"

Jim had to suppress a smile. "Katie, Writer, can you both come here for a minute?"

"Daddy, he has a *name*!" Katie scolded.

"I'm sure he does," Jim said, as Robert walked over to the porch. "He also has some nice clothes, right?"

"Of course he has nice clothes! He doesn't need nice clothes to rake grass, though!"

"Dinner party or something?" Robert asked, sounding as if he already knew the answer. "You need me to dress up while you invite a few folks over?"

"Em is going to invite the neighbor over for dinner tonight. I thought it would be nice if we all dressed up."

"Oh Daddy, we'd love to dress up!" Katie burst into a happy smile.

"Uh yeah…we'd love that." Robert said blandly.

"I don't suppose he's home right now?" Jim asked.

"No, I think he's still at work, or therapy, or whatever he does. I have his cell phone number though if you want to give him a call?"

Robert reached into his pocket and pulled out his cell phone. He found Ben's number, dialed it, and handed the phone to Jim.

"Uh…hi, this is Jim Benson, your neighbor? My wife and I have our daughters and their…uh…writer here with us for a bit. We figured since you were new to the neighborhood, you might like to come for dinner tonight? Go ahead and call the writer back on his cell phone and let him know. Just let us know if you can make it and what time you'd like to eat. Uh…take care."

He handed the phone back to Robert.

"Their *writer*?" Katie yelled. "*Their writer*? Daddy, you can't even use his name? I thought you liked him?"

"Make sure he's dressed up tonight, ok?" Jim pulled her into a hug. He kissed her on the forehead and walked back into the house.

"And you're just going to stand there and let him call you *Writer*, huh?"

"Actually, I'm pretty pleased!" Robert grinned. "He could have called me a lot worse things! Writer sounds pretty nice!"

Twenty Eight

Robert lay on his bed while Katie dug in a suitcase. She pulled out a blue shirt with a black tie. "Try these on, ok?"

Robert folded his hands behind his head. "Why don't *you* try them on, and I'll tell you how they look?"

Katie gave him a dirty look. "This is for *Jill*! I want us to look nice, ok?"

You had me try on the shirt before we bought it, remember? It fits fine."

"I *know* it fits you, I just wanted to see how you looked wearing it! Is it really so hard to try on clothes for me?"

He jumped off the bed and threw his arms around her neck, pulling her toward him. "No, what's hard is keeping my hands off of you! Do you know how fucking horny I am right now?"

"*Robert Wacaster* I can't believe you just said that!" She tried to give him a nasty look, but after a minute broke out into a smile. "Really? You really miss touching me that much?"

He pressed his lips to hers and kissed her softly at first, then more passionately. She pulled him close and they continued to kiss.

"Oh…oh my God, I'm *so* sorry, I didn't mean to…oh man!" Came Jill's voice.

Robert pushed himself away from Katie. "Hi Jill, sorry about that. I didn't mean to do that, I…well, I uh…we…"

"That's ok," she turned around putting her back to them. "I know you and Katie miss…being together at night. I can stay out of here for a while."

"No, no, no! Come on in, we were about finished anyway. If we would have continued, I would have broken some rules."

"Maybe we can break the rules later?" Katie said, running a gentle hand across his back.

Robert tensed up at her touch. "*Please* don't tease me!" He turned to Jill. "Come on in, did you need something in here?"

"No, actually…actually I came to tell you I was sorry about how I was acting. I appreciate you offering me the baseball ticket. I just…I'm just not ready for that yet."

"I understand, I think. No problem."

"Well…" Katie started.

Robert shook his head at her.

"Yes, we understand." Katie finished.

"I guess she had you trying on all kinds of clothes?" Jill asked. She turned around and was looking at the clothes Katie set out on the nearby bed. "The blue shirt there looks nice."

Robert sighed. "Yeah, trying on more clothes." His cell phone began to ring. He pulled it out of his pocket and looked at it. "Hello?"

Both women watched him closely, straining to hear every word. They could barely hear a voice coming through the phone, but couldn't make any words out clearly.

"That's great! That sounds really good! Is there anything you'd like to drink?"

Katie looked at Jill and mouthed, "It's Ben!"

"Well, I'm a recovered alchie, so I don't really drink. No, no, it's not a problem! You remember the bar, right? I'm fine with other people drinking around me, it's been a while."

Katie moved over next to Robert and leaned near the phone trying to hear the other side of the conversation. Robert gave her an annoyed look and turned to walk out of the room. Both women followed him.

"Yeah, yeah, six is fine! I'll let Jim and Emily know. Are you allergic to anything? I'd hate for her to cook something with peanut butter, or something, and then have to call an ambulance!" He began to laugh.

"Yeah no problem, I'll let them know. Oh, by the way, I'm sure Katie will make me wear a tie tonight, so you might want to wear one, too? I see, yeah. Ok then, see you tonight, bye!"

Robert hung up and shoved the phone back into his pocket.

"That was Ben, wasn't it?" Jill asked.

"And he's agreed to come for dinner!" Katie said happily.

"That was Paul, he just bought himself a cow and is starting a farm." Robert said flatly. He walked down the stairs with both Jill and Katie right behind him.

He got to the bottom of the stairs glancing over at Jim who was sitting in his favorite chair, watching TV. "Where's Emily?" He asked nicely.

"She's in the kitchen. Are you writing a book, or something?" Jim said, and began to laugh at his own joke.

"What did he say, Robert?" Katie asked again.

"I told you, he bought a cow and is starting a farm."

Katie reached out and grabbed his shoulder. He stopped as she turned him around to face her. "Don't play with me!"

Robert began to laugh. "Yes honey, it was Ben. I need to pass on a message, ok?"

He walked into the kitchen and smiled at Emily. "Ben returned my call. He said he would be happy to join us for dinner tonight. He gets home somewhere around five and will probably make it here sometime around six."

"Oh, that's wonderful!" Emily's eyes sparkled. Robert could see part of Katie in them. "Did you ask him if he wanted anything special?"

"He said he'd bring some kind of red wine, if you guys didn't mind. I told him that would be fine. I honestly don't know what kind of food goes with that, though."

"He said he'd bring wine?" Jill asked. "What kind?"

"I just told you, red." Robert said looking from Emily to Jill.

"But what kind of red, Robert? There are different kinds of red wine! It *does* make a difference!" Jill scowled.

"I don't know. I don't even drink anymore. Wine is wine to me."

"Yeah, and shoes are shoes, and a dress is a dress. Go tell Katie that!"

Katie frowned at the remark. "Don't even go there, I tried to teach him about clothes, but he just doesn't care!"

Emily pulled Jill into a hug. "I have a few recipes we can look through."

Jill hugged her back. "Thanks Mom." She looked over toward Katie. "Would you please do my hair and make up again tonight?"

"Of course…once I finish wrestling Robert and Daddy into some decent clothing."

"We get to wrestle? Oh I am *so* up for that!" Robert laughed.

Katie ignored his comment. "What else did he say?"

"What do you mean?" Robert asked.

"What did he say to you over the phone?" Katie asked again.

"I just told you, he said he'd be happy to come for dinner and would bring some wine!" He turned and walked back into the living room and sat down on the couch.

Katie followed him and sat down next to him. "He had to have said more than that. You talked to him for a few minutes."

"Honestly, that's all he said!"

"Is she trying to analyze a conversation you had?" Jim asked.

"I guess so."

Katie scowled at him. "Why do you always insist on doing this? I just asked what he said to you. Why can't you tell me?"

Robert began to laugh. "Katie…what do you want from me? He just said he'd be happy to come over. There's nothing else, honestly! No secret codes, no hidden messages. That's it!"

"I heard you tell him I was going to make you wear a tie!"

"Yeah."

"And?"

"And what? He said ties are fine, he's a doctor and wears them all the time anyway!"

"He said that? That he always wears a tie? You see, you *are* leaving things out!"

"I'm not leaving things out! For God's sake, would you like me to call him back and you can ask him to repeat everything he said?"

"I just wanted to know if he said anything about Jill!" Katie whispered to him.

"Don't bother whispering Katie, I can still hear you." Jim muttered.

"No, he didn't say anything about Jill."

"Are you sure?"

"Yes, I'm sure. When he comes tonight, you be sure and dig into him with the third degree, ok? You make sure you ask him everything you want to know! I'm sure your dad can bring out a heat lamp we can make him sit under it, if you want?"

"I *do* have a lamp that puts off a lot of heat in the closet. We can put him under that." Jim said, not bothering to even look away from the television.

Katie scowled at both men. "You two had damned well better behave tonight! I mean it, Daddy! And *you*," Katie said, glaring at Robert. "If you step out of line and embarrass my sister, I will make your life a living hell, do you understand me?"

Jim began to laugh, and smiled at Robert. "Good luck, Writer!"

Robert had finished showering and shaving. He walked into the bedroom to dress. Katie had already laid out some clothes. He began to put them on. While he was dressing she knocked on the door and stuck her head in. "Are you decent, can I come in?"

"I'm probably not decent, but come on in anyway!"

She came in and sat down on her bed. She quietly watched him put on the clothes she had laid out. After putting on the shirt and pants, he picked up the tie and placed it around his neck.

Katie stood up and pulled the tie away from him. "You don't have to wear this, if you don't want to."

Robert looked at her, confused for a minute. "Its fine, you laid it out and I know that means it's something you want me to wear. Really Katie, it's ok."

She smiled and slipped the tie back around his neck. She began to tie it and let out a quiet sigh. "I actually came in here because I wanted to say I'm sorry."

"Sorry for what?"

"I shouldn't have said I would make your life a living hell, you didn't deserve to be threatened like that. I don't even know why I said that to you."

"I think you're just worried about Jill. Don't blame you for wanting everything to be perfect, it's who you are."

"But you're always so nice to everyone. I never have to tell you to behave!"

"Yeah, I'm always so nice. Remember me throwing that coaster out of the car?"

"I forgot about that! Maybe you should be threatened?" She giggled.

She finished with his tie. He stood up straight, waiting for her to inspect him. "Well, how do I look?"

"Always so handsome, I'm so proud of you!"

"I may have to propose pretty soon, we've been getting along pretty well!"

She put her arms around his neck and kissed him gently on the lips. "You propose when you think it's time, I trust your judgment."

"Uh huh, so you really wouldn't mind if I waited say… another year? See how things go?"

"If you wait much longer, I may just ask *you*!"

"Ask me? You would actually as me to marry you? How progressive of you!" He began to laugh. "Any clue as to what your answer will be when I propose?"

She pressed her lips to his again, taking her time with the kiss. "My answer is supposed to be a surprise, isn't it?"

"Yes, I guess it is." He pulled her close and they continued to kiss.

Robert walked downstairs and into the kitchen. The wonderful smells made his stomach growl. Jill and Emily were checking different pots and plates around the kitchen.

"Oh Robert, good! We can use you for a second!" Jill said. "Can you come here and taste this, please? Tell me if it has too much salt?"

She dipped a small spoon into one of the pots and held it out towards him. He looked at the white liquid on the spoon and then opened his mouth for the taste. He swallowed and then looked at her with his eyes wide.

"That was fantastic! What is it?"

"It's home made cream of mushroom soup. We thought we could serve it just before the main course, which is going to be a bit of braised beef and broccoli. So you don't think it has too much salt? Sometimes I put in a bit too much."

"Oh my God, that was *fantastic*!" He grinned widely. "You really made that from scratch?"

"Yes, Mom taught me the recipe a few years ago. Do you think Ben will like it?"

"If he doesn't, then he doesn't have any taste buds! Wow, I can't believe you made this, wow!"

She smiled and went back to checking several other pots. "Is Katie busy?"

"Just chasing me around, why?"

"Well, I didn't plan on wearing what I have on now! But most of the food is under control, I thought maybe she could help me get ready?"

"Sure, why not? She's out in the living room with Jim. She seems pretty excited about the dinner guest."

"Can you stay here and help Mom?" Jill asked as she held out a large, wooden spoon towards him.

"I certainly can't cook like you two! I guess I can stay and help, but…uh…"

"He's already all dressed up, honey. I can handle things by myself. You go ahead and get ready." Emily said, kissing Jill on the cheek. She found a nearby stool and pointed at it. "You can certainly keep me company while Jill gets ready, though."

"Well that, I can handle!" Robert smiled.

Jill sat on her bed as Katie brushed her hair. "Katie...how did you know?"

"How did I know what?"

"That Robert was...you know, The One?"

"I just knew. Even from when we first met, it was like we shared a connection. Even now, part of me gets so excited whenever we look into each other's eyes."

"So you just...knew he was The One, huh?"

"I didn't know at first, but after my trip to California, I knew. But you're a completely different person. You have to judge things for yourself, Jill."

"I didn't mean...well, maybe it isn't Ben, but..."

"He *is* cute. Be careful, sometimes you have to really watch the cute ones."

"Robert's cute."

Katie began laughing. "Yes he is, and I have to watch him every minute! Did you see Daddy sneaking him bacon yesterday?"

"You trust him though, right?"

"Yes, I trust Robert. I feel jealous sometimes, I can't help that, but I know he's loyal. He won't cheat on me."

Robert sat at the kitchen table watching Emily. She moved around checking things and occasionally stirring pots.

"I guess we're eating a big dinner tonight, huh?" He asked.

"It just looks big. It's not really that much. Some soup to start, a couple vegetables and a pot roast." Emily reassured him.

"I put on a tie for a pot roast." Robert laughed.

"You'll use your manners while we have a guest, right?" Emily asked. "I know you've been on your best behavior since you've gotten here, but you have that little sparkle of trouble in your eye that I see in Jim's sometimes."

"I always behave around Katie." Robert frowned.

"I'm just making sure. Trust me when I say you won't like having both my daughters mad at you at the same time!"

The doorbell rang and Robert stood up. "Well, I guess I should go and help Jim say hello."

"Just a second and I'll go with you. Let me just set the soup to simmer a bit." Emily finished adjusting a knob on the stove and took Robert's arm. "Shall we?"

They walked into the living room just as Jim was opening the door. He shook hands with Ben and invited him inside. Ben handed Jim a bottle of wine as he walked in.

"Feel free to take a seat anywhere you'd like. It's always nice to have a neighbor come by. This is my wife Emily, and you remember the writer?"

"Emily, very nice to meet you!" Ben said shaking her hand. "And yes, I do remember Robert, nice to see you again!" He shook hands with Robert and walked towards the living room.

"My two daughters should be down in a few minutes. You know women, they think they have to dress up for everything." Jim said, as he sat down. Ben sat down on the couch and Robert plopped down next to him.

"Oh, of course! I really appreciate the invitation, I don't get very many home cooked meals. I usually end up just finding a TV dinner somewhere, or reheating some left over fast food. Things are starting to pick up with my new practice!"

"Is that so?" Robert asked. "Lots of whackos here in Florida?"

"*Robert!*" Emily glared at him. "Was that nice to say? Maybe you should go upstairs and check on the girls?"

"I was just joking!" Robert frowned as he got up. He walked grumpily towards the stairs.

Ben watched him and laughed quietly. "I like Robert. He doesn't hold back, does he?"

Robert walked to the spare bedroom and knocked on the closed door. "We'll be out in a minute!"

"Are you decent, can I come in?" Robert growled.

Katie opened the door and looked out at him. "Did you need something in here, sweetheart? I told you we'll be down in a minute."

"I kind of…I was sent upstairs. I don't really want to go back down there by myself. Can I just wait for you guys?"

The smile dropped from Katie's lips. "Why were you sent upstairs, what did you do?"

"I didn't *do* anything! I was…they just sent me up here to check on you."

Katie watched him suspiciously. "Uh huh, you didn't do anything. You'd better be behaving! Yes, come on in and you can wait for us, we're almost ready."

She opened the door and let Robert walk into the room. He walked over to his bed and sat down.

Jill was wearing some slacks and a purple, long sleeved, silk shirt. She smiled at him. "Is Ben here? How does he look?"

"Like he shrank too many heads today." Robert scowled. "He's carrying this big walking stick with a human skull on the top."

Katie stopped fussing with Jill's hair and glared at him. "Ok, I see why they sent you up here! If you can't say anything nice, Robert…?"

"No, no, I'll be good! I know I probably sound rude but joking helps me deal with stress sometimes."

"Well *stop it*! You need to deal with stress some other way, understand? At least for tonight! Behave yourself!"

Robert began looking her up and down. "You aren't dressed up! Why are you wearing jeans, Katie? You had me put on a tie!"

"We need to go downstairs!" Katie said as she rolled her eyes. "I'll explain things to you later, if I have to, ok?"

"Explain things to me? Why would I have to have things explained to me?"

Katie and Jill both walked towards the door. "Are you coming, or not?"

Robert sighed. "Yeah, I guess so. We certainly invited the right kind of guy to dinner! I think we all could use a bit of therapy."

They came downstairs and could hear Jim, Emily, and Ben laughing. They walked into the living room. Ben and Jim stood up.

"Ah, here are my two girls, my pride and joy!" Jim smiled. "This is my oldest, Katie. And my youngest, Jill."

Ben reached out and shook Katie's hand. Then he shook Jill's hand, smiled, and looked into her eyes. There was an almost magnetic pause as they looked at each other. Robert turned to look at Katie with his mouth open. He was about to say something but Katie grabbed his arm so he stayed quiet.

They all sat back down. Ben was in the easy chair in the corner with Robert, Katie, and Jill on the couch. Jim sat back down in his chair while Emily remained standing.

"I'm going to go and check on dinner. Jill, let me know when everyone's ready to eat and we can start serving, ok?"

Jill smiled shyly. "Ok, Mom."

Ben glanced over at Robert. "Have you decided whether or not to take me up on the pre-marital counseling?"

Robert glanced quickly at Katie. "Yeah, I would like to take you up on that as long as it's ok with Katie? We really haven't talked about it yet."

"Certainly, we'd be happy for any help you can give us!"

"Is tomorrow too soon?" Ben asked, "I have an opening in the morning."

"Tomorrow," Robert asked. "Uh...I don't think we have anything planned for tomorrow. Is tomorrow ok, Katie?"

"You just tell us where, and what time, and we'll be there!" Katie smiled. She reached out and took Robert's hand.

"How about nine o'clock? You can be my first appointment of the day! I don't have anyone else until noon."

"That would be wonderful, thank you for this!" Katie said politely.

"And where is it?" Robert asked.

"My office is in the Paramount Medical Center." Ben said, reaching into his pocket for a card.

"That's over on Bay Avenue, right?" Jim asked. "The big complex on the corner?"

"Yes, exactly! So you already know where it is! Very good! I'm up on the third floor. If you have any trouble finding it, just call the office and my receptionist can help you out."

"His…*Executive Assistant* can help us?" Robert snickered into Katie's ear. She drove her elbow into his stomach, and he let out a loud, "Oof!"

"Oh Sweetheart, did I get you?" Katie scowled at him. "I'm so sorry!"

Ben tried to hide a smile and looked over at Jill. "It's really nice to see you again, Jill! I was looking forward to hearing more about how your classes were coming! You sound so happy when you talk about teaching!"

Jill began to blush. "Well, I just…I do love to teach. And sometimes, you know when you see that interest in learning… in one of the little ones, I mean…I really like that."

"She was given a teaching award by the city of New York." Robert said quietly. "A very nice plaque."

Jill looked over at him. "How did *you* know about that, did Katie tell you?"

"It's hanging in your room. I looked at the pictures and awards you have on your wall while I was using your computer. It looked pretty important."

"I didn't...I didn't even know you saw that. I didn't know you cared about what I did. I always thought you were just focused on Katie."

"An award from the city?" Ben smiled. "That sounds very impressive! If I'm ever in New York, you'll have to have me over sometime to see it!"

Jill continued to blush. "I'd like that. I think I'd better help Mom with dinner." She jumped up from the couch and walked quickly into the kitchen.

"Well..." Ben smiled. "Any other thoughts, Robert?"

Katie squeezed his hand and glared at him. "Yes *Robert*, would you like to say anything else?"

Robert looked embarrassed. "Uh...dinner's about ready, isn't it? Can we go and eat?"

"Yes, I'm sure dinner is almost ready, we can move into the dining room." Jim and Ben got up and walked towards the dining room. Katie lagged behind, holding onto Robert's hand. "If you embarrass her, I will *never* forgive you!"

"I just mentioned her award!" Robert whispered back. "What was so wrong about that? I'm behaving, honey, I really am!"

Katie led him into the dining area alongside the kitchen and they sat down at the table. Emily smiled as they sat down.

"I'm sorry there isn't much room, things might be a bit cozy for us. But usually it's just Jim and me here."

"Oh, no problem, I'm willing to squeeze in for a home cooked meal." Ben said happily. Robert opened his mouth to say something but after a look from Katie, closed it again without a word.

"I thought we'd start off with some soup." Jill said, as she began filling up bowls for Emily to pass around the table.

"Oh, this is *good*!" Robert said as he licked his lips. "They let me taste it earlier, I love it!"

Katie watched him closely. "Jill's always been a good cook."

The bowls were passed out and Robert began to eat his soup quickly. He shoveled spoonful after spoonful into his mouth and quickly emptied his bowl. Katie reached beneath the table and squeezed his leg hard, as she glared at him. He looked over at her and she mouthed the words, *slow down*!

"Oh, this is good! Is this made from scratch?" Ben asked as he slowly finished his bowl.

"Yes, we use mushrooms from a can, but the broth is made from scratch." Jill answered quietly. "You really like it?"

"Oh, it's wonderful! Obviously, Robert likes it, too!" He let out a small laugh.

"Robert shouldn't wolf down his food, it's rude!" Katie growled.

Ben continued to laugh. "It's actually a compliment. It shows how good the soup is."

Everyone ate quietly through the rest of the dinner. Jill served several more courses which Ben complemented and then ate quietly.

After sitting down and finishing her helping of pot roast, Jill sighed. "I'm sorry we don't have any desert. We didn't think about it until it was too late."

"You should open his bottle of wine." Robert said quietly.

"Oh my gosh; the wine!" Jill said clapping a hand to her forehead. "I completely forgot you were bringing wine for your dinner, I'm so sorry!"

"Don't be sorry, the meal was fantastic. I really enjoyed it without the wine. Thank you."

"Maybe we could open the bottle in the living room and talk some more?" Jim smiled. "Robert and Katie can start on the dishes, they were kind enough to volunteer, and we can have a nice chat?"

Ben stood up from the table. "Why not? That sounds like the end to a perfect visit!"

Jim found the bottle Ben had brought over, got a corkscrew out of a kitchen drawer, and opened the bottle. "Jill, would you mind escorting our dinner guest to the living room and making him comfortable? Your Mom and I will get some glasses and be right out!"

Jill looked at Ben nervously. "I'd like that...did you really enjoy the dinner, Ben?"

"Oh, that was the best dinner I think I can ever remember having. You're a tremendous cook, thank you again!" Jill led him into the living room as Robert and Katie still sat at the table.

Jim pulled the cork out of the bottle and leaned over the table towards Robert. "I know how much you like helping out, Writer! Don't have too much fun, now!" He walked out of the kitchen laughing.

Emily got down four glasses from a cupboard and put a hand on Robert's shoulder before leaving the kitchen. "You don't need to do the dishes, come into the living room and visit with us."

Robert sighed and stood up. "No, that's ok. We want to help out, we'll do the dishes. That was a fantastic dinner, you deserve a break. Go have some wine and relax."

Katie sat at the table, still glaring at him. Emily left and she finally spoke. "You just had to wolf down your meal, didn't you?"

He began picking up dishes from the table and carrying them to the sink. "I just ate my food! I didn't think I was wolfing down anything! You know you're always telling me to slow down!"

"And then when you couldn't be polite, you just quit talking, huh?"

"Why are you so shook up about tonight? He came and had dinner with us. I didn't hear him talking anybody's ear off!"

"You really don't understand what tonight means to her, do you?" Katie said, finally getting up and bringing more dishes over to the sink.

Katie put down the dishes and Robert put his hands on her shoulders. "Katie, you're right, ok? I don't understand. Yes, she likes him and is nervous. But you dress me up, then *you* don't dress up, you get all bent out of shape when I eat fast, you hit me when I make a joke…that was just supposed to be just between you and me by the way, that's why I whispered it!"

"You don't whisper jokes in front of company!" Katie yelled at him. She tried to pull away from him but he held her fast.

"Talk to me, ok? Will you please just talk to me? You know what communication means to us. It's been falling apart ever since we arrived!"

Katie sighed and looked at the floor. A few seconds later she looked back up into his eyes. "She's…she's never been on a date before, ok? I didn't dress up because I've always been the pretty, popular one. I wanted him to notice *her* tonight! I put my hair in a ponytail because I wanted to look as plain as I could, so he'd notice how pretty *she* is! I didn't want him laughing at your jokes, or paying attention to you the famous author. I wanted *her* to be the popular one for once!"

"I think he likes her." Robert smiled. "He seems to like hearing about her. He keeps asking about her teaching, her schooling, and what not."

"She thinks things were always so easy for me with men." Katie said, as she leaned forward and pressed her forehead into his chest. "And until you…well…"

Robert laughed and wrapped his arms around her, hugging her close. "And now here you are, with a prince charming who wolfs down soup!"

She kissed him and then picked up a large pan on the stove. "Ok Prince, pull out the garbage can so we can dump out the leftover soup."

"What?" Robert looked shocked. "You can't dump that out! The soup was a masterpiece! Don't you have some kind of container or something we can put it into? I'll eat it later, you can't just toss it!"

She set the pan back on the stove and put her hands on her hips. "So you want to dirty another dish just so you can wolf down a little bit of leftover soup later, huh? We're on a diet, remember? Even though we've cheated a little the last couple of days."

He smiled crookedly back at her. "How about we keep the soup and I touch you in that spot you love?"

He moved towards her and grabbed her up in his arms as she let out a loud, squealing, giggle. "Stop that! They're going to hear us!"

"Then tell me we can keep the soup!"

She continued to giggle as he kissed her. "You are *so* lucky you're cute!"

Just as Robert and Katie finished cleaning up and came out to the living room, Ben was standing in the doorway, ready to leave.

"I'm sorry I'm so busy this week," He was saying as he smiled at Jill. "But I'll see what I can do. Maybe we can squeeze in a quick lunch sometime? I'll call you!"

"You're welcome back for dinner anytime you'd like!" Emily smiled. "You just come on over. Our door is always open for you!"

He noticed Robert and Katie coming into the living room and waved. "I'm sorry I didn't get to visit with you guys longer! I'll see you two tomorrow morning, though. I have a bit of work to finish and then I need some sleep! Goodbye!"

Robert and Katie waved as he walked out the door.

Twenty Nine

Robert was on his bed staring at the ceiling. He glanced over at Katie after a couple of minutes. She was also lying on her back, watching the ceiling, in the same position he was.

He sat up on his bed. "Are you ok?"

She looked over at him. "Of course, I'm fine."

"Are you sure? You don't look fine."

She sighed. "What if tomorrow...what if he asks us what we do together?"

"What if he does? We do everything together. We eat breakfast together, we spend the day together, we eat dinner together...we're always together."

She sat up on her bed. "That's not what I meant, what if he asks about our dates?"

Robert rolled off his bed and sat next to her. "What do you mean our dates?"

"Well...we never really dated, did we? I mean we just... fell in love and then...?"

"Would you like to date? Should I be taking you bowling or something?"

She turned and gave him a dirty look. "I'm trying to be serious! What if he asks us about...*things we haven't done*?"

"Katie, he's not going to try and break us up, ok? He's just going to talk to us and probably help us make our relationship better, if it can even be better."

"I just...you know I just worry!"

He kissed her cheek and hugged her. "I know. But relax, if you feel uncomfortable at all tomorrow, we'll just leave."

"You mean just walk out of his office? We can't do that! How do you think that would look?"

"Ok, we won't just walk out. But if you aren't comfortable with something, just tell him you aren't comfortable. Leave it at that, ok?"

"When we were in the living room he seemed kind of... shy." Jill said quietly.

"What was that, honey?" Katie asked, as Robert moved back to his own bed laid down.

"He seemed kind of...shy when we were talking. He looked a little nervous."

"Probably scared out of his wits." Robert laughed.

Jill sat up on her bed. "And what's that supposed to mean?"

"I was so scared when I went to pick up Katie for the first time. I was so nervous, my hands wouldn't stop shaking!"

"You didn't seem that nervous." Jill frowned. "At least I don't remember it that way. You seemed pretty confident to me."

"Well, when you first talk to a girl you really like, at least for me, you're scared to death. I think Ben likes you a bit, he's nervous around you. Did you know he told me he was never very good with women?"

"I...I asked if he wanted to have lunch but he said he's really busy. He said he'd call me."

Robert laughed again. "That's a tough call to make! You really like the girl but don't know what to say."

"Do you really think he's really busy or maybe he just didn't want to have lunch with me?"

"I can tell you tomorrow. I'll just poke through his appointment book while we're there."

"You will *not!*" Katie frowned. "You need to behave while we're there, not act like some nosy jackass!"

Robert laughed again. "Good night, Sweetheart. Goodnight, Jill."

Thirty

Robert opened his eyes to sunlight. He yawned and sat up on the bed. Katie and Jill were gone. He found some slacks and a nice shirt and put them on before heading downstairs. He walked into the kitchen to find Katie, Jill, and Emily sitting at the table sharing coffee.

"Well, good morning ladies!"

They all smiled up at him as Katie pulled out a chair next to her. "Honey, Jill's offered to drive us over to Ben's office and wait for us to finish."

"Lovely, thank you Jill."

"Would you like some coffee?" Jill asked. "I know you don't drink it, but I still thought I'd ask."

"No, but do you have a thermos around here somewhere?"

"Would you like to take some coffee with you?" Emily asked nicely. "I can lend you one of Jim's old thermoses?"

"No, but Ben really liked the soup last night, too. At least he said he did. We put the leftover soup in the thermos. Since he's supposed to be so busy we'll bring it with us to his office. He can heat it up later."

Jill smiled widely at the suggestion. "That's a wonderful idea! Mom, can you get Dad's thermos for me? I'll get the soup!"

Katie leaned over and kissed him. "That's very thoughtful of you."

He frowned back at her. "Are you sure you're sleeping ok? I know I hear you tossing and turning at night."

"I'll be ok, it's just…I haven't been away from New York for a while, that's probably it."

"You're sure?"

"Yes, I'm fine. You don't need to worry."

He watched her suspiciously as she got up and got him a fruit cup and a glass of milk. She set his breakfast down in front of him and kissed his cheek again. "I'm fine, really!"

Robert looked over at Emily. "Where's Jim?"

"He had some policeman thing to go to. He's had it planned for a while now and he said he'd be back later. I asked him to take you but he got all huffy because you weren't a police officer. He said no."

Robert began to laugh. "Well, thank God for small favors!"

Everyone was quiet on the way to Ben's office. The girls would usually be chatting about something. The silence began to make Robert nervous. They arrived at the medical center a little before nine and found Ben's office. Robert and Katie walked quietly up to the receptionist while Jill found a nearby seat.

"Good morning," Robert started. "We're here to see Dr. Richards. We have an appointment for nine o'clock?"

The clerk smiled up at him. "You must be Robert and Katie! He's been expecting you. I don't need you to sign in or anything since this is just an informal visit. Please take a seat and I'll let him know you're here."

Robert thanked her. Katie and Robert sat down. She held onto his hand tightly. He could feel how nervous she was. A few minutes later the receptionist came back out of the office. "You can go in now, he's ready for you."

Robert smiled as he stood up and led Katie into the office. It was a large room with degrees and photos hanging on the walls. There were several full bookshelves and Ben sat behind a large desk. There were two large, comfortable looking chairs in front of the desk. Ben came out from behind the desk as they entered and walked over to shake their hands.

"Welcome! It's nice to see you both this morning!"

Robert held out the thermos he had been holding in his free hand. "You liked the soup so much last night and Jill said you were pretty busy all week. We brought you some for lunch. You know, in case you can't get out from behind your desk today?"

Ben's face lit up as he accepted the thermos. "Thank you! I do have a bit of a full schedule later today. Please be certain to thank her for me, ok?"

"She drove us over here and is in the lobby…in case you wanted to say thank you in person?" Katie said quietly.

"I'll have to make a point to do that after we're through!" Ben smiled. "Please, take a seat and we'll get started!"

Robert looked around the office. "Don't we get to lie on a couch? We're here to have our head shrunk, right?"

Katie gave him a worried look and squeezed his hand. Robert leaned back and put his feet up on Ben's desk. "No matter, I'll just make myself comfortable in the chair."

Katie hadn't noticed what he was doing. She looked over and saw his feet on Ben's desk and was horrified. "Oh my God, *oh my God*," she said gritting her teeth. "What is *wrong* with you? Get your feet off his desk! Why are you trying to embarrass me?"

Ben sat down behind the desk, seemingly not taking notice of what Robert had done. Katie looked at him apologetically and tried not to look too embarrassed.

"So Katie, what do you think about what he just did?" Ben asked, looking down at some paperwork on his desk.

"I'm *so* sorry," she answered quietly. "I…I didn't know he was going to do something like that. He shouldn't have done it! I don't know what to say!" She glared over at Robert who had put his feet back on the ground.

"Does what he did make you angry?"

"Yes!" She said, still glaring at Robert.

"And does he know you're angry?" Ben asked. He casually removed the top of the thermos and poured some soup into a small coffee cup on his desk.

"Oh, he knows!" She growled. "He damn well knows!"

"Does he know why?"

She turned towards Ben, an angry look on her face. "Well obviously because he put his feet on your desk and embarrassed me!"

"Are you sure that's why he did it, to embarrass you?"

"It doesn't matter *why* he did it, he should know better!"

He looked at Robert as he sipped some soup from the cup. "Robert, why did you put your feet on my desk?"

"I...I...I just...I thought it was funny. I use humor to..."

"You thought you would be an ass and do whatever you want to, that's why!" Katie finished for him angrily.

Ben looked calmly at Katie. "Is Jill still in the reception room waiting for you? I'd like to thank her for the soup."

"Yes, she should still be there." Katie said quietly. "I can't believe you would do something like that, Robert!"

Ben stood up. "Well, I'm going to go and chat with her for a few minutes if you'll excuse me? While I'm gone Katie, I'd like you to tell Robert you're angry, and then tell him why."

"He knows why!" She said again.

"Just humor me, please?" He said and walked out the office door.

Katie sat with her arms crossed and turned her back to Robert. A few seconds later Robert reached over and touched her shoulder. "Katie?"

She pulled away from his touch. He looked at her sadly. "Are you mad at me?"

She rounded in the chair. "You *son of a bitch*! You just can't help but try to embarrass me, can you? Why do you do things like that?"

"He's a psychologist, they always have couches...I just..."

"You just thought you'd come in here and take control, didn't you? Or maybe you thought you'd keep embarrassing me and then when you finally..." She clapped a hand over her mouth.

"When I finally *what*?"

She was close to tears again. "It doesn't matter."

Robert reached over and took her hand. "Of course it matters! There's more to this, isn't there? I think he sees something I've missed! What's really wrong, Katie?"

"You're…you're right, I don't sleep well at night! I've been having nightmares about you leaving me!"

"Leaving you? I'm not going to leave you!"

"I know we're always together, always so good together, but…"

"But you still dream that I leave, don't you?"

"I keep having this nightmare where you yell and scream at me and then just walk away! I wake up, look over at your bed, and expect you to be gone. You're always still there! But each time…" Tears began to stream down her face.

He reached over and pulled her into a hug. "I should have known. I knew you weren't sleeping well. You've never tossed and turned when we've slept together. Its ok honey, I won't leave you!"

"I…I know, but…"

"I think you need a real commitment, don't you? Not just a promise that I'll marry you. You really need to hear me say the words."

"No!" Katie said pulling back from him. "Don't you rush things because of me! I want us to be together but we *do* need to wait until it's the right time!"

"But if you're having nightmares?"

"I think…I think finally talking to you about them will help."

"Why didn't you just tell me in the first place?"

"I didn't want to worry you! I thought they'd just go away!"

"I'll tell you what," Robert said as he wiped a tear from her cheek. "Whenever you have one of those nightmares, you get up and come over to my bed. You touch me, hug me, or whatever you need to do to make you feel better, ok? At least until we're back in the same bed again?"

"But you said Daddy…"

"If you need to do it Katie, do it! Your dad will just have to understand!"

She smiled and hugged him again. He found some tissues on Ben's desk and used them to wipe the tears from Katie's cheeks.

She looked around. "He's not back yet, what do we do now?"

Robert grinned at her. "Want to put your feet up on the desk? I think it's oak!"

Ben walked out of the office and into the reception area. He spotted Jill sitting in one of the chairs, flipping through a magazine. He walked over and sat down next to her.

"Hi," he said, as she looked up. "Robert and Katie told me you were here. I thought I'd come out and thank you for the soup. I really appreciate it."

He was close enough for her to smell his aftershave. She looked into his eyes and didn't know what to say. She shook herself out of the stupor a few seconds later. "Oh, you're welcome! Actually, we had some left over, and it was Robert's suggestion to bring it for you."

"Well, I appreciate the thought. I am going to visit some of my patients in the hospital today. This soup will come in handy. Sometimes I don't get much time to eat."

"In the hospital? I didn't think you were a medical doctor?"

"Oh…uh…I just do some counseling, I don't make medical rounds." He answered uncomfortably.

Jill thought for a minute and then looked concerned. "It isn't like in the movies is it, with all the padded rooms and straight jackets?"

"Sometimes it is. Mostly it's just people with problems. I try to help them work things out. I don't deal with extreme cases though. It still takes its toll."

"I sometimes have kids that act out in class but I'm sure it's not the same thing." Jill let out a small giggle as she said this.

"No, it's probably not. Jill…we've gotten along pretty well. I was wondering if maybe…?"

A loud thump came from the office and they could hear Katie giggling.

An aggravated look crossed Jill's face. "You'd better go check on them before they have sex on your desk!"

"When I left, Katie was upset about…well, upset about something Robert had done. They were supposed to be discussing why she was upset while I was gone."

Katie's giggling began to get louder. Ben got up from his chair and walked to his office as Jill followed. He opened the door and they saw Katie lying across Ben's desk with Robert on top of her.

"Oh…my…*God*!" Jill gasped stomping into the office with her hands on her hips.

Katie looked up at them from underneath Robert. She had a huge smile on her face. She reached a hand up and smacked him on the shoulder, still giggling. "You see? I told you they'd catch us!"

Robert quickly climbed off her and then helped Katie up from the desk. "Oh…uh…hi Ben…uh, Doc? We were just… you see, she fell on your desk and I was trying to help, and…"

Ben glared at them. "Would you like to have a seat?"

Robert and Katie sat down.

"Could you give us a few more minutes, please?" Ben asked, looking at Jill. She nodded and covered her face with her hands as she walked back out of the office.

Ben closed his office door and walked slowly over to sit down behind his desk. He looked at Katie. "Well, I'm guessing you aren't mad at him any more?"

She began to blush a deep red. "Oh…uh…I'm not mad."

He looked over at Robert. "And how about you? What were you doing on my desk?"

"We actually wanted a couch but couldn't find one in here." Robert replied with a smile. Katie burst out laughing. Seeing the look on Ben's face, she covered her mouth and tried to control herself.

Ben smiled at her. "So there really are no major problems between the two of you, are there?"

She looked over at Robert, and reached for his hand. "Not really, no."

"We're really sorry," Robert said. "We got used to always sleeping together. Since we've been staying with her parents, her father wants us in separate beds. We just got carried away while you were gone. It was really my fault. I just…I got kind of frisky with her."

Katie smiled lovingly at him. "No, it wasn't just your fault, I could have told you no. We both got carried away!"

Ben laughed. "You know, this will probably be the highlight of my day? I think you're both fine. You two get along, you stick up for each other. You're not shy about sex in someone else's office. I think you'll make a wonderful couple!"

"So our heads are now shrunk and we're done?" Robert asked. Katie began to giggle again.

"Yes, I think your heads are as small as they can possibly be. Take care and I'll see you Friday for the game, ok?"

"Hell yeah!" Robert said, as he stood up. Both he and Katie shook Ben's hand and headed out of the office.

Jill didn't speak to them until they were in the car. Both Robert and Katie sat in the back seat. Jill turned around and glared at them. "I have *never* in my entire life been as *embarrassed* as I was today! How could you two *do that*?"

Robert began to grin. "Oh come on! We just…"

"I am really not in the mood for your smart assed mouth!" Jill growled. She turned back around and started the car.

"You don't need to be so mad, we didn't really do *anything*!" Katie snarled back.

Jill fumed, but didn't answer. For the rest of the drive, she refused to say anything.

Thirty One

Jill climbed out of the car and slammed the door. Robert had to lean up from the backseat to let Katie and himself out. Jill walked inside and slammed it behind her. Katie stopped and looked sadly at Robert. "I'm not really like that when I'm mad, am I?"

"It'll be ok honey, I think she just needs some time to be mad at us."

"I am, aren't I?" She asked sadly. "I treat you just the way she's treating us right now. I'm so sorry!"

Robert gave her a hug and they walked inside. Jim was sitting in his usual chair reading a paper, while Emily was sitting on the couch, watching TV.

He sighed as Robert and Katie came in. "What's all the fuss about *this time*?"

"What fuss?" Katie asked quietly.

"You sister comes in and stomps past us without even so much as a hello. You think I won't figure out there's something wrong?" Jim asked, finally putting down his newspaper.

Katie sat down in a nearby chair. "Well, we…we didn't really mean it, we just…"

"I think it has something to do with the shrink." Robert finished for her.

"Did he say something to her?" Jim growled. "Insulted her, or something? Maybe he thinks he's too good to have anything to do with a cop's daughter?"

"No, he was out in the reception area talking to her and then…" Robert started. He glanced quickly over at Katie. "He had to come back in the office with us. I think she's upset about that. I think she maybe wanted more time to talk to him."

"We were fooling around, and they *heard us*!" Katie blurted out. "We've been so close lately, talking about clothes, shoes, and hair; now she's mad at me!"

"Katie, calm down." Robert said as he put his hand on her shoulder. "Give her some time and she'll be fine. I think she just needs to sort out a few feelings."

"What do you mean you were *fooling around*?" Jim asked, glaring at Robert.

"We were just having some fun!" Robert tried to explain. "We ended up on his desk. He came back in and caught us."

"You were having fun with *my daughter* on a doctor's desk?" Jim yelled. "Well isn't that just special?"

Emily got up from the couch and walked over to his chair. "Will you leave them alone, Jim? They're allowed to have fun, if they want to! You need to accept the fact that Robert is going to be a part of this family and your daughter loves him!"

"Well one daughter's upstairs, and all upset! What are we going to do about that?" He fumed back.

Emily let out a small laugh. "How you survived these girls going through puberty, I'll never know! One of them was always upset about something! If it will make you feel any better, I'll go and talk to Jill."

"Would you mind if I tried first?" Robert asked quietly. "I'm part of the reason she's upset, I think. I'd like to at least try and apologize to her."

"Yes," Katie agreed. "We'll go and talk to her first!"

Robert sighed. "Just me Katie, ok? Give me a chance to talk to her alone and we'll see what happens."

"Robert, I think you should..." She started.

"Katie, please? Will you just trust me?"

Emily smiled. "Let him try, Katie. He might be able to make her feel better. If not, we can go up after he tries."

Katie sat down on the couch next to her mother. "Fine! You go and talk to her. Don't be surprised when she just throws you out of the room and tells you to get lost!"

"Thanks."

Robert knocked softly on the door to their room. There was no answer so he opened it slowly. He could see Jill lying on her bed her face buried in a pillow.

"What do you *want*?" She asked into the pillow.

"I just wanted to talk for a minute, do you mind if I come in?"

She rolled over and he could see she had been crying. "Oh, that's nice; they sent *you* up instead of Katie this time? Can't you just leave me alone?"

He walked over and sat on the edge of her bed. "I'm really sorry about today. I know we embarrassed you. I never meant for that to happen."

"What difference does it make? You can just run back to Katie, and everything goes back to being a fucking fairy tale for you! Just go *away*!"

"You know, when Katie and I had our first fight, you were there for me. There to talk, and I really appreciated it. It meant a lot. But if you want me out, I'll go." He got up from the bed and walked towards the door.

"Robert…? I…I think…I think he was just about to ask me out when…"

"We knocked that book off his desk."

She let a small smile cross her lips. "It was a book? We heard a thump but I didn't know what it was. I just remember Katie giggling."

He walked back over and sat back down on the bed next to her. "And you think we ruined your chances with him?"

"I don't know. He was…he wanted to ask me something. After we caught you two, I just felt…well…?"

"Every time you see him, you get interrupted by the Robert and Katie show. We embarrass you somehow, and scare him off, don't we?"

"I think I was more upset that he went into his office. He didn't come back out to finish asking me what he wanted to ask! When I heard him start, I was so excited! And then…I was just so mad."

"Katie's really upset. She said in the last week or so you two have gotten pretty close talking about clothes and things."

Jill giggled. "I guess we have. We never really had anything to talk about. She was always into the girly girl things, and I was always taking some kind of class. And now when I wanted to get prettied up…?"

"Yeah," He put his arm around her and gave her a hug. "You know, when guys like a girl, they don't usually give up. I'm sure he'll talk to you again."

She hugged him back. "Yes; maybe. I don't know. I've been so confused the last couple of days, I can't figure out what I want!"

He got up from the bed and walked over to where his suitcase was. He reached inside and pulled out the baseball tickets. "Here, you take these."

She looked at him, but didn't take the tickets. "I told you, I don't like sports, and I don't want to go to your stupid game!"

He smiled back at her. "Jill, this isn't just a baseball game. It's a night alone with Ben. No Robert, no Katie, no Mom and Dad, just you and him. A baseball game can last three hours or more; that doesn't even include drive time! You go to this game tomorrow night and see if you can sort things out with him, ok?"

"I can't take those! You worked so hard to get them and you really wanted to go to the game!"

Robert laughed. "Worked hard? Honey, after my book first made the best seller list, I spent ten hours sitting in a book store in Seattle signing books! The few I signed here were nothing, believe me!"

"But you made all those phone calls…"

"Take the tickets, Jill!"

"What if he doesn't want to go with me?"

Robert pulled his cell phone out of his pocket and dialed. A surprised look crossed his face. "Doc, is that really you? I thought I'd have to leave a message!"

Jill leaned back from him, looking shocked.

"What? No, no, no problems with Katie. I just wanted to let you know I can't make the game tomorrow so I'm going to send Jill along with you, if you don't mind? What difference does it make? I can't go! Sure, she loves baseball. Ok…no… yeah, Doc, I understand, but…I just can't go, ok? You're ok with taking her for me? Yes, she…ok fine, she doesn't know much about baseball, but you can explain things to her, can't you? She can tell her kids about the game. Yes Doc…yeah, ok…*Ben*! You're welcome, bye." He hung up the phone and held the tickets out towards Jill again.

She reached for them, her hand shaking slightly. "What did he say?"

"He told me to stop calling him Doc and call him Ben."

"I mean about taking me to the game, stupid!" Jill said, as she looked at the tickets.

Robert got up from the bed and walked towards the door laughing. "He told me thanks. Be prepared, I'm sure Katie will be running up here shortly, demanding to know what happened."

Jill gave him a smile. "Thank you, Robert. Thank you for everything."

"Like I keep telling Katie; I haven't given you everything yet!" He smiled as he closed the door and headed back downstairs.

Katie was waiting for him halfway up the staircase. "What happened? What did she say?"

"She's fine, let's go back downstairs."

"What did you say to her, Robert?"

"Sweetie," he laughed. "She's fine now. She was just a bit upset about something, but she's ok now. We had a talk and she forgives us, ok?"

"I should go talk to her, too!"

Robert put his arm around Katie and began moving her back down the stairs. "She's fine, give her a little space, ok?"

"She's really ok? You really made her feel better?" Katie asked with a sad look. "I feel really bad about what we did!"

"It's ok. I tried to make things up to her. I gave her the baseball tickets."

"I thought she didn't want them?"

"He changed my mind." Jill said from behind them. "After talking to him, I decided that maybe I did want to go see some baseball."

"Oh Jill, are you really ok?" Katie said and pushed Robert aside to hug her sister. "I didn't mean to make you feel bad!"

Jill rolled her eyes at Robert as she hugged Katie. "Yes Katie, I'm fine!"

The two women followed Robert back downstairs. The three of them sat on the couch with Robert in the middle.

Jim glanced up at the three of them. "Are we still all upset? Do I have to listen again to how the writer is using my daughter for a *plaything*?"

"Oh Daddy, don't be so melodramatic!" Katie said, glaring at him.

"I'm fine, Dad." Jill smiled. "Robert gave me his ticket to the baseball game. I guess I should think about what to wear?"

"Oh, we can dress you all up!" Katie said, grinning from ear to ear. "I can do your hair and make up, we'll get you all fixed up!"

Jill looked at Robert. "Uh…Katie, I really don't want to dress up this time. I don't think too many people go to a baseball game wearing a dress."

"No, not really," Robert smiled at Katie. "But if you want, we can take you shopping and get you a sweatshirt and hat, or something?"

"I don't understand any of this," Jim said, glaring at Robert. "So which one of you is upset now?"

"None of us are upset, Daddy!" Katie answered, glaring back. "We were just deciding to go shopping again!" She smiled at Robert, "Right, honey?"

"Uh…yeah, I guess so."

Emily walked over and put her hand on Jill's shoulder, "Is this what you really want?"

Jill patted her mother's hand. "Yes, I think it's what I need for now. I need time to talk to Ben without being bothered by *The Robert and Katie Show*."

Emily smiled. "Then you know that both your father and I are behind you!"

"So now they're a show?" Jim growled.

Thirty Two

Robert and Jill stood outside a shoe store as Katie browsed inside. He glanced at Jill and muttered, "Sorry, I didn't realize she'd take over the shopping."

"Oh don't worry, I expected this." Jill smiled. "It's still nice to go out with you two, though. She's always been like this, taking her shopping with you is an all day experience, usually."

"Yeah, but we were supposed to be buying *you* something to wear to the ballgame!"

"We can get to that, but for now, she's happy and bothering some sales person, and not us!"

Robert laughed as he looked back inside the store to see Katie lecturing a clerk about a pair of boots she had tried on. She waved for him to come into the store.

He walked in, heaving a large sigh. "Yes, what do you need?"

"Do you believe they want $350 for these?" Katie said, pointing at the boots.

He reached down and touched the boots. "Real leather, right? It looks like they're pretty well made, how do they fit?"

"Not leather, they're calfskin. They fit really well, but $350? That's *so* expensive!"

"Would you like the boots?"

"Oh, we shouldn't be spending that kind of money! Maybe for Jill, but…?"

"Jill doesn't want boots," Robert sighed. "But if you like them…?"

"Well of course I *like them*! But honey…"

"I'll take the boots!" Robert yelled over at the clerk. "Help me get them off her and into a box!"

Katie happily took off the boots and placed them neatly in a nearby box. "Robert, are you sure? I know I've spent a lot while we've been here."

Robert picked up the box. "Go out and wait with Jill, ok? See if you can find a shop that sells sweatshirts or something."

Katie kissed him and bounced happily back out of the store. The clerk smiled at him from behind the counter. "Oh, we actually have a few sweatshirts, would you like to see what we have?"

"Quiet!" Robert scowled. "Do you want her back in here yelling at you about how much your shirts are? I just need to pay for the boots and leave!" He handed the clerk a credit card.

He had to search a bit to find Jill and Katie. He checked several other stores and found the two sisters in a small sports clothing store. They were looking at some shirts with football logos on them.

"How about this one? This looks cute." Katie was asking, holding up a sweatshirt with a New York Jets logo.

"That's a football team honey; she's going to a baseball game." Robert said as he walked into the store.

"Well of course I know it's a football team!" Katie said as she hung the shirt back up and put her hands on her hips. "I used to watch them with Daddy when I was little! I thought it looked nice!"

He walked across the store and found a t-shirt that said *Tampa Bay Rays* across the front. "This is who you're going to see play, how about this one?"

Katie looked at him skeptically. "I don't know. I'm not sure how much style that one has."

Robert couldn't stop a small laugh from escaping his lips. "Katie…it's not about…this is who she's going to see play in their home stadium!"

"I know that, *Robert*! But she needs to look good!"

He continued to laugh as he looked over at Jill. "Do you like this one or would you like to keep looking? You don't need something with a logo on it. I'm happy to just buy you any kind of shirt you'll be happy with!"

"The shirt's nice, but I will look around some more if you don't mind?"

"Not a problem." He held the shirt up to himself and looked at the size. He walked up to the clerk and paid for the shirt.

He walked out of the store as Katie glared at him. "She *said* she wanted to look around some more!"

"That was for me, Katie. You don't mind if I buy myself some clothes, do you? I liked the shirt!"

"Oh, you should have told me you wanted more clothes, honey! You don't need more t-shirts, do you? We can look for some more shirts and things for you!"

Robert sighed and they began walking through the mall again.

"Hey, why don't we go back to that little bar in the mall and have lunch?" Robert asked.

"I guess we could do that." Katie smiled.

"I'll tell you what; you girls go and get us a table, I will put these bags in the car, and then meet you there, ok?"

Katie reached out for the bags he was carrying. "I can do that if Jill will give me the keys? I need to return the boots anyway."

Robert looked at her. "Return them, why? I thought you liked them?"

"I do like them, honey. But $350 is too expensive. I can't let you spend that much on boots for me."

Robert looked over at Jill, who smiled back at him. "She does this. She'll see something she likes, buy it, and then take it back when she feels guilty."

"He just doesn't need to spend that much on boots!" Katie insisted, still holding out her hands for the bags.

Robert kept a hold of the bags and held out his hand towards Jill. "May I have the car keys, please? I'll meet you girls in the bar."

Jill handed him the keys as Katie tried to protest again.

"Sorry sweetheart," Robert said, laughing. "But you get to keep the boots. I'll be right back!"

He walked out to the parking lot and placed the bags in the car's trunk. He took his time heading to the bar, wondering to himself if Katie would still be upset about the boots. He walked into the bar to find the two girls sitting at a table, food orders already in front of them. Each one had a fruit salad. Sitting in front of an empty chair was a cheeseburger and fries. He sat down in front of the cheeseburger and smiled at the two women.

"You even ordered for me! Outstanding! And I get a cheeseburger and fries, no diet stuff? This day's turning out to be pretty good so far!" He took a bite of the burger and as he was eating, slowly noticed that both women were sitting with their arms crossed, watching him.

"Uh…is something wrong?" He asked, after a second bite. "Why are you guys looking at me like that? Why aren't you eating, too?"

"It's not fair that you do so much for us, buy us things, but you don't ever get anything yourself!" Katie answered.

"What do mean? I get plenty myself! I just bought that t-shirt! You're always picking out clothes for me!"

"You hate clothes." Katie said, still watching him. "I don't even know what you really like!"

"We just…we think you need something special for yourself, ok?" Jill said. "You put up with us buying clothes or going out to eat with us. We never see you do anything *you* want to do. You always just go along with what we want."

"I'm fine. I like shopping with you guys and seeing how happy Katie is when I buy her something."

"No it isn't!" Katie insisted, leaning across the table. "I don't even know what you like, Robert! Where would I even start, if I wanted to buy you something?"

He looked from Katie, to Jill, and back to Katie again. "You guys are serious, aren't you? You're really upset because I haven't shopped for myself since we've known each other? I don't think either of you would even like the same things I do!"

Jill smiled at him. "Try us. You go along with what we like, why not give us the chance to go along with what you like?"

"And you won't get upset?"

"*No* we won't get upset!" Katie smiled. "Why would you think that?"

"Ok, maybe we can go to Disneyworld sometime? I like Disneyworld. I've taken a few vacations there."

Katie broke into a surprised look. "You like Disney, really?"

"Oh yeah, I love the animated features, you know, the cartoons? I also like a lot of the Pixar stuff that's been done. I love movies!"

Katie watched him for a minute and then began to slowly eat her fruit salad. "So you like Disney cartoons, huh?"

Robert laughed and quickly finished off his burger. "Maybe we can forget the diet for today and get some ice cream on the way back home?"

Jill began to giggle. "I don't have a problem with that as long as someone doesn't eat out of the carton!"

"Well, I was thinking of an ice cream cone, not a carton."

Katie gave Jill a dirty look. "She means me. When I get really depressed, I go into the kitchen and eat ice cream out of the carton."

Robert stopped stuffing fries into his mouth and gave her a serious look. "Have you been depressed lately?"

"No, the last time was while you were in California."

He finished off the fries and sat there sipping his drink until Katie and Jill finished eating.

Thirty Three

Jill eventually found herself a nice outfit to wear to the game and they stopped at a small ice cream place on the way home. They each had a cone and Robert also bought a half gallon of chocolate to put in the freezer for later. They sat in the living room.

"Hey Katie, let's play a game." Robert suggested as he finished off the last of his cone. Jim was sitting in a nearby chair, reading Robert's book. He looked up curiously.

"A game," she asked. "What do you mean?"

"Well, you said you didn't know what I liked. So let's play a little game and see how much we really know about each other, ok? I'll tell you something I know about you and then you tell me something you know about me."

She looked around nervously. "But…what if…what if I can't think of anything?"

"We'll help each other. Here, I'll start. You really like clothes and love to shop."

She smiled. "I *do* like clothes. Very good, honey!" She clapped her hands a few times.

"It's your turn, tell me something about me."

Jim watched her curiously.

"You're a writer and like to write." She said, nervously. "And you like Disney stuff!"

Jim let out a small snort.

Robert glared over at him. "She's right, I love Disney! How about you, Jim? Are you into Disney, living here in Florida?"

"No, not especially. You've got a lot of people dying in this book! You wrote about people getting killed and you like Disney?"

"You're reading my book? I'm pleased! When you finish let me know what you think." He turned back to Katie. "You have really beautiful hair and always take your time styling it. I know you like to dress up and look good."

Katie sighed. "You don't like to dress up and have short hair. Are we really learning anything by doing this, Robert?"

He looked at her for a few seconds, thinking. "I like 80's music and some country music. How about you, sweetheart? I don't even know what you like to listen to."

Katie scrunched up her face. "You like country music? Oh, I hate that! All the songs are about cheating, how my honey left me, and things like that!"

Robert began laughing. "Oh they are *not*! There are some good songs out there that don't have anything to do with depressing things!"

Jim put down his book. "You remember me telling you how I used to take your Mom dancing? We went to places that played country music, sweetheart."

"Yes, yes, I can remember you playing it when I was little! It was always about things I didn't like!"

"I'll bet I know one you'll like." Robert smiled. "Wait here a second." He ran up the stairs towards their room.

"There's a country place close by, maybe we could go dancing?" Jim asked Katie. "I'll bet your Mom would love to go out with you and Robert! Maybe we can even get Jill to come?"

"Dad; Are you even listening to me? I said I don't like that music! If you want to go out, we should find some kind of salsa place. Some place with happy music?"

Jim stood up from his chair. "Em? Em, where are you? Do you remember going dancing when we were younger? Would you like to go out dancing with our daughter and the writer?"

Emily came out of the kitchen just as Robert was coming back down the stairs. "What was that? They're going dancing? Oh Jim, I always loved when you took me out dancing!"

"Mom, don't tell him yes, I hate country music!" Katie pleaded. "I'd just be miserable all night!"

Robert handed her some headphones. "Here, put these on and we'll see how you like this one, ok?"

She sighed and crossed her arms. "Did any of you listen to anything I just said?"

Robert put the headphones on her head. "Please?"

Katie adjusted the headphones over her ears. "Fine, you start playing your song about cheating. When I can't stand it anymore I'll tell you to stop, ok?"

Robert just smiled and started the song. After listening for a bit, Katie's eyes began to tear up, and she reached out to hug Robert.

"What'd you play?" Jim asked.

"Can I have this dance for the rest of my life?" Robert replied.

Thirty Four

They put off going dancing for another night so Robert put on his pajamas. Katie was in the bathroom brushing her hair. He walked in and smiled at her as he pulled down his pajama bottoms and began to pee.

"What do you think you're *doing*?" She asked, shocked.

"Oh come on, it's not anything you haven't seen on me! I had to go!"

"And you couldn't wait for me to finish in here?"

"No, couldn't wait. I need to fart too so hold your nose." He let out a large fart and began to laugh.

"Oh my God, I don't believe you just did that!" Katie shouted. "What is *wrong* with you?"

"It's a bathroom!" Robert giggled. "And why are you in here brushing your hair when we're getting ready for bed? It's just going to get messed up again while you sleep!"

Katie sighed and put her hands on her hips. "You know I love you, but you really need some lessons in hygiene!"

"Yeah, I know. Let me give you a hand with that hair." He walked up behind her and began to ruffle her hair with both hands. He ran out of the bathroom and down the hall to their room, laughing hysterically. Katie chased him down the hall. He made it to the room and fell on his bed giggling. She stopped in the doorway and threw her hairbrush at him.

"You son of a bitch!" She screamed.

He put up his arm and batted the brush away. "*Ow*, that *hurt*! Geez, I was just playing with you!"

Katie quickly covered her mouth and nose with her hands. "Oh my God, are you ok? Oh honey, I didn't mean to hurt you!" She rushed over to his bed and sat down beside him. "Are you ok? Let me see your arm! It's not broken, is it?"

Jill was lying on her bed, reading a magazine. "Throwing things now, are we?"

Robert cringed as Katie touched his arm. "Ow, easy there, it still hurts a bit! That was a hard brush!"

She began to gently caress his arm. "Do we need to take you to a doctor? Oh honey, I'm *so sorry*!"

He pulled his arm away from her and put it around her shoulders. He leaned in and kissed her. "I'm fine, Katie. I probably deserved that."

"Yup, you deserved it." Jill agreed.

"You *hush*!" Katie glared over at her. "You don't even know what he did!"

"Does it matter? He's a Sex Fiend." Jill giggled.

"Maybe Mr. Right will get hit with a foul ball tomorrow. You'll be fussing over him the same way Katie's fussing over me, won't you?" Robert laughed.

"No one ever said Ben is Mr. Right, ok?" Jill scowled at him. "Why do you people all seem to be pushing me at him?"

"We've just seen the way you look at him." Robert smiled.

"Uh huh, and how do I look at him?"

"Like the sun rises and sets on him." Katie smiled.

"*I don't*…he's just really cute." She protested. "And he's educated, and interesting, and smart and…" She stopped as she saw both Robert and Katie smiling at her.

"We're behind you in this," Robert said, hugging Katie close. "You like him and are going out. Maybe something will happen, maybe it won't. Either way though, you have a date with a cute, educated, interesting guy."

"*I* think you two would make a really cute couple!" Katie smiled as she kissed Robert and moved over to her own bed.

Jill sat up and looked over at Robert. "What do I say tomorrow? What do I do, I'm really nervous about this!"

"Just pretend he's Robert. You aren't nervous around him!" Katie smiled.

Robert got up from his bed and walked over to sit down next to Jill. "No, don't pretend he's me. Just be yourself. When it's time to say something, you will. You just need a little confidence in yourself. You were always so confident when you talked to me!"

"I...I've never really..." She looked over at Katie. "I haven't been out on a lot of dates."

"Neither have I." Robert smiled.

"Really? I find that hard to believe! You asked Katie out and then things just worked out like magic! It was almost like you knew all the right things to do and say!"

"For her, maybe I did? But I never had too many dates before. I was never any good with women. When the right person comes along things just work out."

"Do you think he'll notice how nervous I am?"

"Not if he's as nervous as you are." Robert laughed.

"Yeah right, an educated doctor like him nervous about going out with me!" Jill said, looking at her lap.

"Well, *I* think you're one of the prettiest girls I've ever seen. He should be plenty nervous!" Robert said, kissing her on the cheek. He walked back over to his bed and lay back down.

Jill smiled and lay back on her own bed, "Thank you, for everything. *Both of you!*"

Thirty Five

Robert opened his eyes and saw Katie sitting on his bed. It was still dark and he tried to blink away the sleep. She reached down and caressed his cheek.

"Katie…are you ok? Did you have the nightmare again?" He asked sleepily.

She leaned down and kissed him. "Yes I…I did have a…dream, honey."

He sat up on one arm and put the other one around her. "I'm right here for you, I'm not going anywhere."

She leaned down and kissed him again. "I know. This time I dreamed about our wedding. It was so…beautiful!"

"Our wedding? You dreamed about…Katie, are you sure you're ok?" He asked as he sat up in the bed.

"I'm fine. I'm sorry for waking you, I just…I do love you *so much*! I just wanted…I needed to touch you. I wish you could have seen the dream, everything was so perfect!"

He smiled and hugged her. "I will get to see it! I'll get to see it when it happens for real! We'll both get to see it together!"

She hugged him close and sniffed as a tear rolled down her cheek.

"Can you people maybe have your wedding in the *daytime*?" Jill's voice said from across the room. "Some of us are trying to *sleep*!"

"Sorry." Robert said as he eased down onto his back. He pulled Katie down next to him. She put her head on his chest closing her eyes.

"I know we're not supposed to, but…but can I maybe just stay here with you for a few minutes?" Katie asked.

Robert took in a deep breath and let it out slowly. "I think that's probably ok."

Thirty Six

"Hey! Hey, you guys need to wake up!" A voice was saying. Robert felt a nudge on his shoulder. He opened his eyes to see Jill standing next to his bed. "You guys need to get up before Dad comes in here and sees this!"

He suddenly realized daylight was streaming through the window and Katie was still sleeping happily in his arms. He smiled up at Jill and then kissed Katie's forehead. "Sweetheart, it's time to wake up."

She snuggled closer to him, if that was even possible. Then, after a small yawn, she opened her eyes and smiled at him. "Oh that was so nice. Are you sure I can't maybe sneak into your bed every night?"

Robert laughed. "Not yet, honey. Eventually, you can sleep with me every night but you know your dad's rule."

"Yes, but we've already broken it and…"

He didn't let her finish. He sat up. "Time to get up, let's go!"

"Atta Boy!" Jill giggled. "Don't give in to her!"

"You hush up!" Katie said, glaring at her. "You just mind your own business! Robert's done a lot for you but you don't need to be on his side for everything!"

Jill walked away, still laughing. Robert and Katie got up from the bed and got ready for breakfast.

Robert sat down at the table. Katie hugged him from behind and kissed his cheek. "Would you like some bacon and eggs for breakfast again, sweetheart?"

Jim was sitting in his usual spot and glared over at them. "She's being nice again writer. What do you suppose she wants today?"

"Some bacon and eggs sound nice." Robert smiled back at her. He looked back over at Jim. "She's fine, she just…she's ok."

Jim looked from Robert, to Katie, and back at Robert again. "You've been behaving in that bedroom, haven't you? You know the rules!"

"Behaving? Oh, of course we've…yeah, we always behave, don't we Katie?"

"Behaving, what's that mean?" Katie giggled. She walked over behind Jim and hugged him. "I love you too, Daddy!"

Jim sighed and looked over at Jill, who sat down quietly at the table. "Have they been following my rules? I know I can trust *you* to tell me!"

"Yes Dad, they've followed your rules." Jill smiled. "Sex Fiend has actually been quite a gentleman since we've been here. It's quite a change from all the noise they usually make in their bedroom back home!"

Jim glared back over at Robert.

"That was lovely, thanks for that." Robert scowled at her. Katie set a plate down in front of him.

"Not to change the subject," Jill smiled back. "But what time do you think…I mean when should I, well…?"

"Go over and bother him at about four. That should give you guys enough time to get to the stadium, find your seats, and maybe even see a bit of the warm ups." Robert answered shoveling eggs into his mouth.

"But is that when he said to come?"

"Who cares?" Robert grinned with his mouth full. "Just go over, bang on his door, and tell him you're ready to go!"

"I'm a college graduate, not some thug!" Jill shot back.

"Yeah, she's not some thug!" Jim smiled.

Emily was sitting next to Jill and put a hand on her arm. "Maybe Robert can call and ask what time he'd like to meet up with you?"

"Yeah, I'll call and tell him when you want to show up." He mumbled.

"*I* can call him for you and ask *nicely*!" Katie said, giving Robert a dirty look.

He reached into his pocket, pulled out his cell phone, and handed it to Katie. "Knock yourself out, sweetie!"

"And you were being so sweet! Can't you be sweet *all day* once and not just at random intervals?"

Robert leaned over and kissed her cheek. "Maybe just once. I'll save the once for Christmas or something, ok?"

Katie pushed a few buttons on the phone and held it back out towards Robert. "How does this phone work? I can't even find his number!"

He calmly pushed a couple of buttons and handed the phone back. She held the phone up to her ear and listened.

"It's going to voice mail I'll have to leave a message. Ben? It's Katie Benson, I'm just calling for Jill to find out what time you'd like to meet up with her for the baseball game?"

"Four o'clock, we'll push her in your door at four!" Robert tried to yell with his mouth full.

Katie glared at him. "If you wouldn't mind, please call us back when you get some free time. Let us know when and where you'd like to meet. Thanks Ben, I hope you have a good day!"

"Four o'clock!" Robert yelled again just before she hung up. She pushed his phone into her pocket. "Hey, don't I get my phone back?"

"Why, so when he calls back you can be rude and try to tell him what he's going to do? I don't think so. I'll hold on to this until he calls back."

Robert began to laugh. "Ok, but sometimes I get a lot of calls. Feel free to handle them however you like."

"Oh you do *not!*" Katie giggled. "I almost never see you on your phone! We're always together Robert; I know what goes on in your life now!"

"Do you now?" He laughed, looking over at Jim. "I just don't answer most of the calls."

As if on cue, the phone in her pocket began to ring. Katie pulled it out, smiling. "I'll bet this is Ben calling back!" She put the phone to her ear, "Hello?"

Robert watched as the smile left her face. He glanced over at Jill. "I don't think that's him."

"I'm sorry?" Katie said wrinkling her brow. "No, I'm *not* some *floozy* he just picked up! Who *is* this?"

Robert began laughing. "I wonder…?"

"No, you may *not* speak to him until you tell me who this is!" Katie began shouting. "You're…John? John, is that *you*? This is Katie, from Mr. Goldstein's office!"

"Oh no, it's New York. They always want something." Robert smiled.

"Yes, I'll ask him, and have him call you back later." Katie said sternly. "No, you may *not* speak to him! Because I said you can't, that's why! How *dare* you say those things to me when I answered his phone!" She angrily hung up and pushed the phone back into her pocket.

"Uh…who was that?" Robert asked trying not to laugh.

"That was a pig from our legal department back in New York. He wanted to tell you he received the signed contract and asked how the next book was coming."

Robert could no longer contain himself and began laughing. "You employ pigs there?"

"When I answered the phone he asked if you had just picked me up! Then he had the nerve to say, '*Ok Toots, roll off him and give him the phone!*'"

"You didn't want to roll off me and give me the phone, huh?"

Katie gave him the dirtiest look she could. He ignored it and continued eating.

Thirty Seven

After breakfast, Katie, Jill, and Emily went upstairs. Jim was in his favorite chair reading Robert's book, while Robert sat on the couch watching TV. An hour later Katie came downstairs and held Robert's phone out for him to take.

"I've had it with this thing!"

"You don't like my phone?"

"Honey, I thought you were joking about getting a lot of calls! How come I never see you answering it?"

"I keep it on vibrate and only answer calls from people I want to talk to. Why, who called?"

"Paul called, your brother called, and then agent! You don't bother to answer your phone for these people?"

"Carl called?" Robert smiled. "You talked to my brother?"

"Yes, I spoke to him. He sounded very nice and said he can't wait to meet me. I've met Paul and we chatted a bit. Your agent wanted to know who she should be contacting to help out promoting your movie."

"Oh, I don't even know. I guess I could give her the director's number?"

"I put her in contact with the publishing promotions department. They've been working with the movie people and will know what to tell her."

"Really? They've been...?"

"Can you please just tell us when Ben calls?"

Robert jumped up from the couch and hugged her. "Of course I will!" Katie hugged and kissed him and walked back upstairs.

"So you ignore business calls?" Jim asked after she had left.

"Well, sometimes. I just write the books, I don't do the other stuff! Since the book did so well, they always ask me about this or that. I usually let them try to make up their own minds."

Jim shook his head. "But you're sure you can support my daughter, huh?"

Robert laughed. "Yeah, I'm sure I'll get by."

His phone began to ring again, and this time it was Ben. Robert answered, "Hello?"

"Hi Robert; It's Ben. I was returning Katie's call. The game's at six, right?"

"Yeah, I thought I'd send Jill over to your place at about four. Then you can take your time getting to the stadium and parking, and finding the seats."

"Four sounds good so I'll see her then?"

"Uh…well, Katie told me I wasn't supposed to force a time on you. Would you mind if I run the phone upstairs to Jill, so you can talk to her?"

"That would be fine."

Robert ran upstairs and knocked on the bedroom door. Katie opened it and Robert held out the phone. She reached for it but he shook his head and pointed into the room at Jill.

"*Me*?" Jill asked nervously. "He wants to talk to *me*?"

She walked over and took the phone. Robert turned and walked back downstairs. He could hear Katie behind him whispering his name loudly.

"*Robert*! Don't you want to hear what he says to her?"

He turned and smiled back up the stairs. "It's their business, Katie. Show some trust in her, she'll be fine!"

She waved her hands at him and hurried back to the room. Robert walked back out to the couch and went back to watching TV.

"What have you gotten my daughters into?" Jim asked, as he sat back down. "Everything's such a fuss over this guy now!"

"Yeah, I know. I don't understand it much either. They're so worked up! I just wanted to see a baseball game and everything turned into such a production!"

"If you want to go to the game, then go. I'll go up and tell Jill she can't go out with this guy!" Jim scowled.

"You really are uptight about who your daughters see, aren't you?" Robert asked. "For God's sake Jim he's a psychologist! I'm sure Jill will be fine with him!"

"Yeah, tell me that after you've been a cop for twenty five years! These guys always seem normal until one day…then they just snap. And I don't want anyone snapping on my girls! Speaking of which, if something is going on at night with you and Katie up in that room, it had better *stop*! If I have to, I'll start doing bed checks at night!"

"Oh you will *not*!" Emily said, walking down the stairs. "You leave the kids alone! What goes on between Robert and Katie is their business and you will *not* interfere. Do you understand me?" She sat down next to Robert and crossed her arms.

"Em, I just worry, and if bed checks…"

"You *will* leave them alone and that's the end of it!" Emily chastised him. "Robert has been a perfect gentleman since he's been here. He's even put up with all the crap you've given him! Now you leave him and Katie alone!" She turned and smiled at Robert. "Honey, don't you worry about Jim!"

Robert smiled back. "He's ok, he's just watching out for his daughters."

"There, you see?" Jim laughed. "The writer's on my side! I'm just trying to take care of my daughters!"

Emily gave him a dirty look, and for a few seconds, Robert could see so much of Katie in her mother. He had been on the receiving end of several of those looks before.

Just before four o'clock, Jill and Katie came downstairs. Jill was wearing a very nice white outfit. Katie styled her hair and done her make up. She stepped into the middle of the living room and looked around.

"Well, how do I look?"

"You look *wonderful*, honey!" Emily beamed. "I hope you have a great time tonight!"

"Dad?" She asked, looking over at Jim.

He looked her up and down, and then sighed. "You look beautiful, sweetheart. Just be careful for me, ok?"

"Robert?"

He sat on the couch, staring at her. "Wow. I mean, *wow*! You know, I can hardly believe you're the same girl who answered the door when I came to pick Katie up for our first date. You're stunning."

Katie beamed at her and fussed a bit more with Jill's hair. "You see? I told you, you look great! Now go and have a wonderful time!"

She smiled as Jim got up to walk her to the door. "Would you like me to walk you over there, honey?"

"I'll be fine Dad, I promise! And before you ask, yes I have my phone and I'll call you if I have any problems at all, ok?"

Jim hugged her as they reached the front door. "Ok, just… just be careful, ok?"

Jill kissed him and walked out the door.

"Hey, bring me back a bat, or something!" Robert yelled after her. "I like bats!"

Thirty Eight

Robert sat on the couch watching TV as Katie sat next to him. He leaned forward, squinting. "You know, I really miss my TV back home."

Jim looked up from his book. "You miss your TV? Was it wall sized, or something?"

"No, I was living in a small condo back in Vegas. Once I made a bit of money with the book, I bought a nice high definition flat screen for my living room. Surround sound, speakers everywhere, it was really cool! Even back when I was first writing the book I had a flat screen in my bedroom. Nothing fancy back then, but it was always really cool to watch sports on."

"Does high definition really make that big of a difference?" Jim asked. "I never thought it looked that different?"

"It really does for sports. You get a wider view of the field and the grass looks greener, at least to me."

"We thought about getting a new TV but have been waiting for them to go on sale." Emily smiled.

"I'd be happy to buy you a new TV." Robert said, looking at Katie. "Honey, you don't mind if I buy your parents a new TV do you? I mean we have a couple of hours before the game. We could find a nice flat screen and have it set up for when the game comes on."

Jim put down his book and looked from Robert, to Emily. "I'd love a high definition TV, especially for football season! We could let him buy us a TV, can't we, Em?"

Emily gave Robert a worried look. "You really don't have to do that."

"I'd really like to! Look how excited Jim is! And then I'd get to watch the ball game on a new TV, too!"

Katie leaned over and kissed his cheek. "Always for someone else."

"Yeah, right," he laughed. "I just want to see the game in high definition. Not selfish at all, is it?"

Jim was nodding, looking over at Emily. "Em?"

Emily sighed, giving in. "Fine, you boys go and buy a new TV. But I think Katie and I should come along to make sure you don't buy some monstrosity that won't fit in the living room!"

Jim jumped happily to his feet. "Oh no, we won't get anything too big, will we writer? I'll get my car keys!"

"He has a *name*, Daddy!" Katie scowled as Jim walked past her.

Jim kept pulling a cell phone out of his pocket and looking at it.

"She's fine." Robert said, watching him. "She'll be ok with Ben, don't worry so much."

Jim scowled at him. "She'd better be. I just…it's hard for me to accept that my little girls are old enough to date now, ok?"

"One's old enough to be engaged."

"You're not *helping*!"

"Yeah, I'm sorry. So, what do you think? Nice TVs, huh?"

"Pretty big. Now that I really look at them, they are… pretty big."

"Well, it'll be your living room it's going to set in, so let's find one you like."

Katie came up next to Robert and took his hand. "This is what you guys want, one of these huge TVs?"

"I don't know…I wouldn't mind a big one, but like your mom said, we really don't need one that's *too big*." Jim said. He pulled his cell phone out of his pocket and glanced at it again. He noticed Robert watching him and quickly pushed it back into his pocket. "Sorry."

Emily put her arms around Jim and hugged him. "She's fine, Jim. Jill's a big girl and can take care of herself."

"I know, I know! Can I just be a father and worry a little, though? Please?"

Emily smiled and began to laugh. "Of course you can worry! That's our job to worry about her! But she'll be fine with Ben. We did get to meet him at dinner the other night."

"Yeah, I guess you're right. Besides, I know where he lives." He picked up a remote in front of one of the TVs, "I kind of like this one, what do you think, Em? You see, you can open up a little window and watch two channels at once!"

"Why on earth would you want to watch two TV channels at the same time?" She asked.

"Well, you know, maybe if there's a commercial on, or...I don't know, it just looks fun!"

She glanced at Robert. "It's so big, though...and expensive."

"It's not so bad. The one he likes says it comes with a blueray player. You can watch dvd or blueray movies on it."

"I'm not sure we'd know how to work one of those." Emily frowned. "Are they like a vcr at all?"

"Almost like them, except they play dvds."

"We'd have to put this big thing on a wall though, right?" Emily asked. "I'd have to take down some of our pictures."

"No, I can get you a stand for it, just like the one it's sitting on now. It can sit right where your other TV is. It'll be ok. If this is the one Jim wants we should get it. I think it's a good choice!"

Katie looked closely at the TV. "Maybe we should get one for back in New York? It might be nice to watch when we're home?"

"I still have all my stuff back in Vegas, honey. I'll need to take a trip back there and get it eventually, if we're going to stay in New York. I can just bring my TVs back from there."

Katie looked at him blushing slightly. "Oh sorry, I forget you lived somewhere else before we met. I just can't picture us not being together anymore."

He smiled. "I know what you mean." He glanced over at Jim. "So is that the one you want? I'll go and find a sales guy."

Jim stopped him. "This isn't some credit card scam or anything like that, right? You really have this money in the bank?"

Robert began laughing. "Yes, I really have the money in the bank. I know it seems like a dream. Sometimes I can't believe it myself but I do have the money."

Jim watched him for a minute, and then let him go. "Ok, I believe you. Especially since the book hasn't been half bad! And thank you for the TV, I do appreciate it!"

Robert purchased the TV and made arrangements for it to be delivered and set up within the hour. They would cut it close to game time but would at least get to watch part of the game on the new TV. On the way home, they stopped and bought some snacks for the game. As they got home the truck with the TV was pulling up.

"That was a pretty fast delivery!" Robert smiled, greeting the driver.

"We were told this was a priority; that you wanted to watch the baseball game." The driver smiled. "We understood that and made you our first stop."

Robert and Jim moved the old TV and stand out of the living room while the driver and his partner unloaded the new TV.

Katie took Robert's hand as they were setting up the TV. "Come into the kitchen with me and help me sort through all the food you and Daddy had to have for this game!"

"No Katie, I want to watch them set all this up. I need to make sure the cable is plugged in right for the high definition to work."

"Oh come on, they know what they're doing!"

"No, go sort through the stuff yourself, ok? I'll be in and help after they finish."

She sighed and let go of his hand. She started towards the kitchen but then turned and sat down on the couch instead.

"Watch that cable," Robert instructed the deliver men. "I don't want anyone tripping on that. Yeah, yeah, that's good over there."

It didn't take them long before the TV was up and running with still plenty of time before the game would start. Jim was sitting in his favorite chair once again, and Robert sat on the couch next to Katie.

"Can we go into the kitchen and get all your snacks ready yet?" She scowled at him.

"Just a minute honey the pregame show is on. I can meet you in the kitchen when a commercial comes on, if you want?"

Katie got up from the couch and walked towards the kitchen. She looked at the bags sitting on the counter and unloaded them. Emily helped her quietly.

"Why did they have to have V8 Juice?" Katie asked, shaking her head.

"I think your dad wants some with his beer, and Robert said he was going to make a bloody mary without any alcohol in it." Emily explained. "He said they go good with the peanuts they bought."

Katie poked her head back into the living room. "Robert, are you really going to drink this V8 Juice? Mom said you were going to make bloody marys?"

Robert's attention was focused on the TV. "Huh? Yeah, yeah, I'll be there in a minute. Just a few more minutes, ok?"

Finally a commercial came on. Instead of going into the kitchen Robert ran upstairs to their room and came back down wearing the Tampa Bay Rays shirt he bought. "Look," he showed Jim proudly. "I found this at the mall today! I love this!"

"He didn't even come to the kitchen like he said he was going to!" Katie said angrily.

"Oh honey, let them enjoy the new TV, and their game!" Emily said, putting a hand on Katie's shoulder. "I'm sure he doesn't mean to ignore you."

"*Robert*," Katie yelled into the living room. "You said you would come in here with me for the commercial!"

Jim began laughing. "Better go writer, your little precious is calling you!"

Robert scowled back at him and walked towards the kitchen. "Yes sweetie, what did you need?"

"Mom said you wanted bloody marys for the game?"

"Oh yeah, I forgot about that! It was neat watching them set up the TV! I'll come in and make one in a bit. Go ahead and put everything in the refrigerator, ok?"

"I can make one and bring it out to you, if you want?" She said, with a sigh.

"No, that's ok. I put Tabasco and a few other things in and taste as I go. I can do it."

He walked out into the living room and sat back on the couch. Katie began helping Emily put the groceries away. Emily kept watching her, and after a few minutes, spoke.

"Are you ok, honey?"

"Yes, I'm ok. I just…I guess I'm just used to him always showing me a lot of attention. I guess now I'm jealous of a new TV and…and my own father. I'm a horrible person, aren't I?"

"No, you aren't a horrible person!" Emily laughed. She hugged Katie. "He's just very special to you. I think you just want to be special to him, too. Don't worry honey, he'll be back to spoiling you before you know it!"

"I love him, Mom. I really do, and I know I shouldn't be jealous. He's actually the first man I've ever been with that I know I can trust completely. But it's hard to see him so focused on something other than me."

Emily kissed her on the cheek. "Let's make them drinks and take them out some of the snacks. I know Robert said he would make his own but let's surprise him, ok?"

"You don't think he'll mind?"

"Not at all, look how interested he is in the TV."

Katie smiled and began mixing the V8 in a glass with some Tabasco. She broke off a celery stalk and used it to stir the drink. She took it out into the living room for him as Emily followed her with a glass mixed with beer and V8 Juice for Jim.

"Oh, thanks, Em!" Jim said, without taking his eyes off the TV. "You should sit down and see this TV! It's almost like really being there! The writer really did good for us!"

"Apparently *The Father* approves." Katie said sourly, as she handed Robert his drink. He took a sip and then held the glass back out to her.

"Good try sweetie, but maybe a bit more Tabasco? Not too much though, just a bit."

Katie scowled at him as she took the glass back. His attention was still focused on the TV, though. She stalked back into the kitchen and opened the bottle of Tabasco. She put a bit more into his drink and glanced out into the living room, watching him laughing and talking with Jim and Emily. She poured most of the drink into the sink and emptied the Tabasco bottle into the glass. She walked back out into the living room and handed Robert the glass.

"There you are sweetheart, just a bit more Tabasco."

He put the glass to his lips and gulped down a mouthful. His eyes widened, and he immediately began to choke. "Katie…how much…oh geez, what the hell?" He sputtered and choked as she stood in front of him and watched.

"Oh honey, did I put in too much? I'm *so sorry*!" She said as sweetly as she could.

Jim began to laugh. "Better keep an eye on her, writer!"

Robert set the glass on table next to the couch and then ran to the kitchen. He turned on the sink and began to gulp water from the faucet. Katie followed him into the kitchen.

She watched him for a minute, feeling guilty. "Are you ok?"

He turned towards her after a minute or so. His face was beet red. "Why did you do that?"

"I…I'm…sorry." She said looking down at the floor. "I was…I'm sorry."

"Writer, they're singing the National Anthem!" Jim yelled from the living room.

Robert put his arm around Katie's shoulders. "Come on; sit next to me on the couch, ok? Please?"

She allowed him to lead her back to the living room and sat down on the couch next to him.

"Something you drank?" Jim laughed.

"That's not funny!" Katie said glaring at him. "I didn't mean for that to happen! I just put too much Tabasco in his drink!"

"Like drinking pepper spray, wasn't it?" Jim continued to laugh.

Robert put his arm around Katie's shoulders and pulled her close. He kissed her on the cheek. "It was just an accident. It's ok."

Feeling really bad now, Katie kissed Robert back. "I really am sorry! I shouldn't have done that!"

"It's ok honey, no harm done." Robert said, his attention back on the TV.

The game started and Katie was quiet for a little bit. Once or twice she mentioned how good the TV looked, and how real the grass color was, but she mostly stayed quiet.

Finally around mid game, Jim spoke up in between innings. "Where were your tickets, writer? Maybe we can see Jill on TV?"

"I don't know, somewhere behind home plate, but I'm not exactly sure where. I haven't seen her yet, but I've been looking, too."

Jim pulled his cell phone out of his pocket and looked at it. "Maybe I should call and ask how things are going?"

Emily reached out and took the phone away from him. "You don't need to call your daughter, she's fine!"

Katie ignored him and began looking at Robert's shirt. "Isn't this the shirt you bought at the mall?"

Robert smiled at her. "Yeah, I love it! It even fits good!"

Katie rolled her eyes. "You mean it fits *well*. For a best selling author your English is horrible sometimes, Robert!"

He began laughing. "Yeah, sometimes it ain't so good!"

She looked over at the glass full of Tabasco and V8 still sitting on the table next to him. "Can you hand me that drink? It doesn't need to sit there! I can at least go and pour it out."

"What? Yeah, yeah," he replied as the game began again. "Here you go." He picked up the glass and handed it to her. Just as she took the glass, a homerun was hit, and Jim suddenly yelled, holding his hands above his head. The yell scared Katie and she dropped the glass on Robert. The reddish liquid quickly covered his chest.

"Oh, oh *shit*!" He screamed as he jumped up from the couch. "Oh no, get it off me, get it *off*!"

He quickly yanked the shirt over his head and ran to the kitchen, throwing the shirt into the sink. He grabbed a towel and quickly wet it with cold water. He then began dabbing at his chest with the towel.

Katie walked into the kitchen behind him. "Where did you put the shirt? We need to soak it so it doesn't get ruined!"

Robert ignored her and kept dabbing at his chest.

She looked closer at him and noticed his chest turning pink. "Are you ok, did you get cut, or something?"

"This is made of the same stuff they make pepper spray from, Katie. It just hurts, but I'll be ok. It was an accident, don't worry about it."

She hurried over to him and put one hand on his shoulder while trying to take the wet towel from him with her other\ hand. "Oh honey, I'm so sorry, let me help!"

Robert took a deep breath and pulled the towel away from her grasp. "Katie, I'm ok. Can you just get me another shirt, please? Another t-shirt, the dirty one's over there in the sink."

She looked at him sadly. "I'm…I'm so…sorry. Yes, I'll get you another shirt." She walked out of the kitchen and slowly up the stairs trying not to cry. A few minutes later, she was back with his favorite, black t-shirt. It was the one that said, *'The Treaty'* across the front. She handed it to him and then began to slowly rinse the Tabasco covered shirt in the sink.

He slipped on the t-shirt and watched her for a minute. "It was an accident Katie, it's really no big deal."

"I know." She said sadly. "It's ok Robert, go back and watch the rest of your game. I'll stop bothering you."

"You don't bother me." He said, hugging her from behind.

"I know; I'm fine. Go back and watch the game, ok?"

He kissed her cheek. "Are you sure? I'm ok honey, it was just an accident."

She looked down at the stained shirt in her hands and could tell it was ruined. She did her best to smile back at him. "Really, I'll clean this up and be back out in a bit, ok? I'm fine, really!"

He looked at her suspiciously for a few seconds before turning to go back to the living room. "Ok, if you're sure?"

"Of course I'm sure." She smiled.

She put down the shirt and walked to the freezer. She took out the chocolate ice cream and sat down at the kitchen table to eat.

Robert walked distractedly back to the living room. He neared the couch and Emily could tell something wasn't right. "Are you ok? Jim said that stuff might burn a bit!"

Robert took in a deep breath. As he let it out, he looked up at Emily with resolve in his eyes. "May I please have my ring?"

Jim looked up from the TV. "Now, in the middle of the game?"

"Yes, now." Robert replied. "I need to change out of this shirt, could you get it for me while I do that?"

"Of course!" Emily said, following him upstairs and heading for her bedroom.

She came out of her room with the ring. Robert was wearing slacks, a dark blue dress shirt, and a black tie. He smiled at Emily as she handed him the ring. He reached out and handed her back a small camera. "She'll probably want pictures. Just push the button. After it focuses it'll take a picture."

"You're going to propose?" Emily asked, covering her mouth. "Right now?"

Without answering, Robert walked back down the stairs and into the kitchen. Katie looked up as he came in and sat down.

"Hi," he said quietly.

"Hi," she answered.

"Having some ice cream, huh?"

"Robert, you don't have to do this, you can go back out and watch the game."

He smiled at her, his eyes full of love. "You don't mind sharing, do you?" He got up and found a spoon before sitting back down. He reached over and scooped out some ice cream. "This makes you feel better, huh?"

"Robert..."

"You know...I think I knew the first time I looked into your eyes."

"You really don't need to do this," she sighed. "I'll get over it. I just need some time by myself."

He let out a small laugh as he got another spoonful of ice cream. "When I first walked into your office, I saw you and thought to myself, '*Man, she's beautiful!*' I love you more than anything, Katie. In the mornings now you're my sunshine. At night, you're my stars, you're my everything. I hate to see you depressed."

She let out a small giggle. "You're my sunshine and stars, too."

"You know, I can't really imagine not having you with me. I really do want to spend the rest of my life with you. I want to raise a family with you."

"I want to raise a family with you too, and we will. But…"

"Let me finish Katie, I need to finish, ok?" He said and got down on one knee in front of her. He heard a quiet gasp from Emily near the doorway.

"Oh Robert, don't do this just because I'm depressed! You don't have to…"

He reached up and took her hand in his. "Sweetheart, I love you more than anything. I do think we belong together. I don't see any reason to wait any longer. We both know we want to spend the rest of our lives together. I said we should wait in case things changed but they won't. We'll always love each other! I need you, love you, and we both need this!"

She looked into his eyes now and began to cry.

"Katie, will you stay by my side through thick and thin, for better or worse? Katherine Ann Benson, will you marry me?" He pulled the ring case out of his pocket and held it out towards her.

Jim stood in the kitchen doorway next to Emily, watching. Emily began to cry quietly. He took the camera from her hand and began to take pictures himself.

Katie burst into tears and threw her arms around Robert's neck, sobbing wildly. He hugged her back laughing and crying. He spoke up again. "Katie, is this a yes?"

She pulled back from him and looked into his eyes. "*Of course* it's *yes*!" She wailed.

He wiped some tears from his own cheek. "Then you need to stop hugging me and let me put the ring on your finger."

Katie continued to cry but held out her shaking hand. He steadied it as best he could and slipped the ring onto her finger. It fit perfectly.

She looked down and for the first time realized it was the ring she had wanted and given to her by the man she wanted. She pulled him back into a hug and continued to cry.

Thirty Nine

A short time later they were back in the living room. Katie sat on the end of the couch as Robert lay with his head in her lap watching the last inning of the baseball game. She reached down and carefully began to loosen the tie he was wearing.

Robert reached towards his tie and looked up at her. "You don't need to take it off honey. I put it on to propose, I know you like ties!"

"You've proposed and now you should be comfortable. You hate ties."

"I just wanted things to be special for you," he smiled. "I knew you were starting to feel left out while we were watching the game."

She pulled the tie away from his neck. "Things are always special with you, I'm sorry I acted so spoiled. Are you really ok? I'm so sorry about putting that awful stuff in your drink!" She set the tie aside and began to unbutton his shirt. A flash went off. Robert turned his head and aimed a quick scowl at Jim, who let out a quiet chuckle.

"Yeah, I'm ok. It was just an accident. You didn't mean to drop the glass."

"I was upset about not getting all of your attention and put that stuff in your drink! I'm so sorry! Are you *sure* you're ok? You said it was like pepper spray!" She reached inside his shirt and began to gently rub his chest.

"I'm fine, honey," He said with a contented sigh. "That feels so good!"

Another flash went off. Katie looked up and noticed her father was taking pictures. "Daddy, why are you taking pictures of us? Where did you even get that camera from?"

Jim smiled widely back at her. "I got the whole thing! I took pictures of everything! The writer gave me this camera. He said you'd want pictures."

Emily was sitting next to Jim looking at the camera. "Oh Katie, the pictures are wonderful, what a beautiful moment!"

Katie looked down at Robert. "You had Daddy take pictures?"

"Of course, I knew you'd want pictures of your proposal. Katie, why didn't you just talk to me? Why didn't you just tell me you were feeling left out?"

"I…I tried, but you weren't paying any attention to me. I just…in some ways I guess I *am* really spoiled and awful. I just wanted you to notice me. You were so focused on the TV, the game, and Daddy…"

He sat up and put his arm around her. "I'm sorry. I didn't even realize you were feeling like that. Next time just tell me you really need to talk and we'll sort things out. Communication, remember?"

She looked down at the ring on her finger. "I'm so sorry I had to rush you into this."

He began laughing. "Sweetheart, you didn't rush me into anything. I bought that the day you picked it out. We both knew what we wanted. The time came and I knew."

A tear fell from Katie's eye, as she kissed his cheek. "Thank you. And I do promise to talk to you when I'm upset, ok?"

He reached up and touched her cheek. "I'll be holding you to that!"

Jim set down the camera and pulled out his cell phone. He glanced at it and then back at Robert and Katie. "Well, one daughter's engaged, where's the other one?"

"She's probably on her way home. Oh, I can't wait to tell her when she gets home. I don't want to spoil her date by making her feel I tried to outdo her again though." Katie smiled.

"Yeah, but we can call her and ask who won, right?" Robert said, winking at Jim. "I mean we were kind of tied up and didn't really get to see the final score."

"You had your head in my lap during the end of the game!" Katie scolded him. "But you can't remember who won?"

He pulled out his cell phone, dialed and held the phone up to his ear. "Jill? Hey, it's Robert! We bought a new TV and a few other things were going on back here. We didn't get to see the final score. Who won? Oh yeah? *What*? How were the seats at least? I see. Yes, I'll let him know. Have a good time, ok? Don't come home too late or he'll have a fit. Ok, bye sweetie." He hung up.

"Well, who won?" Katie asked.

"Oh, um…" He glanced over at Jim. "She ah…she said she didn't know. They were talking and…getting to know each other and are going out for a drink now. They'll be back later."

"A drink?" Jim asked. "And what do you mean by *getting to know each other*? What was he doing with my daughter?"

"Oh, you hush!" Emily smiled. "She had a good time with Ben, though?"

Robert smiled and took Katie's hand. "Yeah, she said she had a great time. I'm sure they'll be fine."

Forty

"Sweetheart, can we see the pictures Daddy took of our proposal?" Katie asked nicely.

"Yeah, let me get my laptop. We can see them better than on the cameras little screen, ok? Take the memory card out for me."

Katie picked up the camera while he went to get his laptop. "Take out the what? I'm not very good with this stuff, remember?"

Robert came back with his laptop and set it down on the coffee table. While it was booting up he showed Katie how to remove the memory card from the camera.

"That wasn't hard at all!" She smiled. "I could get used to stuff like this!"

He slid the card into the laptop and brought up the pictures. He had to admit; Jim really had taken some pretty good shots.

"Oh, you look so handsome." Katie cooed. "I can't believe we're really engaged now!"

"We are. So now all you have to do is plan the perfect wedding."

She covered her mouth and tried not to cry again. "It'll… it'll be perfect no matter what…just because we'll be there together!"

Robert kissed her and hugged her close. "Of course it will."

"Oh, I wish I could show my friends these now!" Katie sniffed.

"We can email them if you want to Katie? I do know how to do that, remember? You just need to tell me what their email addresses are."

"Could you email one to my sister?" Emily asked. "I know some of the rest of the family would love to see these! I can give you her email address!"

"We can email anyone you'd like." Robert smiled. He brought up an email program and placed one of the photos in the email. "Ok, just tell me the email address of everyone you'd like to send this to. I can send it right off!"

"I...I don't remember my friend's addresses!" Katie said, sounding excited. "How do I find them out?"

Robert began to laugh, "How about you call them, honey? Call them up and tell them the news and then they can tell you what their addresses are."

Excitement filled her face. "Oh, I forgot about my phone! I can do that!" She ran back upstairs towards the bedroom. Emily opened a small address book she had retrieved and began looking up email addresses.

"How many can we send this to?" She asked.

"As many as you'd like!" Robert smiled.

"We have a lot of family." Jim warned. "This might take a while!"

"I have all night!" Robert answered happily. "Just tell me who to send it to!"

Robert sent the picture to all the addresses Emily gave him. She seemed almost as excited at Katie. Katie was still upstairs. He finished and walked upstairs to see where was. He found her lying on her stomach still talking on her cell phone.

"Oh, it was so romantic! Oh yes, he's so perfect and did it at the perfect time! He always knows what to say!"

He watched, knowing she didn't even realize he was there. He listened as she went on and on about how perfect he was, how romantic everything had been, relating every detail. He listened for a bit and cleared his throat.

She didn't hear him. He walked into the room, sat down on the bed, and placed a hand gently on her back. She turned and smiled happily at him. "Oh Holly, Robert's here! I've got to go! Yes, I'll call you as soon as we get back to New York! I love you too, sweetie. Bye." She hung up and sat up next to him.

"You've been up here a while. Did you get your friend's email addresses?" He asked.

"My...?" Her face turned to disappointment. "Oh no, I forgot! I was so excited telling them about your proposing. I forgot we had pictures to send!"

"You're excited, huh?" He put his arms around her shoulders and hugged her close. "I'm glad. I'm happy you're excited about marrying me."

"You're excited too, right?"

"Of course. How could I not be excited about marrying the perfect woman? We sent the picture of me proposing to all your aunts, uncles, and cousins."

"Really? Mom gave you everyone's address?"

"I think she's as excited as you are about our engagement."

Katie hugged him again. "Oh Robert! You've made everything...so...so..."

He hugged her back. "I know baby, I know. Come on, let's go back downstairs."

She allowed him to lead her downstairs, clinging closely to him. They walked into the living room and sat down on the couch.

Jim was peeking between the curtains out the front window.

"Jim, will you quit doing that, she's fine!" Emily was saying from a nearby chair.

"Well where is she then?" He asked. "How long does it take to go out for a drink? He'd better not be taking advantage of her!"

"Your oldest daughter just got engaged! Can't you be happy for *her*?"

"I think that's them!" He said anxiously. "Yes, it's them! They're pulling into the driveway next door!" He left the curtains and walked to the front door. Emily got up and cut him off.

"You will not meet her at the door and start in with the third degree!"

"Em!" He complained. "I just want to make sure she's ok! You know, that he didn't drug her, or anything?"

"You will sit down and stop hassling your daughters!" She scolded. "We've met Ben. He's not some thug from an alley! Show some trust in your girls!"

Katie got up and took her father by the hand. "Come on Daddy, sit down. She'll be back in a few minutes if they just pulled in. She can tell us everything." Katie led him to the couch and sat him down next to Robert. She sat down on his other side, still holding his hand.

He looked at Katie for a few seconds and then turned to Robert. "You understand, right? You worked in security! Am I such a bad guy for wanting to know she's safe?"

"We met him, remember? Katie and I were even in his office for marriage counseling. She'll be fine with him." Robert replied, trying to reassure him.

"Where is she? Maybe I should go out there?"

He started to get up but Katie pulled him back down. "Daddy, please don't embarrass her! I'm sure she's just saying goodbye!"

Robert got up from the couch and walked to the front window. He peeked through the curtains and walked to the front door. He opened it and stuck his head out, looking towards Ben's house. He walked back to the couch and sat back down.

"Well?" Jim asked.

"I didn't see them they must have gone inside."

"They *what*?" Jim roared. He pulled his cell phone out of his pocket and began to dial.

Katie tried to grab the phone but he held it out of her reach. "I'm going to find out what's going on!"

Robert put his hand on Jim's shoulder. "I think we can go over looking for her in about thirty minutes."

He stopped dialing. "You'll go over there with me?"

"If you give her thirty more minutes, then yes. I'll go over with you and find out what's going on."

"You *will not*!" Katie scowled over at Robert. "You don't need to be encouraging him!"

"Let's just give her a half hour and then check on her, please?"

Jim looked at Robert for a minute, "Ok…but she'd better not be hurt, drugged, or anything like that! Thirty minutes, not a second less!" He slid his phone back into his pocket.

Forty One

Jim sat between Robert and Katie, looking at his watch every minute or so. He stared intently at the door. Katie held onto his arm, rubbing his shoulder and trying to reassure him.

"Ok writer, it's been twenty five minutes! Get ready to go!"

"Daddy…" Katie pleaded.

Emily walked over towards the couch. "Jim, you don't have to…"

The front door began to open and everyone in the living room jumped to their feet. Jill walked into the living room looking flushed and smiling widely. She hugged Emily, Katie, Jim, and then stopped in front of Robert, smiling dreamily.

"Thank you, *so much* for that! It was perfect!" She put her arms around his neck and hugged him close. She then kissed him on the cheek and walked towards the stairs.

Everyone watched her walk slowly up the stairs.

"Are you happy now?" Jim roared. "He's drugged her! She's all loaded up on something!"

"Oh Daddy, don't be stupid. She looks happy, and tired, not drugged!" Katie glared at him.

Jim headed for the staircase and everyone followed along. They found Jill in the bedroom, lying on her bed. She was on her back, holding a pillow to her chest and smiling up at the ceiling.

Jim went immediately over and sat down next to her on the bed. "Honey, look at me. Let me see your eyes. Can you focus on my finger?"

Jill stopped smiling and glared at him. "What? I'm not on drugs Dad! Can't I just come home and be happy?"

"Focus on my finger, Jill." Jim said again.

Jill held up a middle finger. "Focus on *this* finger, Dad! I'm fine! I just had a really…good night, ok?"

He leaned down near her and sniffed. "How much did you have to drink?"

Jill sat up on the bed. "*Mom?*"

Emily walked over and put an arm around Jim. "Jim, she's fine! Your daughter is home safe and sound, ok? Can you stop bothering her?"

He turned and looked up at Robert who nodded back.

"Fine, you just had a good night. I hope it wasn't *too* good of a night, though!" He scowled.

She went back to smiling at the ceiling. "It was…perfect."

"Jill," Robert said proudly, "Katie has something to tell you, too."

Jill glanced over dreamily. "You do? Did you want to see my finger, too?" she began giggling at her own joke.

Katie held out her hand showing off the engagement ring. "Robert proposed while you were gone. We're really engaged now."

The smile left Jill's face. "He…?" She sat up on the bed and looked up at Robert. "You really proposed to her? Oh Katie, I'm so happy for you!" She put her arms around Katie and hugged her close. She then walked over and hugged Robert. "Congratulations!"

Jim watched her closely. "You're sure you're ok? No drugs, you can remember everything that happened tonight?"

Jill sat back down on her bed. "Yes Dad, I remember everything. Actually," she began to blush, "I don't think I'll be able to ever forget tonight."

"What's that supposed to mean?" Jim asked. "What happened, what won't you forget?"

Emily smiled and began to lead Jim out of the room. "Come on Sherrif, she'll tell you when she's ready."

He looked at Robert as he went out the door. "You find out what that meant for me! What won't she ever forget?"

Robert sat down next to Jill on the bed and Katie sat on her other side. "So it was a good night, huh? You had a good time at the game?"

Jill looked at him and sighed. She smiled dreamily again.

"Yeah, yeah, I get the hint." He said. "Sister thing, right? I'll be downstairs watching TV. Let me know when I can go to bed, ok?" He got up and walked out of the room leaving Katie and Jill together.

Robert came downstairs and saw Jim and Emily sitting on the couch. He walked over and sat down in Jim's usual chair.

"So," Jim asked, "What did you find out?"

Robert began laughing. "They tossed me out, just like you. I guess they want a little sister talk."

Emily smiled. "I think your girls are pretty happy. How long has it been since they've gotten along this well?"

"Yeah, I guess you're right." Jim mumbled. "Somehow, those two getting along like this makes me nervous."

A few minutes later Katie and Jill came downstairs wearing their pajamas.

"Honey, can you show Jill our engagement pictures?" Katie asked.

"Yeah, sure. How about I get them all cued up? You and Jill can look at them while I get ready for bed."

Katie began to giggle. "You know I'm not good with computers!"

Robert ignored her and brought up the pictures on his laptop. "It's easy Katie. Just push these arrow keys to go forward and backwards through the pictures, ok?"

She smiled and kissed him. "Ok, thank you."

Robert walked up the stairs and into the bedroom. He was putting on his pajamas and heard a knock at the door. Katie poked her head in and gave him a serious look. "Can we talk?"

"Of course we can talk, you know that. Come on in."

"I...I kind of agreed to something."

"With who, Jill?" He asked. He glanced at the pajama top he was holding and after a few seconds, tossed it aside.

"I didn't mean to plan something without talking to you first, but she was so excited. Robert, she had such a good time tonight."

He patted the bed beside him. "Ok, sit down and tell me what we agreed to do."

She sat down and looked at her lap. "I know we're supposed to be working on our communication…"

"What did you tell her we'd do, Katie?"

"I didn't really think it would be a problem and you're always so nice when we ask you for something!"

He reached out and gently touched her cheek. He turned her face so she was looking him in the eyes. "It's ok Katie; just tell me what you want."

"Well, she said she was thinking about taking some classes here this summer. I guess Ben knows some people at the college here and she wanted to know if we could fly home to New York? She wanted to stay a bit longer."

"That's it? You just told her we'd be fine with flying home?"

"I didn't think you'd mind! You don't mind, do you?"

"Not one bit! So what happened tonight? What's she all hopped up about? I guess things went well for her?"

Katie's face filled with excitement. "Oh Robert, he kissed her! He kissed her and she said she knows how I feel about *you* now! She feels so connected to him, just like I do to you!"

"So that's why she wants to stay, because they're involved now?"

"You don't have to de-personalize it like that!" Katie giggled. "But yes, I think they're falling in love, just like we did that first weekend! Isn't it exciting? Listening to her, it's like I get to fall in love all over again, too!"

"So tonight you got engaged and your sister fell in love, huh? What a night!"

Katie smiled but looked down at her lap. "Yes, what a night. What I really wanted to talk to you about is our engagement."

"You didn't want to get engaged?"

She looked back up at him. "Yes, I did want it to happen, with all my heart. But I feel like I pushed you into this. You gave me the ring because I was in the kitchen feeling sorry for myself."

He pulled her close. "I gave you the ring because I love you and want to marry you. You didn't push me into anything, Katie. You were right that day at the mall. I didn't really go to the bathroom. I went back to the jewelry store and bought you the ring you wanted."

"I know…but…"

"But *nothing*! If you want to wait longer we can certainly do that. I do want to marry you and I think tonight was the perfect time to propose."

Tears began to fall from Katie's eyes. "Really? You didn't just do it because I was acting spoiled?"

"Of course I didn't do it just because you were acting spoiled!" Robert laughed. He kissed her gently. "You *are* spoiled but I still love you and want to marry you."

She kissed his cheek. "Thank you. You're sure I didn't pressure you into this, though?"

"No you didn't pressure me. If you feel really bad though, you can give the ring back and we can pretend I didn't propose?"

"Absolutely not," she said, glaring at him. "I'm ready to plan our wedding!"

There was a soft knock at the door and Jill stuck her head inside. "Are you guys ok? Can I come in?"

"She keeps trying to give the ring back!" Robert smiled.

"Oh I do *not*!" Katie giggled. "But you just think you have to be so funny saying that, don't you? It's too late, you're marrying me!"

"And how about you?" Robert asked, looking at Jill. "I hear you've *connected* with Ben now?"

"Shh," Katie scolded him. "That was just supposed to be between us!"

Jill walked over and sat down on the bed next to Robert. "Yes, since you asked, I *do* feel connected to him. He was so sweet tonight, so…understanding."

"Understanding is overrated, isn't it Katie? We don't understand anything!" Robert laughed.

"You joke and laugh all you want!" Jill smiled. "But I'll never be able to pay you back for giving me those tickets. For letting me have the night I had."

"Sure you can, just buy me tickets sometime."

Katie pushed him playfully. "Be nice! She's trying to thank you, asshole!"

"So tell me honey, how long does it take to plan a wedding?"

"You're probably safe for about six months or so. It's not something you can just plan over a weekend. Unless… Did you want to have a quick ceremony somewhere?"

"I want you to be happy. You plan whatever you want to for us, ok?" We get to invite Jill and the shrink, right?"

"Yes, of course we'll invite Jill! She is a bride's maid! And if she's still together with Ben, then yes, we'll invite him too."

"Wow, a shrink at our wedding. He'll probably try to analyze everything."

Jill giggled and moved over to her own bed. "You joke all you like, writer." She lie back on the bed and sighed.

Robert stood up. "I'm going to go downstairs and tell your Dad you let the shrink kissed you!" He began laughing.

Katie pulled him back down onto the bed. "No, what you are going to do is stay here with me! And you *won't* be telling Daddy anything about Jill's night! That's for her to tell him, if she wants to!"

"Hey, he told me he wanted…"

"I don't care what he told you! You'll listen to *me*, Robert! As your future wife, you'd better start listening to me!"

"Yes Dear. Can we at least go back downstairs and say goodnight?"

Katie gave him a stern look. "Sure. If you behave. You listen to what I said, it's her business."

He stood up and pulled Katie up with him. "Yes, I promise to be good."

Katie led him back downstairs. They walked into the living room to see Jim and Emily looking at the pictures on Robert's laptop.

Emily smiled widely at them. "I hope you don't mind, we were a bit nosy and ended up looking at some of your other pictures."

"I don't mind at all." Robert smiled, as he, and Katie sat down on the couch next to her parents.

"Where are these from? You look so nice in a tie! You're both so dressed up!"

"Those were taken at the airport after our first weekend together." Robert smiled. He put his arm around Katie and pulled her close. "She was dropping me off and we didn't have any pictures of each other. So I used my digital camera and took a few. Then I emailed her the pictures. She has copies of those somewhere."

"I printed them out at work. They're at home on my dresser." Katie smiled. "I meant to buy some frames for them."

Emily kept looking through the pictures on screen. She noticed several taken in what looked like a bookstore.

"Oh, those are kind of embarrassing. Those are pictures of some of my book signings. In one or two you can kind of see how tired I am."

"Oh my God! You look exhausted in that one!" Katie gasped. "You should have left and gotten some rest!"

"Rest doesn't sell books, sweetheart. I did what I had to do. Signing books helped make me a popular author."

They looked through some more pictures and Robert stood up. "Well, you're welcome to keep looking through the pictures, use my laptop for whatever; I'm beat. It's been a long day and I'm ready for bed."

Katie stood up with him, "I can tuck you in, if you want?"

"I'd like that."

"You two behave up there!" Jim snarled. "Don't make me have to come up there and check on you! You aren't married yet!"

Emily glared at him. "What did I tell you? Now stop this!"

"Rules are rules." He mumbled back as Robert and Katie made their way upstairs.

They got to the bedroom door and Robert stopped Katie. "How about I kiss you goodnight out here so we don't bother Jill?"

She put her arms around his neck and gazed into his eyes. "You can kiss me anywhere you want sweetheart." He leaned in and kissed her slowly, very passionately. After the kiss they walked into the room and laid down on their separate beds.

"So, what did Dad say?" Jill asked.

"Oddly enough, he didn't say anything!" Robert answered. "He didn't even ask me what I found out about your night."

"Mom had a hold of him." Katie giggled. "He knows not to ask you if she told him not to. And you'd better mind *me* the way he minds *her*!"

"I think we'll be ok, honey." Robert laughed. "We *connect*, just like you said."

Forty Two

Robert opened his eyes to Katie sitting on the side of his bed. She kissed his cheek and ran a hand through his hair.

"Good morning, sunshine." She smiled.

He looked around and saw sunlight streaming through the window. "It's morning already? Wow, last night went quick, what time is it?"

"Its eight o'clock sweetheart, everyone's getting ready for breakfast."

He yawned. "Ok, I'll get up."

She put her arms around his neck and kissed him as he sat up. "What's all this for?"

"I just love you." She smiled. "Last night meant so much. You've made me so happy and I just wanted to kiss you."

"I love you, too. I'd be happy to just sit her and kiss you all day honey but I need to go to the bathroom." He laughed.

He got up and walked to the bathroom with Katie following. She closed the door and watched as he began to pee.

"Robert, would you mind if…if we flew home tomorrow?"

He looked over at her. "Tomorrow? Are you in a hurry to get out of here?"

"No, it was nice to see Mom and Dad, but…"

"But?"

She smiled and began to blush slightly. "But I've been away from work for a while, and…and I'm actually kind of anxious to get started on the wedding plans. It'll be easier to do that in New York."

"Have you told your parents we're ready to leave?"

"Well…I was thinking we could maybe do that at breakfast?"

"Yes, I think we can do that. If that's when you want to leave honey, we can certainly do that!"

She reached over and put her hand on his arm as he was pulling up his pajama bottoms. "Thank you. I'll be downstairs when you're ready, ok?"

"Ok."

He took a quick shower, put on his worn jeans and a t-shirt, and headed downstairs. He sat in the empty chair next to Jim, who smiled widely at him and held out a plate full of bacon.

"Bacon this morning, writer?"

Jill was sitting nearby and watched the two men closely. Katie was helping her mother and set down a glass of milk in front of Robert.

"Daddy, he's not going to tell you anything about Jill's night!"

"I didn't ask him anything! I just offered him some bacon! Is he still on a diet and can't have any? Are you still on a diet, writer?"

Robert looked from Jim, to Katie. "I…uh…I can have some bacon, can't I Katie?"

She put a hand on his shoulder and glared at Jim. "Yes, you may have some bacon. Now drink your milk, sweetheart."

"We…uh…we were thinking about leaving tomorrow." Robert stuttered.

"Tomorrow?" Emily asked. "Why so soon? It seems like you guys just got here!"

"Well yeah, but…uh…Jill was going to, uh…did you ask them yet, Jill?"

A large smile crossed Jill's lips but she didn't say anything. Instead, she shook her head.

"Ask us what?" Jim growled, looking at Jill. "What went on last night? What aren't you telling me?" He looked over at Robert. "Writer?"

Katie stood behind Robert's chair and put her arms around him. "*He* won't tell you Jill's business Daddy! I've told him to be quiet about it! He listens to me, just like you listen to Mom!"

"But it was ok for you girls to tell him about last night, huh? Why don't you girls ever trust me with anything?"

Jill continued to grin widely. "I'll tell you what happened, Dad. He kissed me. He kissed me and I kissed him back!"

"And you couldn't tell me *that*?" Jim exclaimed. "You couldn't tell me that this guy kissed you on your first date?"

"We knew you'd just get all upset!" Katie said, scowling. "When we tell you things like that, you rant and rave and get all upset!"

"I just worry about you! I just want you to be safe! You were in high school the last time you told me something like that, for crying out loud!"

"I was safe with Ben, Dad. I do appreciate you worrying, but I was fine. We were at the baseball game, talking, and… and it just happened. We kissed. After the game he took me to this beautiful, little bistro and bought me some sparkling wine and cheesecake."

"So that's why you took so long getting home, isn't it?" Jim asked.

Jill sighed deeply. "I know I probably worried you sick but I lost track of things. I was having such a wonderful night!"

"I've tried to be understanding." Jim frowned. "I thought I've been doing good dealing with Katie marrying the writer."

"You just can't use his name, though!" Katie said, as she let go of Robert and put her hands on her hips. "How do you think that makes him feel? How do you think that makes *me* feel?"

Jim let out a small snicker. "Are you enjoying breakfast *Robert*? Would you like some more milk; maybe some eggs to go with that bacon, *Robert*?"

Robert smiled and let out a small laugh as he looked behind him at Katie.

Jim looked back over at Jill. "And you really like this guy, this Ben?"

"Yes Daddy, I do really like him." She answered quietly. "He said he knew some people at the university who could help me with a few classes. Would you mind if I stayed here for a few classes during the summer and keep seeing Ben?"

"And he treated you well, he was a gentleman? He didn't force himself on you last night?"

"He was a *perfect* gentleman. I think you might even like him, if you give him a chance. Just like you gave Robert a chance?"

"You know you're always welcome wherever we are, sweetheart. Of course we wouldn't mind you staying for the summer! And Katie and the wri…*Robert* are both welcome here anytime, too!"

Katie smiled and walked over to hug Jim. "Thank you, Daddy!"

"I just want you girls to be happy and safe, you know that, right?"

Katie kissed him on the cheek. "We know Daddy, and we are!"

Robert looked across the table at Jill. "He *kissed* you? At the *ballgame*? Please at least tell me it was between innings?"

Jill began to blush. "I don't know, I didn't pay much attention to the game. I don't know if Ben did, either."

"You didn't even watch the game? You just went there and…and *kissed*?"

"Oh Robert, now you're starting to sound like Daddy! So they kissed a little, so what?" Katie said, glaring at him.

"I just…well I wanted to see the ballgame! And…she just…?" He looked at Katie and sighed. "Yeah, I guess you're right. No big deal."

Jim began laughing. "Don't let her take control, Writer! You can't let her be the boss all the time!" He smiled over at Jill. "You used the writer here so you could kiss that…*guy*?" Both he and Robert began to laugh. Jill tried not to smile and began to blush a deep red.

Emily crossed her arms. "Ok, you two have harassed Jill long enough! You leave her alone now!" She walked over behind Jill's chair and leaned down to kiss her on the cheek.

"Don't you let them bother you, sweetheart!" She looked back up at Robert. "Do you and Katie have any plans for today? If you're leaving, can we spend today together?"

"I don't know," Robert replied, "Katie, did you have any plans for today?"

"Well, if we're going to fly back we should probably make some plane reservations. I'll have to see if someone can pick us up at the airport."

"I can get plane tickets online, honey. That shouldn't take very long. After that, maybe we could find some nice, little bistro and get some wine and cheesecake?"

Jill glared at him. "Do you know any nice bistros near here?"

"I thought maybe...?"

"That's a special place, just for us. Sorry *writer*." She smiled widely again.

"Maybe I could call the shrink? I'll bet he can recommend someplace for us to go."

Jill looked up at Katie with a panicked look on her face. Katie returned her look with a smile. "Don't worry. I'll make sure he doesn't call Ben." She glared at Robert. "You behave!"

"Hey, I just thought..." He stopped in the middle of his sentence when Katie began shaking her head. "Yeah, fine, I won't call."

Jim began to laugh again. "I told you writer, don't let her run you too much!"

"Daddy, you need to behave, too! Stop telling him that! We're *partners*, we don't run each other!"

"Well, I think I'll see when we can get a flight. Thanks for the bacon, Jim." Robert stood up, and there was suddenly a small, musical, sound. He looked down at his pocket and pulled out his cell phone.

"It's me." Jill smiled. She pulled her cell phone out of her pocket. After looking at it, she held it to her chest. She smiled excitedly and excused herself from the table also.

Forty Three

Robert sat next to Katie in the living room, looking at his laptop computer. "How about we leave tomorrow night? We can spend the day here and then fly out at about six. I can pay for the first class tickets right now if you're good with that?

"First class is so expensive, why can't we just buy regular seats?" Katie asked.

"Regular? Honey, I'm a best selling author! Why shouldn't we fly first class?"

"Because it's too expensive, Robert! Look, we can save around $600 if we fly coach."

"Katie, we have plenty of money, what's $600?"

"It's $600 that could be saved for our children's college fund! Or $600 we can put down on a new house or buy furniture with! I'm going to have to sct a budget for you, aren't I?"

He looked at her and sighed. "Fine, we can fly coach. It's a big difference from first class, you'll see! We can take the direct flight, and…"

"Pick that one, it's the cheapest." Katie said, pointing at the screen.

"Katie, that one isn't a direct flight. It stops in North Carolina."

"So? It's the cheapest one, we can save some money. Besides, I won't mind stopping in North Carolina while we're together! It'll be like a little mini trip for us!"

"Fine, fine! We'll save a few dollars and stop in North Carolina. Don't be crying to me when you're bored, though!"

Katie smiled and hugged him. "Thank you, sweetheart!"

Jill walked into the living room followed by Jim and Emily. "Ben sent me a message to call him. I told him about you guys getting engaged, I hope you don't mind!"

"Yeah, whatever." Robert shrugged.

"Thanks for the enthusiasm!" Katie said, giving him a playful shove. "No, we don't mind at all! How's he doing?"

"Well, I told him you wanted to go to the bistro. He said he knew another one nearby that is really nice and I should take you there."

"I see. The place won't shrink our heads, will it?"

Katie smacked him. "*Stop that*, she really likes him, you need to be nice!"

"We thought maybe we could all go there for lunch. Ben has invited us all over for dinner tonight to celebrate your engagement!"

"He cooks?" Robert asked. "I remember him telling me he ate a lot of take out and frozen stuff."

"Well…I've given him a shopping list and will probably go over and cook for everyone."

"You're going over there to cook?" Robert asked, surprised. "Jim, you're letting her go over to the shrink's house to cook?"

Jim nodded. "I know she can take care of herself. If she tells me that's what she wants to do then I'm fine with it. Besides, we'll be over later to check on things."

Robert smiled at Katie. "Is this the same guy? Are you guys sure this is your dad? Are you going to ask him if he slept with your daughter? Can I be there for your talk with him?"

Jim glared at him and looked over towards Emily. "Are you sure I have to get along with him? He's starting to get nasty!"

"Yes, I'm sure you need to get along with him." She smiled back. She pointed a finger at Robert. "And you need to get along, too! Don't you be harassing Jim, *or* Ben! I'll be keeping my eye on you!"

Robert opened his mouth to say something but Katie put a finger to his lips. "No honey. You just behave, ok? Remember when you told me we had to sleep in separate beds and I didn't want to? What did you tell me? You said we needed to respect Daddy's rules in his house! Now you need to listen to Mom and me when we tell you to behave!"

He looked over at Jill who crossed her arms and grinned back.

"Yes ma'am, I'll behave. I'll…be nice."

"Good, then everyone's happy! Our flight leaves at 7:05 pm tomorrow night. We have tonight and tomorrow to spend together!" Katie said, clapping her hands. "Oh, and I'm getting so in the mood for cheesecake, too!"

"Yeah, cheesecake, yay." Robert said, quietly.

Jill drove them all to a small place with tables and umbrellas in a small garden in the back of the restaurant. A waitress seated them and Jill ordered them each a piece of cherry cheesecake and a bottle of wine for the table.

Robert stopped the waitress. "Oh, uh…could I have a coke instead of the wine?"

"Oh no, you don't drink, do you?" Jill asked, concerned. "I got so wrapped up in Ben, the cheesecake, and everything, I totally forgot! I'm so sorry!"

"It's not a problem."

"Hey, can I have a beer then, if we can order different drinks?" Jim spoke up.

"Oh, I don't think I want any wine, either." Katie said quietly.

"Oh, don't skip trying it just because of me!" Robert said, putting his hand on her back. "You have some with your cheesecake and tell me how it is, ok?"

"But you don't drink! I'll feel bad drinking in front of you!"

"Honey, I knew what we were coming here for! Jill wants you to taste this special wine with the special cheesecake. I want you to try it, too!"

She looked over at Jill and Emily. "Are you sure?"

"We don't have to have wine. I completely forgot you don't drink!" Jill said again.

Robert looked up at the waitress, "The cheesecakes, the wine and three glasses, one beer, and one coke, please"

She looked around the talbe waiting for more argument. After a few seconds, she said, "Ok then, I'll be right back with your order."

Robert broke the silence first, "So, he told you to bring us here, huh?"

He *suggested* I bring you here." Jill corrected him, "He said I could take you to the other place, but I still wanted it to be just for us. It really was..." she looked at Katie as she said the next part, "Special for me."

He gave Katie a confused look, and she leaned over and whispered, "I'm always telling her that *you're* special, honey."

"And he couldn't come, huh?" Jim snorted, "Working, I guess? Counseling someone?"

"Yes Dad, he's working. I told you, he invited us all over later ronight! And *please* be nice when we go, I *really* do like him!"

"We've been nice so far, haven't we, writer? We took him to get his tire fixed!"

"Daddy..." Katie growled.

Robert reached over and took Katie's hand, "It's ok, he says it with affection, I think."

"Why won't he use you name? It's like he doesn't respect you!"

"It doesn't bother him when I call him writer," Jim said, "Are you really bothered by that nickname, *Robert*?"

Robert smiled back, "Not at all, sir. I'm used to it now, kind of like I got used to Jill calling me Sex Fiend."

A small giggle escaped from Jill's lips.

"And since you two are engaged, I suppose you slept together last night?" Jim scowled.

No, still separte beds." Robert smiled back.

"Robert said we needed to respect *your* rules in *your* house, and we have!" Katie said proudly, "We *wanted* to sleep together, but we followed your stupid rules!"

"Really?" Jim asked. He glanced over at Jill.

She nodded, "They cuddle once in a while, but you can't blame them for that, they're in love! But no Dad, they don't sleep together."

"I'm impressed! I thought when your mother told me to stay out of the room and stop bothering you guys, you were sleeping together!"

"They wouldn't do it in the same room as me, Dad!" Jill smiled, "They do have one or two morals!"

The waitress brought over their order and Katie picked up Robert's napkin and began situating it in his lap.

"Hey, what're you doing? I don't want that there!" he protested.

"Use your manners, Robert! Your napkin goes in your lap!"

"I'll be careful, I don't want it in my lap!"

"That's where it goes! Will you just listen to me?"

"Fine, would you like to cut my cheesecake up for me, too?"

"Ok, ok, I get it! You don't want any help!" Katie said. She turned to eat her cheesecake with a foul look on her face.

Robert reached out and handed her a wine glass, "Try this and let me know how the wine goes with the cheesecake, ok?"

"Are you sure you want my opinion on that?" she scowled back, "You don't seem to care what I think about manners!"

He sighed, and placed the napkin on his lap, "Ok, I'm sorry. I didn't mean to hurt you, honey. You know I love you! I'm just not used to having it there."

As she looked into his eyes, her look softened, "I know, and I'm...sorry, too. Of course I'll try the wine!"

Forty Four

After they had returned from the restaurant, Katie and Robert walked upstairs to decide what they would wear to Ben's party.

"What are you going to wear: probably a dress, right? Did you think about what colors you want us wearing? I know colors are important to you in clothes."

Katie stood beside him and looked at him without saying a word.

"I know you probably want me in a tie, maybe I could...Katie? Are you ok, honey?"

"We can talk, right?" she asked.

"Of course, you know we always want to communicate!" He led her over to sit on the bed. "What's wrong? You aren't getting cold feet already, are you?"

"No, I just...I've been thinking about things I've said to you since you proposed, and...well..."

"Things you said? Like what?"

"I nag you, don't I?"

"You *what*?" he asked, chuckling.

"I'm a *nag*! At breakfast I kept telling you to be nice, and you're always nice! At lunch I nagged you about your napkin and manners, I just feel like..."

Robert looked down at his lap. You were right."

She looked over at him. "What? I was right about what, nagging you?"

"No, you and your mom were right, I was going to harass Jill and I wanted to call and bother Ben."

"Why? Why would you do that?"

He looked up into her eyes. "I...it's you and me talking, right? And we're always honest with each other? I was...jealous."

"Jealous, what do you mean?"

"Since we first met, Jill was always around. She was there to talk to me for our first fight. She was telling you to talk to me about wanting to go back to work. I got used to having her around, you know? Don't take that the wrong way honey, ok? I love *you* more than anything, and I do want to marry you and spend the rest of our lives together. I just kind of got used to having Jill around, too. And thinking about some other guy...getting her attention, I just... Have you ever had a feeling you didn't understand? Did something stupid based on that feeling and then felt bad about it later?"

Katie took his hands in hers and smiled sweetly at him. "I gave the man I love a glass full of Tabasco to drink."

"You were jealous of me showing your paretns so much attention and ignoring you, right? I'm so sorry, Katie!"

"Don't worry about Jill. She still loves you, too! I know you mean the world to her, you've done so much for her, for both of us!"

He sighed. "Thanks for understanding. Maybe we just need a bit more counseling? I liked the counseling we got from Ben!" He slid his arms around her waist and pulled her down onto the bed, kissing her neck. She pulled him close, giggling.

"Oh, oh geez, I'm *sorry*!" came Jill's voice. "I just wanted to change my shirt! I always seem to be interrupting you guys, don't I?"

Robert sat up smiling. Katie sat up next to him, looking a bit flushed, but happy. "That's ok. We were just talking about you."

"Yes, I could hear! I must have done something really funny for you to be giggling like that, huh?"

I'm really sorry; sorry about everything I said and did." Robert said quietly.

"Messing around with your fiance is expected, Sex Fiend, you don't need to apologize for that." Jill laughed.

"I'm sorry about everything I said about you and Ben. I'm sorry if I treated you badly at lunch and breakfast." Robert continued sadly. "I was...a bit jealous of you giving attention to another guy."

She looked at him curiously. "What? I don't remember you saying anything to apologize for."

"I shouldn't have teased you about kissing him at the ballgame. I shouldn't be calling him a shrink and making comments about him shrinking heads. It wasn't appropriate. It was just kind of a shock for you to...well...I think I'll really miss you when we go back to New York tomorrow."

Jill sat down next to him on the small bed. She looked at him for a minute and put her arms around his neck, hugging him close. She then kissed him on the cheek. "I'll really miss you guys, too! And you know what? I think I kind of know how you feel. I was so mean to you when you and Katie first met, remember? And when she flew to California, I was so jealous! And when we were driving here, you were always so good with her! Sometimes I was so jealous that I didn't have what you two have."

"We'll have to eat out all the time now when we get back home." Katie smiled. "Jill always did all the cooking."

"Jill returned her smile. "Well, I guess someone will just have to learn how to cook then, won't they?"

Robert put an arm around Jill. "I really will miss you!"

"I'm not going to prison, or dying, you idiot!" she scolded him. I expect to get a lot of phone calls from *both* of you! Just because you don't see me every day doesn't mean you can't dial a phone!"

"And you can call us, too!" Robert smiled.

Jill stood up. "Ok, let me get my shirt changed so I can get over to Ben's place to start dinner before you people make me start crying. He'll think something's wrong. I want you two to have a wonderful engagement party!"

"Thanks, Jill." Both Robert and Katie said at the same time.

Katie walked out of the bathroom wearing the same red, sleeveless, dress she wore for the first party thrown for Robert back in New York. Her hair was in a French braid.

"Do you remember this dress?" She asked, as he finished buttoning up the shirt she had picked out for him, "I was wearing it when you and Jill came back from the store that first weekend. You almost dropped the groceries?"

He smiled widely. "Oh my God, yes I remember that one! You still look beautiful wearing it! And you...went with a braid, huh?" His smile dipped slightly.

Her face changed at his reaction. "You don't like the braid? I can take it out, just give me a minute." She turned and headed back towards the bathroom. Robert followed and stopped her.

"Your hair is fine, sweetheart. I've just never seen you with it braided like that."

"If you don't like it, I'll take it out! I want to wear my hair the way *you* like it!"

"I like *you*!" He said putting his arms around her waist and looking into her eyes. "I love you, actually. I'll like your hair however you want to do it, ok?"

"But..." She started.

He interrupted her by putting a hand gently to her cheek and kissing her. "You're *beautiful*! I think you're perfect just the way you are!"

She kissed him back. "Thank you, you know I love you, too! I think Mom and Dad are waiting, we'd better go."

"Yeah, let's go and see the shrink and his girlfriend!" He laughed.

Forty Five

Jim, Emily, Robert, and Katie stood on Ben's porch. Jim rang the doorbell. After a few seconds, Ben opened the door smiling widely.

"Welcome, everyone! Please, come on inside!" As Robert and Katie entered, Ben held out his hand. "Congratulations! I guess you two got engaged while we were at the ballgame last night?"

Robert reached out and shook Ben's hand. "Yes, we sure did. It's official. She has a ring and everything!"

Robert finished shaking hands and Katie held out her left hand proudly. "Oh, it was *so* romantic, too! Robert had my Dad take pictures!"

Ben smiled at Robert. "Really, pictures? I'd love to see them some time. Everyone, please make yourselves at home. We have champagne for the occasion, I know you don't drink Robert but Jill insisted you wouldn't mind."

"Nah, what do I care?" He answered with a touch of sarcasm.

Jim and Emily sat down on a large couch and Robert plopped down in a nearby overstuffed chair.

Katie sat down on the couch with her parents. "*Robert*, you should sit next to me on the couch!"

"I like this chair. You can sit on my lap if you want?"

Jim glared at him and crossed his arms.

"Yeah, yeah, ok! I'm moving over to the couch!"

He moved over to sit next to Katie and Jill came out from the kitchen. "Hi everyone! Sorry I wasn't able to meet you at the door with Ben but I had some things to tend to in the kitchen. We're having spaghetti tonight because I know Katie doesn't like meat."

Jim looked over at her. "Still? I thought it was just some phase you were going through? You had some of the pot roast the other night!"

"No it's not a phase!" Katie scowled back. "I just don't like meat very much! So I don't usually eat it!"

"And you're going to put up with that, writer? With not having any meat when you go back to New York?"

"I've eaten meat when I've been out with him, so there!" Katie answered.

"Is that a fact?" Jim laughed. "You've eaten meat for the writer, huh?"

Jill ignored them and smiled at Katie. "Have you two set a date yet?"

"No, we haven't really talked about it." Robert said thoughtfully. "I just proposed and she said yes. We'll let you know as soon as we figure out the when, ok?"

"I'd better be one of the first to get an invitation!" Jill said, as she put her hands on her hips. She leaned down and kissed both Robert and Katie. "Well, I know I've already said it, but congratulations again!"

"Thank you." Both Robert and Katie said together.

"And I guess you've taken a shine to my other daughter?" Jim asked, standing up.

Ben took a deep breath. "Yes I have. Jill warned me you'd want to have a talk with me. Would you like to step into my office for a few minutes?"

"Jim...?" Emily said quietly.

"I want to have a chat, too!" Robert said, standing up. "I'd like to find out your intentions with my future sister in law, too!"

Jim turned and shot him a scathing look. "You sit down and mind your own business!"

"Mind my...?"

"Your fiancé is right there on the couch! You take care of *her*!"

Robert sat back down and looked at Katie. She smiled back at him and kissed him on the cheek. Ben and Jim walked towards a nearby room and closed the door.

"How do you think he'll do with Daddy?"

"Oh, Ben will be fine. I've already told him everything Dad will probably ask. He's ready." Jill giggled.

"I just don't know what to do with your father sometimes," Emily sighed. "I'm sorry about this."

Katie began looking around the room. "Oh my God, where is that music coming from?"

"Ben has a stereo hooked up, there are speakers hidden all over. He thought it might be nice to play some quiet music for our little party."

Katie took several deep breaths. "Oh, that's our song! Can you turn it up?"

"Is it really?" Jill asked, looking at Robert. "I didn't even know you two *had* a song! I'm not sure where the stereo is but I can see if I can find it."

Robert stood up and held out his hand. "Well, since it's our song I guess we should maybe dance? Like the song says: Can I have this dance for the rest of my life?"

Katie took his hand and they moved to an empty piece of the living room. They began to hold each other and dance.

She looked into his eyes and smiled. "Thank you for this. I know I keep saying that, but your coming into my life has been like a dream."

Robert held her close. "A dream, huh? Well if this is a dream, I hope we never wake up."

She kissed him. "You said I'm your sunshine, do you remember?"

"Did I? I said that?"

"You don't remember? It was so romantic and sweet, I can't believe you don't remember saying that!"

He watched her for a minute and then said. "In the morning you're my sunshine. At night you're my stars. You're my everything."

She sniffed as a tear fell from her eye. "I knew you wouldn't forget saying something like that. I love you so much!"

"I love you, too."

Jim and Ben came out of the small office. Jim sat next to Emily. Ben smiled and winked at Jill.

Emily looked at Jim. "Well?"

"I think our girls will be ok."

Jill walked over near Ben. "Look at them." She said, pointing at Robert and Katie. "I just can't believe how quickly they fell in love."

"I've counseled couples who were together for years before they got married and still didn't look at each other the way those two do. Sometimes it happens that fast."

"She was with Barry for a couple of years and she never seemed anywhere near as close to him, as she is to Robert."

"I guess she got over being mad at him for putting his feet on my desk?" Ben laughed.

Jill didn't seem to hear him. "Do you think we could ever…?" She looked up at Ben and blushed. "Never mind."

"We've just had one date. We're different people, we can't be exactly like Robert and Katie. But so far, I'd say we're doing ok."

"Just ok?"

"I think our start was a bit slower than theirs was. Our relationship might take a bit more work."

The song ended but Katie kept her arms around Robert's neck. He hugged her close. "I think the song's over, honey."

"I don't care. I just want to stay in your arms forever!"

Her cell phone began to ring from inside her pocket. She ignored it and kept her arms around his neck.

"You aren't even going to see who that is?" He asked.

She sighed. "If I have to, I guess." She reached down and pulled the phone out of her pocket. "Oh, it's Julie. I'd better take this one." She held the phone up to her ear. "Hello?"

As she was talking on her phone Jill called them all to dinner. Katie stayed in the living room for a few minutes while the rest of them walked into the dining room. Jill had lit several candles on the table and began to serve the spaghetti.

"Is Katie coming in to eat?" She asked. "She's not really going to spend dinner time talking to her friends while we eat, is she?"

"She'll be here, she just needs a minute." Robert reassured her. "Give her a break. She's still pretty excited, I think."

"Yeah, yeah." Jill mumbled.

A few minutes later Katie came into the dining room and sat down at her place next to Robert. "Sorry I'm late. My friend Julie called me. She's going to pick us up at the airport tomorrow night."

"Julie? That's one of your friends I've met already, isn't it?" Robert asked.

"Yes. She's one of my best friends. Her boyfriend Joseph will probably come with her to pick us up." She said, making a sour face as she said the name.

"You don't like him?" Robert asked.

"No, he's ok...I guess."

"Are you sure? Why'd you make that face when you said his name?"

"He's fine, I didn't make a face."

Robert looked over at Jill. "Yes you did. She made this horrible face, didn't she?"

"Later, ok?" Katie said with a pleading look.

Robert watched her for a few seconds and then turned to Ben. "So you guys had a good time at the ballgame, huh? I didn't get to see the end, who won?"

"I believe the Yankees won, didn't they?" Ben answered looking at Jill.

"Yes, the Yankees." She said, trying to hide a smile.

"Oh yeah, what was the final score?"

"Well, actually...we...ah..." Ben started.

"Tampa won, three to two." Jim said casually.

"Thanks *Dad*!" Jill scowled over at him. "You're a huge help!"

"You at least had good seats, right?" Robert asked.

"Oh, they were excellent seats!" Ben smiled. "We were right behind home plate, just like you said! I can't thank you enough! If I can ever help you out with something, you just let me know!"

"Is that so? Well actually…" Robert began. Katie reached over and gently put a hand on his arm, shaking her head. He looked down at her hand and then back at Ben, "I appreciate that, thank you. I'll remember."

"Leash is pretty tight there, huh writer?" Jim began to laugh.

Katie gave him a dirty look and smiled towards Ben. "I guess you and Jill had a very nice time?"

"Yes, we did. I guess she's staying here in Florida for a while to take a few classes and we did plan to keep seeing each other."

"Baseball classes?" Robert asked with a smile. Katie kicked him under the table. He looked over at her and mumbled an apology.

Ben watched Robert for a minute. "Does my seeing Jill bother you?"

"I guess it's just kind of a shock. I just didn't really expect this."

"It was probably a shock to her when you and Katie got together."

"Yeah, I guess. Just be nice to her, ok?"

"That's a promise." Ben said and smiled at Jill. She blushed slightly and smiled back.

"Don't worry writer, we had a talk. I'll keep an eye on my daughter while she's here." Jim scowled. "So far I think he's ok."

"Not to change the subject, but did you know when you wanted our wedding to be?" Robert asked Katie. "Did you have a date in mind?"

"If you didn't mind…I kind of wanted to have our wedding at the Queens Botanical Garden. We'd have to see when it's available. There are a lot of things to plan for a wedding."

"A botanical garden? That sounds really nice. I think that will be perfect!"

She looked over at Jim. "Is that ok with you, Daddy?"

Jim had a mouth full of spaghetti and swallowed before answering. "Isn't that the place over in Flushing? You want some kind of garden wedding?"

"Oh yes, that sounds so romantic!"

"I think you have to have reservations six months or so in advance for that place. Is that what you really want? Can you not get her pregnant for that long, writer?"

"Oh, I don't know...I am a sex fiend, you can ask..." Robert began. He stopped as Katie elbowed him in the stomach.

"We can wait. We wanted time together before taking our vows anyway." She smiled.

"I can make some calls and get some dates for you then, if that's what you have your heart set on?"

"Thank you, Daddy."

"I think this calls for a toast," Ben said as he stood up and lifted his glass, "To Robert and Katie: May they have a long and happy life together!"

"Here, here!" Jill said, raising her glass also.

After looking at Robert for a few seconds, Jim lifted his glass too. "Take care of her, writer." He glanced at Katie. "And congratulations, *Robert* and Katie!"

Katie smiled widely and mouthed the words *Thank you* towards her father.

After dinner Ben opened the bottle of champagne and passed around glasses. Robert passed but insisted Katie have some. He gave her an evil little smile as Ben filled her glass.

"You just love this, don't you?" She growled.

After Ben proposed another toast to them he seemed to notice Robert still watching him closely.

"You really *aren't* comfortable with me seeing Jill, are you?"

Robert sighed. "Well...sure I am, I just...ok, no I'm not."

Katie put a hand on his arm. "Robert…"

"No, it's fine Katie." Ben said. "I'd like to hear what he has to say."

"It's not you," Robert began. "It's just…I guess I'm just jealous. For the last month or so, Jill was always there to talk to me when I needed her. And now…"

"And now you kind of feel abandoned?" Ben asked.

"I told you we could talk on the phone all the time." Jill sighed. "I'm not abandoning anyone."

"Like her dad, I just want her safe, I think. I want to make sure she's taken care of, and happy."

Ben looked over at Jill. "Are you happy?"

Jill walked over and put her arms around both Katie and Robert and hugged them close. "I'm more happy than I've ever been, ok? My sister's engaged to a wonderful man and I've met a wonderful man myself."

"If you have doubts about me…" Ben started.

"No," Robert smiled. "I guess I don't have any doubts. If I really was upset about her seeing you, I guess I wouldn't have given her the baseball tickets. But I do appreciate you talking to me about it, though."

"Atta boy writer," Jim yelled. "Make sure you're comfortable with him! You did promise to look out for my girls!"

Robert began to laugh. "Yeah, I guess I did."

Katie got up and walked over to hug Ben. "We know you'll take good care of Jill. Try not to break her heart, ok?"

"I think we'll be ok." Ben smiled and hugged Katie back.

Forty Six

Robert lay on his bed with Katie by his side. She was gently caressing his chest and kissing him.

"Are you going to let him get any sleep at all, Katie?"

"He'll get plenty of sleep, don't you worry. He'll make me go back to my own bed eventually. I can't wait until we're home and can sleep together again!"

Robert began laughing. "You know, I'm kind of looking forward to that myself."

"Could we just sleep together here tonight, maybe?"

"Rules are rules, sweetie. And it's a good test of willpower."

"I guess. I just don't see what the point is."

He looked into her eyes and sighed. "I know you don't. But it makes your dad feel better when we stay in separate beds, ok? Katie...can I ask you something?"

"Of course."

"You said you'd tell me later, and it's later. You don't like the guy your friend's seeing?"

"What? I don't remember saying anything like that!"

"You said Julie and her boyfriend were going to pick us up at the airport, and when you said his name you made this face like you didn't like him. You said you'd tell me later?"

"Oh Joseph, it's no big deal."

"Honesty, communication?"

She sighed. "Ok, if you have to know everything. He just...I don't really like the way he looks at me. He just...makes me nervous."

"Nervous? Like he might attack you, or something?"

"No, nothing like that. He's really nice to me, but he just...sometimes the way he looks at me makes me feel...it's hard to explain."

"How does he look at you, like you're the most beautiful thing he's ever seen?"

"Kind of, but…what did you say?" She began to giggle. "I'm trying to tell you some guy makes me nervous and you turn it into a compliment?"

"I just wondered. I've probably made plenty of girls nervous, too." He began to giggle, too.

"Oh my God, you two *deserve* each other!" Jill said, putting a pillow over her head. "Please tell me you talk about more important things and not stuff like this?"

"The other day we had a discussion about whether or not the grass I raked was ruining my shoes." Robert laughed.

"Oh geez! Good luck with the marriage!" Jill laughed.

"Yeah, good luck." Robert said, as he smiled at Katie. He leaned over and kissed her deeply and passionately, and then sent her off to her own bed.

Forty Seven

"Well this is it, I guess?" Robert said as they stood in the airport. Ben and Jill came along with Jim and Emily to drop off Robert and Katie. "I know Katie was a bit nervous about me meeting her father, but I had a really nice time, and am really glad we met!"

Katie hugged her mother and then her father. Her hug with Jim lasted a while as they held each other.

"Oh Daddy, I'm so sorry I haven't visited you in so long! I really did miss you!"

"You just take care of yourself. And you remember the writer's promise and call me at least once a week, ok?"

"I will! I'm so glad you like Robert, it means a lot to me!"

"Well...he does treat you ok, and he seems like a pretty nice guy. I'm happy you aren't with that last guy."

She kissed him and moved away to see Robert hugging Emily. "Thanks for everything. And if you and Jim ever want to fly out to New York for a visit, you just let me know! We'll be happy to have you anytime!"

Emily hugged him back tightly. "Thank you Robert. I think Katie has found herself a wonderful husband! And don't you think you can't fly back out here again! You know we love having you here!"

Both Katie and Robert moved over to hug Jill.

"Thanks for all the talks we had. I'll probably be calling you for more talks." Robert smiled.

"You'd better! If you're going to marry my sister, I'll have to keep an eye on what goes on between you two! And...I kind of enjoyed our little talks, too."

"You'll just have to learn to talk to *me* now, won't you?" Katie smiled.

"I think we're both on the path to talking to each other. We'll just keep working at it, ok?"

Katie kissed his cheek as Robert turned to Ben. He held out his hand and Ben shook it happily. "Are you still upset about my seeing Jill?"

"No, I'll be fine. I think I'll be ok with it. You know, I kind of got used to having both girls around…Jill watching out for both Katie and me. I'll be fine with you seeing her as long as you treat her right."

Jill put her hand into Bens and her head on his shoulder. "He does, Sex Fiend, he does. We aren't really moving as fast as you and Katie did, but we're doing ok."

"And if you decide you need to talk, I know we don't know each other very well yet but I was your first marriage councilor." Ben smiled.

Robert blushed a bit. "Yeah…sorry about the whole…desk…thing."

Ben began to laugh. "Don't worry about it! You probably won't be the last person to do that. Have a good trip and be sure to call if you need anything! And feel free to call just to say hello, too. If I don't answer, just remember I'm probably busy, but I'll call back as soon as I can!"

"We'll stay in touch." Robert smiled.

After taking a deep breath, Robert took Katie's hand. "Come on, we'd better get moving, the plane will be boarding soon. And I need to get you moving before you cry again."

"Before I…don't be stupid, why would I…?" Katie began. She caught her father's eye and ran back to him again, throwing herself in his arms. "Oh Daddy!"

Jim hugged her close.

"It's ok sweetheart. You know I love you. Go with Robert, you'll be fine. We'll always be there for you. I'll be in back in New York yelling at your writer in no time, ok?"

"Thank you." Katie sobbed, hugging him close. "Thank you for accepting him!"

Jim kissed her, and then eased her back over to Robert. "You take good care of my daughter now!"

"I will. Thanks for everything." He began leading Katie towards their loading gate.

Robert sat looking out the window of the plane. He watched the clouds go by and wondered what was in store for Katie and him.

"Robert," Katie said softly. "I'm…I'm sorry I embarrassed you before we left."

He turned towards her with surprise. "Embarrassed me? What do you mean?"

"You said you needed to get me going before I cried, and…"

"You always cry, honey. I knew you'd get emotional before we left, it was fine. I was really happy to see you that close to your dad again."

"Really? You're sure I didn't embarrass you? I mean, I know you're always so…"

He took hold of her hand and looked into her eyes. "Katie, I do love you. I do want to marry you, and I accept you for who you are. I meant what I said when I proposed, you *are* my sunshine and stars! You never embarrass me, ok? You just be who you are around me. If we just keep communicating, and being honest, and sharing our love, everything will be fine. And no, you didn't embarrass me at all."

Katie smiled, and kissed him. "You are *so* perfect! I can't wait to marry you!"

Robert laughed. "I can't wait either. I'm sure everything will go really smooth, too."

"It will, as long as we're together." Katie smiled, and put her head on his shoulder.

The End…for now. Read about Robert and Katie's wedding in, "A Writer's Wedding" coming soon!

Made in the USA
Charleston, SC
18 May 2010